ONCE STALKED

(A RILEY PAIGE MYSTERY—BOOK 9)

BLAKE PIERCE

ISBN: 978-1-64029-080-8

BOOKS BY BLAKE PIERCE

RILEY PAIGE MYSTERY SERIES
ONCE GONE (Book #1)
ONCE TAKEN (Book #2)
ONCE CRAVED (Book #3)
ONCE LURED (Book #4)
ONCE HUNTED (Book #5)
ONCE PINED (Book #6)
ONCE FORSAKEN (Book #7)
ONCE COLD (Book #8)
ONCE STALKED (Book #9)
ONCE LOST (Book #10)

MACKENZIE WHITE MYSTERY SERIES
BEFORE HE KILLS (Book #1)
BEFORE HE SEES (Book #2)
BEFORE HE COVETS (Book #3)
BEFORE HE TAKES (Book #4)
BEFORE HE NEEDS (Book #5)
BEFORE HE FEELS (Book #6)

AVERY BLACK MYSTERY SERIES
CAUSE TO KILL (Book #1)
CAUSE TO RUN (Book #2)
CAUSE TO HIDE (Book #3)
CAUSE TO FEAR (Book #4)
CAUSE TO SAVE (Book #5)

KERI LOCKE MYSTERY SERIES
A TRACE OF DEATH (Book #1)
A TRACE OF MUDER (Book #2)
A TRACE OF VICE (Book #3)
A TRACE OF CRIME (Book #4)

PROLOGUE

Colonel Dutch Adams looked at his watch as he strode through Fort Nash Mowat, and saw that the time was 0500 hours on the dot. It was a brisk, dusky April morning in Southern California, and all appeared as it should.

He heard a woman's voice yell out sharply …

"The garrison commander is present!"

He turned in time to see a training platoon snap to attention at the female drill sergeant's command. Col. Adams paused to return their salute and continued on his way. He walked a little faster than before, hoping not to attract the attention of other drill sergeants. He didn't want to interrupt more training platoons as they gathered in their formation areas.

His face twitched a little. After all these years, he still wasn't quite used to hearing female voices snapping out commands. Even the sight of mixed-gender platoons sometimes startled him a little. The Army had definitely changed since his own days as a teenaged recruit. He didn't like many of those changes.

As he continued on his way, he heard the barking voices of other drill sergeants, both male and female, calling their platoons into formation.

They don't have much punch anymore, he thought.

He could never forget the abuse spewed by his own drill sergeant so many years ago—the savage invectives against family and ancestry, the insults and obscenities.

He smiled a little. That bastard Sergeant Driscoll!

Driscoll died many years ago, Col. Adams recalled—not in combat as he'd surely have preferred, but of a stroke brought on by hypertension. In those days, sky high blood pressure had been an occupational hazard of drill sergeants.

Col. Adams would never forget Driscoll, and as far as Adams was concerned, that was how things should be. A drill sergeant ought to make an indelible imprint on a soldier's mind for the rest of his life. He ought to present a living example of the worst kind of hell a soldier's life had to offer. Sergeant Driscoll had definitely had that kind of lifelong impact on Col. Adams. Were the trainers under his command here at Fort Nash Mowat likely to leave that kind of impression on their recruits?

Col. Adams doubted it.

Too damn much political correctness, he thought.

1

Softness was now even written into the Army's training manual
…

"Stress created by physical or verbal abuse is non-productive and prohibited."

He scoffed as he thought of the words.

"What a load of crap," he murmured under his breath.

But the Army had been moving in this direction since the 1990s. He knew he ought to be used to it by now. But he never would be.

Anyway, he wouldn't have to deal with it much longer. He was a year away from retirement, and his final ambition was to make brigadier general before then.

Suddenly, Adams was distracted from his musings by a puzzling sight.

The recruits of Platoon #6 were milling around aimlessly in their formation area, some doing calisthenics, others just idly talking among themselves.

Col. Adams stopped in his tracks and yelled.

"Soldiers! Where the hell's your sergeant?"

Flustered, the recruits jumped to attention and saluted.

"At ease," Adams said. "Is somebody going to answer my goddamn question?"

A female recruit spoke up.

"We don't know Sergeant Worthing's whereabouts, *sir*."

Adams could hardly believe his ears.

"What do you mean, you don't know?" he demanded.

"He never showed up for formation, *sir*."

Adams growled under his breath.

This didn't sound like Sergeant Clifford Worthing at all. In fact, Worthing was one of the few drill sergeants that Adams had any real use for. He was a real hard-ass of the old school—or at least he wanted to be. He often came to Adams's office to complain about how the rules reined him in.

Even so, Adams knew that Worthing bent the rules as much as he could. Sometimes the recruits complained about his rigorous demands and verbal abuse. Those complaints pleased Adams.

But where was Worthing right now?

Adams waded among the recruits into the barracks, passing between the rows of beds until he got to Worthing's office.

He knocked sharply on the door.

"Worthing, are you in there?"

No one replied.

"Worthing, this is your CO, and if you're in there, you'd damn sure better answer me."

Again no one replied.

Adams turned the doorknob and pushed the door open.

The office was immaculately neat—and no one was there.

Where the hell did he go? Adams wondered.

Did Worthing even show up on the base at all this morning?

Then Adams noticed the NO SMOKING sign on the office wall.

He remembered that Sergeant Worthing was a smoker.

Had the drill instructor just stepped out for a smoke?

"Naw, it can't be," Adams grumbled aloud.

It didn't make sense.

Even so, Adams stepped out of the office and headed for the back door of the barracks.

He opened the door and stood staring into the early morning light.

He didn't have to look long or hard.

Sergeant Worthing was crouched with his back against the barracks wall, a burned-out cigarette hanging out of his mouth.

"Worthing, what the hell …?" Adams snarled.

Then he recoiled at what he saw.

At Adams's eye level was a large dark wet blotch on the wall.

From that blotch, a continuous smear trailed down to where Worthing was crouched.

Then Adams saw the dark hole in the middle of Worthing's head.

It was a bullet wound.

The entry wound was tiny, but the exit wound had taken off much of the back of Worthing's skull. The man had been shot dead, standing there smoking an early morning cigarette. The shot had been so clean that the drill sergeant had died instantly. Even the cigarette had remained in his mouth undisturbed.

"Jesus Christ," Adams murmured. "Not again."

He looked all around. A large empty field stretched out behind the barracks. The shot had been fired from some great distance. That meant it had been fired by a skilled marksman.

Adams shook his head with disbelief.

His life, he knew, was about to become complicated—and extremely aggravating.

CHAPTER ONE

Riley Paige stood looking out an open window of her townhouse. It was a lovely spring day, one of those storybook days with birds singing and flowers blooming. The air smelled fresh and clean. And yet a lurking darkness kept tugging at her.

She had the strange feeling that all this beauty was somehow terribly fragile.

That's why she kept her hands hanging at her sides, as if she were in a shop full of delicate china, and a single wrong move might break something lovely and expensive. Or maybe it was as if this perfect afternoon were just a paper-thin illusion that would fall away at the touch of a hand only to reveal …

What? Riley wondered.

The darkness of a world full of pain and terror and evil?

Or the darkness that lurked inside her own mind—the darkness of too many ugly thoughts and secrets?

A girlish voice interrupted Riley's musings.

"What are you thinking about, Mom?"

Riley turned around. She realized that she'd momentarily forgotten the other people in her living room.

The girl who had spoken was Jilly, the skinny thirteen-year-old Riley was in the process of trying to adopt.

"Nothing," Riley said in reply.

Her handsome former neighbor Blaine Hildreth smiled at her.

"You certainly seemed to be far away," he said.

Blaine had just arrived at Riley's home with his teenaged daughter, Crystal.

Riley said, "I guess I was just wondering where April is."

It was a matter of some concern. Riley's fifteen-year-old daughter hadn't come home from school yet. Didn't April know that they had plans to go to Blaine's restaurant for dinner shortly?

Crystal and Jilly grinned at each other mischievously.

"Oh, she'll be here soon," Jilly said.

"Any minute now, I'll bet," Crystal added.

Riley wondered what the girls knew that she didn't know. She hoped April wasn't in some sort of trouble. April had gone through a rebellious phase and had endured a lot of trauma a few months ago. But she seemed to be doing much better now.

Then Riley looked at the others and realized something.

"Blaine, Crystal—I haven't asked if you wanted something to

4

drink. I have some ginger ale. And bourbon if you'd like that, Blaine."

"Ginger ale would be nice, thank you," Blaine said.

"For me too, please," Crystal said.

Jilly started to get up from her chair.

"I'll go get some," Jilly said.

"Oh, no, you don't need to," Riley said. "I'll get it."

Riley headed straight to the kitchen, rather pleased to have something like this to do. Serving refreshments would normally be the job of Gabriela, Riley's live-in Guatemalan housekeeper. But Gabriela had the day off and was visiting friends. Gabriela sometimes made Riley feel spoiled, and it was nice be able to fetch drinks for a change. It also kept Riley's mind focused on the pleasant present.

She poured glasses of ginger ale for Crystal and Blaine, and also for herself and Jilly.

As she carried the tray with the drinks back into the living room, Riley heard the front door open. Then she heard April's voice talking to someone she'd brought in with her.

Riley was handing out the drinks when April came in, followed by a boy about April's age. She looked surprised to see Blaine and Crystal.

"Oh!" April said with a gasp. "I didn't expect—"

Then April reddened with embarrassment.

"Omigod, I completely forgot! We were going out tonight! I'm so sorry!"

Jilly and Crystal were giggling. Now Riley understood the reason for their amusement. They knew already that April had a new boyfriend, and that she'd probably forgotten all about dinner because she was so preoccupied with him.

I remember what that was like, Riley thought, wistfully remembering her own adolescent crushes.

Pleased that April had brought him over to introduce him, Riley eyed the boy quickly. She immediately liked what she saw. Like April, he was tall, gangly, and rather awkward looking. He had bright red hair, freckles, sparkling blue eyes, and a goofy, amiable smile.

April said, "Mom, this is Liam Schweppe. Liam, this is my mom."

Liam offered Riley his hand to shake.

"Very pleased to meet you, Ms. Paige," he said.

His voice had an amusing teenaged-boy squawk to it that made

Riley smile.

"You can call me Riley," she said.

April said, "Mom, Liam's—"

April stopped short, apparently not ready to say "my new boyfriend."

Instead she said, "He's captain of the high school chess team."

Riley's amusement was growing by the minute.

"So you're teaching April to play chess, I take it," she said.

"I'm trying," Liam said.

Riley couldn't help but chuckle a little. She was a pretty good chess player herself, and for years she'd been trying to get April interested in the game. But April had always rolled her eyes at the idea and considered chess to be perfectly uncool—a "mom thing" that couldn't possibly interest her.

Her attitude seemed to have changed now that a cute boy was involved.

Riley invited Liam to come and sit down with the others.

She told him, "I'd offer you something to drink, but we're all just getting ready to head out to dinner."

"The dinner that April forgot about," Liam said, his grin widening a little.

"That's right," Riley said. "Why don't you come too?"

April's blush deepened.

"Oh, Mom …" she began.

"'Oh, Mom' what?" Riley said.

"I'm sure Liam's got other plans," April said.

Riley laughed. She was obviously getting into "uncool mom" territory again. It seemed that April was ready to introduce Liam to her, but a family dinner was rushing things as far as she was concerned.

"What do you think, Liam?" Riley asked.

"Sounds great, thanks," Liam said. "Where are we going?"

"Blaine's Grill," Riley said.

Liam's eyes lit up with excitement.

"Oh, wow! I've heard great things about that place!"

It was Blaine Hildreth's turn to grin.

"Thanks," he said to Liam. "I'm Blaine. I own the restaurant."

Liam laughed.

"Cooler and cooler!" he said.

"Come on, let's all get going," Riley said.

*

A little while later, Riley was enjoying a delicious dinner with April, Jilly, Blaine, Crystal, and Liam. They were all sitting on the patio at Blaine's Grill, enjoying the lovely weather as well as the wonderful food.

Riley was talking about chess with Liam, discussing middle-game planning tactics. She was impressed by his knowledge of the game. She wondered how well she'd do in a game against him. She guessed that she'd probably lose. She was a good player, but he was already the captain of a high school chess team and he was still a sophomore. Besides, she'd had few opportunities to play the game lately.

He must be really good, she figured.

The thought pleased her a lot. Riley knew that April was brighter than she realized, and it was good that she had a boyfriend who challenged her.

As she and Liam talked, Riley found herself wondering just where this thing between him and April was going. There were just two months left of the school year. Would they part ways and lose interest in each other? Riley hoped not.

"What are you doing this summer, Liam?" Riley asked.

"Going to chess camp," Liam said. "Actually, I'm going to be a junior coach. I've been trying to talk April into coming too."

Riley glanced over at April.

"Why don't you go, April?" she asked.

April blushed again.

"I don't know," she said. "I was thinking about soccer camp. That might be more my speed. I'd probably be in way over my head at chess camp."

"Oh, no, you won't be!" Liam said. "There will be players from all levels—including some who are just starting to learn the game, like you. And it's right here in Fredericksburg, so you wouldn't have to leave home."

"I'll think about it," April said. "Right now I just want to focus on my grades."

Riley was glad Liam didn't seem to be distracting April from school. Still, Riley wished she'd consider going to the chess camp. But she knew she'd better not push it. That might turn it into another "uncool mom thing." It was best to leave it up to Liam to persuade her if he could.

Anyway, Riley was pleased to see April look so happy. Dark-haired with hazel eyes like Riley's own, sometimes April looked astonishingly grown up. Riley remembered that she'd chosen April's name because it was her own favorite month. And it was her favorite month because of days just like this.

Blaine looked up from his meal at Riley.

He said, "So tell us about this award you're going to get tomorrow, Riley."

It was Riley's turn to blush a little.

"It's no big deal," she said.

Jilly let out a squeal of protest.

"It is so a big deal!" Jilly said. "It's called the Award of Perseverance, and she's getting it because of that cold case she just solved. The boss of the whole FBI is going to give it to her."

Blaine's eyes widened.

"You mean Director Milner himself?" he said.

Riley was feeling truly awkward and self-conscious now.

She laughed nervously.

"That's not as impressive as it sounds," she said. "It's not a big trip for him to come to Quantico. He works right over in DC, you know."

Blaine's mouth dropped open with amazement.

Jilly said, "Blaine, April and I are getting out of school to see her get it. You and Crystal ought to come too."

Blaine and Crystal both said they'd love to come.

"OK, then," Riley said, still feeling embarrassed. "I hope it doesn't bore you. Anyway, that's not the biggest event tomorrow. Jilly's the star of the school play tomorrow night. That's a much bigger deal."

Now Jilly was blushing.

"I'm not the *star*, Mom," she said.

Riley laughed at Jilly's sudden coyness.

"Well, you're playing one of the title roles. You're Persephone in a play called *Demeter and Persephone*. Why don't you tell us the story?"

Jilly started telling the story of the Greek myth—shyly at first, but getting more enthusiastic about it as she continued. Riley felt more and more pleased. One of her girls was learning to play chess; the other was excited about Greek mythology.

Maybe things are looking up, she thought.

Her efforts at marriage and family had been troubled at best. Recently she'd made a bad mistake, trying to let her ex-husband, Ryan, back into the girls' lives and her own. Ryan had proved to be as incapable of commitment as ever.

But now?

Riley looked over at Blaine, and realized that he was already looking at her. He was smiling, and she smiled back. There was definitely a spark between them. They'd even danced and kissed during a date last month—their only one-on-one date so far. But Riley cringed a little inside as she remembered how awkwardly it had ended—with her running off to work on a case.

Blaine seemed to have forgiven her.

But where were things going between them?

Again, that lurking darkness welled up inside Riley.

Sooner or later, this happy illusion of family and friendship could give way to the reality of evil—to murder and cruelty and human monsters.

And she had a feeling, deep inside, that it was going to happen very soon.

CHAPTER TWO

Sitting in the front row of the auditorium at Quantico, Riley felt terribly ill at ease. She'd faced down countless vicious killers without losing her composure. But right now, she felt on the verge of outright panic.

FBI Director Gavin Milner stood at the podium at the front of the big room. He was speaking of Riley's long career—especially the case that she was being honored for, the cold case of the so-called "Matchbook Killer."

Riley was struck by the distinguished baritone purr of his voice. She'd rarely spoken with Director Milner, but she liked him. He was a slight, dapper little man with a flawlessly neat mustache. Riley thought he looked and sounded more like a dean of some fine arts school than the head of the nation's most elite law enforcement organization.

Riley hadn't been listening to his actual words very well. She was much too nervous and self-conscious as it was. But now that he seemed to be nearing the end of his speech, Riley paid more attention.

Milner said, "We all know of Special Agent Riley Paige's courage, intelligence, and grace under pressure. She's been honored for all these qualities in the past. But we are here today to honor her for something different—her long-term tenacity, her determination not to leave justice undone. Because of her efforts, a killer who claimed three victims twenty-five years ago faces justice at last. We all owe her a debt of gratitude for her service—and for her example."

He smiled, looking straight at her. He picked up the box with the award in it.

That's my cue, Riley thought.

Her legs felt wobbly as she got up from her chair and made her way up onto the stage.

She stepped to the side of the podium and Milner hung the Medal of Perseverance by a ribbon around her neck.

It felt surprisingly heavy.

Strange, Riley thought. *The others didn't feel like this.*

She'd received three other such awards over the years—the Shield of Bravery, and Medals of Valor and Meritorious Achievement.

But this one felt heavier—and different.

It felt almost wrong somehow.

Riley wasn't sure just why.

FBI Director Gavin Milner patted Riley on the shoulder and chuckled a little.

He said to Riley in a near-whisper ...

"Something to add to your collection, eh?"

Riley laughed nervously and shook the director's hand.

The people in the auditorium burst into a round of applause.

Again with a chuckle and in a near-whisper, Director Milner said, "It's time to face your public."

Riley turned around and was rather overcome by what she saw.

There were more people in the auditorium than she'd realized. And every face was familiar—a friend, a family member, a colleague, or someone she'd helped or saved in the line of duty.

They were all on their feet, smiling and clapping.

Riley's throat caught, and tears formed in her eyes.

They all believe in me so much.

She felt grateful and humble—but she also felt a spasm of guilt.

What would these same people think of her if they knew all of her darkest secrets?

They knew nothing about her current relationship with a savage but brilliant killer who had escaped from Sing Sing. They certainly didn't suspect that the criminal had helped her solve several cases. And they couldn't possibly know how hopelessly entwined Riley's own life was with Shane Hatcher's.

Riley almost shuddered at the thought.

No wonder this medal felt heavier than the others.

No, I don't deserve this, Riley thought.

But what was she going to do—turn around and give it back to Director Milner?

Instead, she managed to smile and utter a few words of appreciation. Then she stepped carefully down off the stage.

*

A few moments later, Riley was in a large, crowded room that had been set up with refreshments. It looked like most of the people who had been in the auditorium were here. She was the center of a swirl of activity as everyone took turns congratulating her. She was grateful for the stabilizing presence of Director Milner, who stood right beside her.

In the first wave of well-wishers were colleagues—fellow field agents, specialists, administrators, and office workers.

Most of them were visibly happy for her. For example, Sam Flores, the nerdish head of the Quantico technical analysis team, gave her a silent thumbs-up and a thoroughly sincere smile and moved on.

But Riley also had her share of enemies, and they were here as well. The youngest was Emily Creighton, a fairly inexperienced agent who fancied herself to be Riley's rival. Riley had called her out on a rookie mistake a few months back, and Creighton had resented her ever since.

When it came Creighton's turn to congratulate Riley, the younger agent forced a smile through her clenched teeth, shook her hand, mumbled "Congratulations," and wandered away.

A few more colleagues came and went before Special Agent in Charge Carl Walder stepped toward Riley. Babyish both in appearance and behavior, Walder was Riley's idea of the ultimate bureaucrat. She was always at odds with him, and he with her. In fact, he'd suspended and even fired her on a few occasions.

But right now Riley was amused by his expression of cringing goodwill toward her. With Director Milner standing beside her, Walder didn't dare show anything but feigned respect.

His hand was damp and cold as he shook hers, and she noticed beads of sweat on his forehead.

"A well-deserved honor, Agent Paige," he said in a shaky voice. "We are honored to have you on the force."

Then Walder shook hands with the FBI director.

"So good of you to join us, Director Milner," Walder said.

"My pleasure," Director Milner said.

Riley watched the director's face. Did she notice a slight smirk as he nodded at Walder? She couldn't be sure. But she knew that Walder didn't command a whole lot of respect in the Bureau, neither by his subordinates nor by his superiors.

After the last of her Quantico colleagues congratulated her, the next wave of well-wishers stirred up powerful emotions for Riley. They were people she'd met in the line of duty—family members of murder victims, or people she'd saved from becoming victims. Riley hadn't expected them to be here, especially not so many of them.

The first was a frail, elderly man that she'd rescued from an insane poisoner last January. He took hold of Riley's hand with both of his and tearfully said, "Thank you, thank you, thank you," over and over again.

Riley couldn't help but cry herself.

Then came Lester and Eunice Pennington and their teenaged daughter, Tiffany. In February, Tiffany's older sister, Lois, had been murdered by a sick young man. Riley hadn't seen the Penningtons since she'd solved their case. Riley could hardly believe they were here. She remembered them as distraught and grief-stricken. But they were smiling through their tears, happy for Riley and grateful for the justice she had given them.

As Riley exchanged emotional handclasps with them, she wondered how much more of this she could take without fleeing the room in tears.

Finally came Paula Steen, the elderly mother of a girl who had been killed twenty-five years ago in the case that Riley was being honored for today.

Riley felt truly overwhelmed now.

She and Paula had been in touch for many years now, talking by phone on every anniversary of her daughter's death.

Paula's presence here today took Riley completely off guard.

She clasped Paula's hands, trying not to break down uncontrollably.

"Paula, thank you for coming," she managed to stammer through her tears. "I hope we can still stay in touch."

Paula's smile was radiant, and she wasn't crying at all.

"Oh, I'll keep calling once a year as always, I promise," Paula said. "As long as I'm still in this world, anyway. Now that you've caught Tilda's killer, I feel ready to move on—to join her and my husband. They've been waiting for me for a long time. Thank you so much."

Riley felt a sudden pain deep inside.

Paula was thanking her for the peace she now felt—thanking her for allowing her to die at long last.

It was too much for Riley to process.

She simply couldn't speak.

Instead, she clumsily kissed Paula on the cheek, and the elderly woman walked away.

People were leaving now, and the room was markedly less crowded.

But the ones who most mattered to her were still here. Blaine, Crystal, Jilly, April, and Gabriela had stood nearby watching her this whole time. Riley felt especially good about the look of pride on Gabriela's face.

She also saw that the girls were smiling, while Blaine's

expression was one of awed admiration. Riley hoped that this whole ceremony didn't intimidate him or scare him off.

Coming toward her were three people whose faces she was especially happy to see. One was her longtime partner, Bill Jeffreys. Standing right beside him was Lucy Vargas, an eager and promising young agent who looked up to Riley as a mentor. Next to her was Jake Crivaro.

Riley was surprised to see Jake. He'd been her partner years ago and had long since retired. He'd come out of retirement just to help her on the Matchbook Killer case, which had haunted him for years.

"Jake!" Riley said. "What are you doing here?"

The short, barrel-chested man let out a raspy laugh.

"Hey, what kind of welcome is that?"

Riley laughed a little too and hugged him.

"You know what I meant," she said.

After all, Jake had headed back to his apartment in Florida as soon as the case was over. She was glad he was back, even if it was a lot sooner than she'd expected.

"I wouldn't have missed this for the world," Jake said.

Riley felt a renewed wave of guilt as she hugged Bill.

"Bill, Jake—this isn't fair."

"What isn't fair?" Bill asked.

"My getting this award. You two did as much work as I did."

Lucy took her turn to hug Riley.

"Sure, it's fair," Lucy said. "Director Milner mentioned them. He gave them credit too."

Bill nodded and said, "And we wouldn't have done anything at all if you weren't so damned stubborn about reopening the case."

Riley smiled. It was true, of course. She'd reopened the case when nobody else had thought it was possible to solve.

Suddenly she felt a new wave of confusion over what had just happened.

She looked around and said to Bill, Jake, and Lucy, "All these people—how did they know about this?"

Lucy said, "Well, it was in the news, of course."

That was true, but it didn't explain things as far as Riley was concerned. Her award had been announced in tiny news items that scarcely anyone would have noticed unless they were looking for it already.

Then Riley noticed a sly grin on Bill's face.

He contacted people! Riley realized.

He may not have reached out to every single person from her past, but he'd put the wheels in motion.

She was startled by the contradictory emotions she felt.

Of course she was grateful to Bill for making sure that this day was nothing short of extraordinary.

But to her surprise, she was angry too.

Without seeming to realize it, Bill had set an emotional ambush for her.

Worst of all, he had made her cry.

But she reminded herself that he'd done it out of friendship and respect.

She said to him, "You and I are going to have a little talk about this later."

Bill smiled and nodded.

"I'm sure we will," he said.

Riley turned toward her waiting family and friends, but she was stopped in her tracks by her boss, Team Chief Brent Meredith. The big man with black, angular features didn't appear to be in a celebratory mood.

He said, "Paige, Jeffreys, Vargas—I need to see you in my office right away."

Without another word, Meredith walked out of the room.

Riley's heart sank as she headed over to Blaine, Gabriela, and the girls to tell them to wait a little while for her.

She remembered that lurking sense of darkness she had felt over dinner yesterday.

It's here, she thought.

Some new evil was about to enter her life.

CHAPTER THREE

As Riley followed Bill and Lucy down the hallway toward Chief Meredith's office, she tried to figure out why she felt so unsettled. She couldn't put her finger on just what was troubling her.

She realized that it was partly a sensation she was long since used to—that familiar heightened apprehension she got whenever she was about to get new orders.

But something else was mixed in with that feeling. It didn't feel like fear or foreboding. She'd been on too many jobs in her career to be unduly worried about what was ahead.

It was something she barely recognized.

Is it relief? Riley wondered.

Yes, maybe that was it.

The ceremony and the reception had felt so bizarre and unreal, stirring up conflicting thoughts and waves of emotions.

Heading to Meredith's office was familiar, comfortable ... and it felt like an escape of sorts.

But an escape into what?

Doubtless into a well-known world of cruelty and evil.

Riley felt a shiver go up her spine.

What did it say about her that she was more comfortable with cruelty and evil than she was with celebration and praise?

She didn't want to dwell on that question, and she tried to shake off that anxious feeling as she walked. But she couldn't quite do it.

It seemed that she was feeling less and less comfortable in her own skin these days.

When Riley, Bill, and Lucy reached Meredith's large office, the chief was standing beside his desk.

Someone else was already there—a young African-American woman with short straight hair and large, intense eyes. She stood up at the sight of Riley and her companions.

Meredith said, "Agents Paige, Jeffreys, and Vargas, I'd like you to meet Special Agent Jennifer Roston."

Riley eyed the woman she'd spoken to on the phone right after solving the Matchbook Killer case. Jennifer Roston wasn't tall, but she looked athletic and completely competent. The expression on her face was that of a woman who was secure in her own abilities.

Roston shook hands with each of them.

"I've heard great things about you," Lucy told her.

"You've reset some records at the Academy," Bill said.

Riley had also heard great things about Agent Roston. She already had an amazing reputation and had received some excellent commendations.

"I'm so honored to meet all of you," Roston said with a sincere smile. Then, looking Riley straight in the eye, she added, "Especially you, Agent Paige. It's great to meet you face to face."

Riley felt flattered. She also felt a slight, nagging concern.

As they all made their way to chairs and sat down, Riley wondered what Roston was doing here today. Was Meredith going to put her on an assignment with Riley and her two colleagues?

The thought made Riley a little uneasy. She, Bill, and Lucy had built an excellent rapport, a seamless working relationship. Wouldn't a new addition to their little team disrupt that, at least temporarily?

Meredith answered her question. "I wanted the three of you to meet Agent Roston because I've got her working on the Shane Hatcher case. The bastard has been at large for way too long. Headquarters has decided to make him a priority. It's time to bring him in, and we need fresh eyes assigned to that specific case."

Riley squirmed a little on the inside.

She already knew that Roston was working on the Hatcher case. In fact, that was what they had discussed over the phone. Roston had asked for access to Quantico's computer files about Shane Hatcher, and Riley had given her that access.

But what was going on right now?

Surely Meredith hadn't brought them all together to work on the Hatcher case. She wasn't sure how much Meredith actually knew about her own connections with Hatcher. She would have been arrested if her boss was fully aware that she had let the escaped killer go because he'd helped her out.

She knew perfectly well Hatcher was probably up in the mountains hiding in the cabin she had inherited from her father— staying there with Riley's full knowledge and approval.

How could she possibly even pretend to be trying to bring him to justice?

Bill asked Roston, "How is it going so far?"

Roston smiled.

"Oh, I'm just getting started—I'm only doing research at this point."

Then looking at Riley again, Roston said, "I appreciate the

access you gave me to all those files."

"I'm glad to help out," Riley said.

Roston squinted a little at Riley, her expression turning vaguely curious.

"Oh, it's been a great help," she said. "You've put a lot of information together. Even so—I thought there'd be more about Hatcher's financial dealings."

Riley suppressed a shudder as she remembered doing something rash right after that phone call.

Before giving Roston access to the Hatcher files, she'd deleted one called "THOUGHTS"—a file that not only contained Riley's personal thoughts and observations about Hatcher, but also financial information that would likely lead to his capture. Or at least make it possible to cut off his resources.

What a crazy thing to do, Riley thought.

But it was done, and it couldn't be undone even if she wanted to change that.

Riley now felt distinctly uneasy under Roston's inquisitive gaze.

"He's an elusive character," Riley said to Roston.

"Yes, so I take it," Roston said.

Roston's eyes stayed locked on Riley's.

Riley's discomfort grew.

Does she already know something? Riley wondered.

Then Meredith said, "That will be all for now, Agent Roston. I've got another matter to discuss with Paige, Jeffreys, and Vargas."

Roston got up and politely took her leave.

As soon as she was gone, Meredith said, "It looks like we've got a new serial case in Southern California. Someone has murdered three drill sergeants at Fort Nash Mowat. They were shot at long range by a skilled marksman. The most recent victim was killed early this morning."

Riley was intrigued, but also a little surprised.

"Isn't this more of a case for the Army Criminal Investigation Command?" she asked, noting the other name for the Army's Criminal Investigation Division. She knew the CID typically investigated felony crimes that were committed within the US Army.

Meredith nodded.

"The CID is already working on it," he said. "There's a CID office in Fort Mowat, so they're up and running. But as you know, Provost Marshal General Boyle is in charge of the CID. He called me a little while ago to ask the FBI to pitch in. This is looking to be an especially nasty case, with all kinds of negative PR repercussions. There's going to be a lot of bad press and political pressure. The sooner it gets solved, the better for everybody."

Riley wondered if this was a good idea. She'd never heard of the FBI and CID working together on a case. She worried that they might wind up stepping on each other's toes, doing more harm than good.

But she didn't raise any objection. It wasn't up to her.

"So when do we head out?" Bill asked.

"ASAP," Meredith said. "Do you have your go-bags here?"

"No," Riley said. "I'm afraid I wasn't expecting this so soon."

"Then as soon as you can pack your things."

Riley felt a sudden burst of alarm.

Jilly's play is tonight! she thought.

If Riley left right now, she'd miss it.

"Chief Meredith—" she began.

"Yes, Agent Paige?"

Riley stopped short. After all, the FBI had just given her an award and a raise. How could she back out of this now?

Orders are orders, she told herself firmly.

There was nothing she could do.

"Nothing," she said.

"OK, then," Meredith said, rising to his feet. "The three of you get moving. And solve this thing fast. Other cases are waiting."

CHAPTER FOUR

Colonel Dutch Adams stood staring out his office window. He had a good view of Fort Nash Mowat from here. He could even see the field where Sergeant Worthing had been killed only this morning.

"Damn it to hell," he muttered under his breath.

Less than two weeks ago Sergeant Rolsky had been killed in exactly the same way.

Then a week ago it was Sergeant Fraser.

And now it was Worthing.

Three good drill sergeants.

Such a stupid waste, he thought.

And so far, the agents from the Criminal Investigation Command hadn't been able to crack the case.

Adams stood wondering ...

How the hell did I wind up in charge of this place?

He'd had a good career overall. He wore his medals proudly—the Legion of Merit, three Bronze Stars, Meritorious Service Medals, a Meritorious Unit Commendation, and a hefty batch of others.

He looked back over his life as he stared out the window.

What were his best memories?

Surely his wartime service in Iraq, both in Operation Desert Storm and Operation Enduring Freedom.

What were his worst memories?

Possibly the academic grind of piling up enough degrees to get a commission.

Or maybe standing in front of classrooms giving lectures.

But even those weren't as bad as running this place.

Driving a desk and filing reports and presiding over meetings—all that was the worst of it as far as he was concerned.

Still, at least he'd had the good times.

His career had come at a personal cost, though—three divorces and seven grown children who scarcely spoke to him anymore. He wasn't even sure how many grandchildren he might have.

That was just how it had to be.

The Army had always been his true family.

But now, after all those years, he was feeling estranged even from the Army.

So how was his parting from military service going to feel in the end—like a happy retirement, or just another ugly divorce?

He breathed a bitter sigh.

If he achieved his final ambition, he'd retire as a brigadier general. Even so, he'd be all alone after he retired. But maybe it was just as well.

Maybe he could just quietly disappear—"fade away" like one of Douglas MacArthur's proverbial "old soldiers."

Or like some wild animal, he thought.

He'd been a hunter all his life, but couldn't remember ever having run across the carcass of a bear or a deer or any other wild animal that had died of natural causes. Other hunters had told him the same thing.

What a mystery that had always been! Where did those wild creatures go to die and rot away?

He wished he knew, so he could go where they did when his time came.

Meanwhile, he had a hankering for a cigarette. It was a hell of a thing, not being able to smoke in his own office.

Just then his desk phone buzzed. It was his secretary in the outer office.

The woman said, "Colonel, I've got the provost marshal general on the line. He wants to talk to you."

Colonel Adams felt a jolt of surprise.

He knew that the provost marshal general was Brigadier General Malcolm Boyle. Adams had never talked to him as far as he could remember.

"What's it about?" Adams asked.

"The murders, I believe," the secretary said.

Adams growled under his breath.

Of course, he thought.

The provost marshal general in Washington was in charge of all Army criminal investigations. Doubtless he'd gotten word that the investigation here was lagging.

"OK, I'll talk to him," Adams said.

He took the call.

Adams immediately disliked the sound of the man's voice. It was too soft for his taste, didn't have the proper bark for a high-ranking officer. Nevertheless, the man vastly outranked Adams. He had to at least feign respect.

Boyle said, "Colonel Adams, I just wanted to give you a heads-up. Three FBI agents from Quantico will be arriving there soon to help with the murder investigation."

Adams felt a surge of irritation. As far as he was concerned, he already had too many agents working on it. But he managed to keep his voice calm.

"Sir, I'm not sure I understand why. We've got our own Criminal Investigation Command office right here at Fort Mowat. They're on the case."

Boyle's voice sounded a little tougher now.

"Adams, you've had three murders in less than three weeks. It sure sounds to me like you folks could use a little help."

Adams's frustration was growing by the second. But he knew he mustn't show it.

He said, "Respectfully, sir, I don't know why you're calling me with this news. Colonel Dana Larson is the CID commander here at Fort Mowat. Why aren't you calling her first?"

Boyle's reply took Adams completely aback.

"Colonel Larson contacted me. She asked for me to call in the BAU to help. So I put in a call and arranged it."

Adams was aghast.

That bitch, he thought.

Colonel Dana Larson seemed to do everything she could to annoy him at every opportunity.

And what was a woman doing in charge of a CID office anyway?

Adams did his best to swallow down his disgust.

"I understand, sir," he said.

Then he ended the call.

Colonel Adams was seething now. He banged his fist against his desk. Didn't he have any say in what went on in this place?

Still, orders were orders, and he had to comply.

But he didn't have to like it—and he didn't have to make anybody comfortable.

He growled aloud.

Never mind people getting killed.

Things were going to get very ugly.

CHAPTER FIVE

As she drove Jilly, April, and Gabriela home, Riley couldn't bring herself to tell them she was heading out right away. She was going to miss Jilly's very first major event, a starring role in a play. Would the girls be able to understand that she was under orders?

Even after they all got home, Riley couldn't tell them.

She burned inside with shame.

Today she'd earned a medal for perseverance, and in the past she'd been honored for valor and bravery. And of course, her daughters had been in the audience watching her receive her medal.

But she sure didn't feel like much of a hero.

The girls headed outside to play in the backyard, and Riley went up to her bedroom and started packing her things. It was a familiar routine. The trick was to pack a small bag with enough necessities to last for a couple of days or a month.

While she was laying things out on her bed, she heard Gabriela's voice.

"Señora Riley—what are you doing?"

Riley turned and saw Gabriela standing in the doorway. The housekeeper was holding a stack of clean linen that she was about to put in the hall closet.

Riley stammered, "Gabriela, I've—I've got to go."

Gabriela's mouth dropped open.

"Go? Where?"

"I've been assigned to a new case. In California."

"Can't you go tomorrow?" Gabriela asked.

Riley swallowed hard.

"Gabriela, the FBI plane is waiting right now. I've got to go."

Gabriela shook her head.

She said, "It is good to fight evil, Señora Riley. But sometimes I think you lose sight of what's good."

Gabriela disappeared into the hallway.

Riley sighed. Since when did Riley pay Gabriela to be her conscience?

But she couldn't complain. It was a job that Gabriela was getting to be all too good at.

Riley stood staring at her unfinished packing.

She shook her head and whispered to herself …

"I can't do this to Jilly. I just can't."

All of her life she had sacrificed her kids for work things.

23

Every time. Not once had she put her kids first.

And that, she realized, was what was wrong with her life. That was a part of her darkness.

She was brave enough to face down a serial killer. But was she brave enough to put work on the back burner and make her kids' lives her number one priority?

At this very moment, Bill and Lucy were getting ready to fly out to California.

They were expecting to meet her at the Quantico airstrip.

Riley sighed miserably.

There was only one way to solve this problem—if she could solve it at all.

She had to try.

She took out her cell phone and dialed Meredith's private number.

At the sound of his gruff voice, she said, "Sir, this is Agent Paige."

"What's the matter?" Meredith asked.

There was a note of concern in his voice. Riley understood why. She had never used this number except in dire circumstances.

She gathered up her nerve and came right to the point.

"Sir, I would like to delay my trip to California. Just for tonight. Agents Jeffreys and Vargas can go ahead of me."

After a pause, Meredith asked, "What's your emergency?"

Riley gulped. Meredith wasn't going to make this easy.

But she was determined not to lie.

In a shaky voice she stammered, "My younger daughter, Jilly—she's in a school play tonight. She's—she's playing the lead."

The silence that fell was deafening.

Did he just hang up on me? Riley wondered.

Then with a growl Meredith said, "Would you repeat that, please? I'm not sure I heard you correctly."

Riley stifled a sigh. She was sure that he'd heard her perfectly well.

"Sir, this play is important to her," she said, growing more nervous by the second. "Jilly's—well, you know I'm trying to adopt her. She's had a hard life, and she's coming out of a very difficult time and her feelings are very delicate and…"

Riley's voice faded off.

"And what?" Meredith asked.

Riley swallowed hard.

"I can't disappoint her, sir. Not this once. Not today."

Another grim silence fell.

Riley was starting to feel more determined.

"Sir, it won't make any difference in the case," she said. "Agents Jeffreys and Vargas will go ahead of me, and you know how capable they are. They can get me up to speed when I do get out there."

"And when would that be?" Meredith asked.

"Tomorrow morning. Early. I'll head for the airport as soon as the play's over. I'll take the first flight I can get."

After another pause, Riley added, "I'll go on my own dime."

She heard Meredith grunt a little.

"You certainly will, Agent Paige," he said.

Riley gasped and caught her breath.

He's giving me permission!

She suddenly realized that she'd barely been breathing during the conversation.

It took a lot of effort not to burst out into uncontrolled gales of gratitude.

She knew Meredith wouldn't like that at all. And the last thing she wanted was for him to change his mind.

So she simply said, "Thank you."

She heard another grunt.

Then Meredith said, "Tell your daughter to break a leg."

He ended the call.

Riley breathed a sigh of relief, then glanced up and saw that Gabriela was standing in the doorway again, smiling.

She'd obviously been listening to the whole call.

"I think you are growing up, Señora Riley," Gabriela said.

*

Sitting in the audience with April and Gabriela, Riley was thoroughly enjoying the school play. She'd forgotten how charming events like this could be.

The middle-school kids were all dressed in makeshift costumes. They had painted flat scenery to look like scenes from the story of Demeter and Persephone—fields full of flowers, a volcano in Sicily, the dank caverns of the Underworld, and other mythical places.

And Jilly's acting was simply wonderful!

She played Persephone, the young daughter of grain goddess

25

Demeter. Riley found herself remembering the familiar story as it unfolded.

Persephone was outside picking flowers one day when Hades, the god of the Underworld, rode by in his chariot and snatched her away. He took her down into the Underworld to be his queen. When Demeter realized what had happened to her daughter, she wailed with sorrow.

Riley felt chills at how convincingly the girl playing Demeter expressed her grief.

At that point, the story started getting to Riley in a way she hadn't expected.

Persephone's story seemed eerily like Jilly's own. After all, it was the story of a girl who lost part of her childhood to forces much greater than herself.

Riley felt herself tearing up.

She knew the rest of the story very well. Persephone would regain her freedom, but only for half of every year. Whenever Persephone was gone, Demeter let the earth grow cold and dead. Whenever she came back, she brought the earth back to life, and springtime came again.

And that was how seasons had come into the world.

Riley squeezed April's hand and whispered, "Here comes the sad part."

Riley was surprised to hear April giggle.

"Not so sad," April whispered back. "Jilly told me they changed the story a little. Just watch."

Riley sat and paid close attention.

Fully in character as Persephone, Jilly cracked Hades over the head with a Grecian urn—actually a pillow in disguise. Then she stormed out of the Underworld and back to her overjoyed mother.

The boy playing Hades threw an enormous tantrum and brought winter to the world. He and Demeter then fought a tug-of-war, changing the seasons from winter to spring and back again, and so on again and again for the rest of time.

Riley was delighted.

When the play ended, Riley led the way backstage to congratulate Jilly. On their way, she ran into the teacher who had directed the play.

"I love what you did with the story!" Riley told the teacher. "It was so refreshing to see Persephone turned from a helpless victim to an independent heroine."

The teacher smiled broadly.

"Don't thank me," she said. "It was Jilly's idea."

Riley rushed over to Jilly and gave her a big hug.

"I'm so proud of you!" Riley said.

"Thanks, Mom," Jilly said, smiling happily.

Mom.

The word echoed through Riley. It meant more to her than she could say.

*

Later that night when they were all at home, Riley finally had to tell the girls she was leaving. She poked her head in Jilly's door.

Jilly was fast asleep, exhausted from her great success. Riley loved the look of contentment on her face.

Then Riley went to April's bedroom and looked in on her. April was sitting up in bed reading a book.

April looked up at her mother.

"Hey, Mom," she said. "What's up?"

Riley stepped quietly into the room.

She said, "This is going to seem weird but … I've got to leave right now. I've been assigned to a case in California."

April smiled.

She said, "Jilly and I both pretty much guessed that was what your meeting back in Quantico was all about. And then we saw that go-bag on your bed. We actually thought you were going to leave before her play. You usually don't pack it unless you're out the door."

She stared at Riley, her smile widening.

"But then you stayed," she added. "I know you delayed the trip, at least for the play. Do you know how much that meant to us?"

Riley felt herself tear up. She leaned forward and the two of them embraced.

"So it's OK if I go, then?" Riley asked.

"Sure, it's OK. Jilly told me she hoped you'd catch some bad guys. She's really proud of what you do, Mom. So am I."

Riley felt moved beyond words. Both of her daughters were growing up so fast. And they were becoming really amazing young women.

She kissed April on the forehead.

"I love you, dear," she said.

"I love you too," April said.

Riley wagged her finger at April.

"Now what are you doing up?" she said. "Turn off that light and go to sleep. It's a school night."

April giggled and turned off the light. Riley went to her own bedroom to get her bag.

It was after midnight and she had to drive to DC in time for a commercial flight.

It was going to be a long night.

CHAPTER SIX

The wolf lay on his stomach on the rough desert soil.

That's how the man thought of himself—a beast stalking his next kill.

He had an excellent view of Fort Nash Mowat from this high place, and the night air was pleasant and cool. He peered at tonight's prey through the night-vision scope on his rifle.

He thought back to his hated victims.

Three weeks ago it had been Rolsky.

Then came Fraser.

Then came Worthing.

He'd taken them out with great finesse, with shots to the head so clean they surely hadn't even known a bullet had hit them.

Tonight, it would be Barton.

The wolf watched Barton walking along an unlit path. Although the image through the night scope was grainy and monotone, the target was sufficiently visible for his purposes.

But he wouldn't shoot tonight's prey—not yet.

He wasn't far enough away. Someone nearby might be able to figure out his location, even though he had attached a flash hider to his M110 sniper rifle. He wasn't going to make the amateurish mistake of underestimating the soldiers on this base.

Following Barton through his scope, the wolf enjoyed the feel of the M110 in his hands. These days the Army was transitioning toward using the Heckler & Koch G28 as a standard sniper rifle. While the wolf knew the G28 was lighter and more compact, he still preferred the M110. It was more accurate, even if it was longer and harder to conceal.

He had twenty rounds in the magazine, but he only intended to use one when the time came to fire.

He was going to take out Barton with one shot, or not at all.

He could feel the energy of the pack, as though they were watching him, giving him their support.

He watched as Barton finally arrived at his destination—one of the base's outdoor tennis courts. Several other players greeted him as he stepped onto the court and unpacked his tennis gear.

Now that Barton was in the brightly lit area, the wolf had no further need of the night scope. He detached it to use the day optical sight. Then he took aim directly at Barton's head. The image was no longer grainy, but crystal clear and in full, vivid color.

Barton was about three hundred feet away now.

At that range, the wolf could depend upon the rifle's precision down to an inch.

It was up to him to stay within that inch.

And he knew that he would.

Just a slight squeeze of the trigger, he thought.

That was all that was needed now.

The wolf basked in that mysterious, suspended moment.

There was something almost religious about those seconds before pulling the trigger, when he *waited* for himself to will the shot, waited for himself to *decide* to squeeze with his finger. During that moment, life and death seemed strangely out of his hands. The irrevocable move would happen in the fullness of an instant.

It would be his decision—and yet not his decision at all.

Whose decision was it, then?

He fancied that there was an animal, a true wolf, lurking inside him, a remorseless creature that took actual command over that fatal moment and movement.

That animal was both his friend and his enemy. And he loved it with a strange love that he could only feel toward a mortal enemy. That inner animal was what called out the best in him, kept him truly up to the mark.

The wolf lay waiting for that animal to strike.

But the animal didn't.

The wolf didn't pull the trigger.

He wondered why.

Something seems wrong, he thought.

It quickly occurred to him what it was.

The view of the target in the glaring tennis court floodlights through the regular scope was simply too clear.

It would take too little effort.

There was no challenge.

It wouldn't be worthy of a true wolf.

Also, it was too soon after the last killing. The others had been spaced out to stir up anxiety and uncertainty among the men he loathed. Shooting Barton now would disrupt the psychological rhythmic impact of his work.

He smiled a little at the realization. He got to his feet with his gun and started to walk back the way he'd come.

He felt right about leaving his prey undisturbed for now.

No one knew when he'd strike next.

Not even he himself.

CHAPTER SEVEN

It was still dark when Riley's commercial flight took off. But even with the time change, she knew it would be daylight in San Diego when she got there. She was going to be in the air for more than five hours and she was already feeling quite tired. She had to be fully functional tomorrow morning when she joined Bill and Lucy for the investigation. There would be serious work to do, and she needed to be ready for it.

I'd better get some sleep, Riley thought. The woman seated next to her already seemed to be dozing.

Riley tilted her chair back and closed her eyes. But instead of falling asleep, she found herself remembering Jilly's play.

She smiled as she recalled how Jilly's Persephone had bonked Hades over the head and escaped the Underworld to live life on her own terms.

Remembering how she had first found Jilly made Riley's heart ache. It had been night in a truck stop parking lot in Phoenix. Jilly had run away from a miserable home life with an abusive father and climbed into the cab of a parked truck. She had fully intended to sell her body to its driver whenever he came back.

Riley shuddered.

What would have become of Jilly if she hadn't stumbled across her that night?

Friends and colleagues had often told Riley what a good thing she'd done by bringing Jilly into her life.

So why didn't she feel better about it? Instead, she felt pangs of despair.

After all, there were countless Jillys in the world, and very few of them were ever rescued from terrible lives.

Riley couldn't help all of them, any more than she could rid the world of all vicious killers.

It's all so futile, she thought. *Everything I do.*

She opened her eyes and looked out the window. The jet had left the lights of DC behind, and outside there was nothing but impenetrable darkness.

As she peered into the black night, she thought about her meeting that day with Bill, Lucy, and Meredith, and what little she knew about the upcoming case. Meredith had said that the three victims were shot from a long distance by a skilled marksman.

What did that tell her about the killer?

That killing was a sport to him?

Or that he was on some kind of sinister mission?

One thing seemed certain—the killer knew what he was doing, and he was good at it.

The case was definitely going to be a challenge.

Meanwhile, Riley's eyelids were feeling heavy.

Maybe I can get some sleep, she thought. Again she leaned her head back and closed her eyes.

*

Riley was staring at what looked like thousands of Rileys, all of them standing at odd angles toward each other, becoming smaller and finally vanishing into the distance.

She turned a little, and so did all the other Rileys.

She lifted her arm, and the others did as well.

Then she reached out, and her hand came in contact with a glass surface.

I'm in a hall of mirrors, *Riley realized.*

But how had she gotten here? And how was she going to get out?

She heard a voice call out ...

"Riley!"

It was a woman's voice, and somehow familiar to her.

"I'm here!" Riley called back. "Where are you?"

"I'm here too."

Suddenly, Riley saw her.

She was standing directly in front of her, in the midst of the multitude of reflections.

She was a slight, attractive young woman, wearing a dress that looked many decades out of style.

Riley immediately knew who it was.

"Mommy!" she said in a stunned whisper.

She was surprised to hear that her own voice was now that of a little girl.

"What are you doing here?" Riley asked.

"I just came to say goodbye," Mommy said with a smile.

Riley struggled to understand what was happening.

Then she remembered ...

Mommy had been shot to death right before Riley's eyes in a candy store when Riley was only six years old.

But here Mommy was, looking exactly the same as when Riley

32

had last seen her alive.

"Where are you going, Mommy?" Riley asked. "Why do you have to go?"

Mommy smiled and touched the glass that stood between them.

"I'm at peace now, thanks to you. I can move on now."

Little by little, Riley started to understand.

Not long ago, she had tracked down her mother's killer.

He was now a pathetic old vagrant living under a bridge.

Riley had left him there, realizing that his life had been punishment enough for his terrible crime.

Riley reached out and touched the glass that separated her from Mommy's hand.

"But you can't go, Mommy," she said. "I'm just a little girl."

"Oh, no, you're not," Mommy said, her face radiant and blissful. "Just look at yourself."

Riley looked at her own reflection in the mirror next to Mommy.

It was true.

Riley was a grown woman now.

It seemed strange to realize that she was now much older than her mother had lived to be.

But Riley also looked tired and sad in comparison with her youthful mother.

She'll never grow any older, Riley thought.

The same was not true for Riley.

And she knew that her world was full of trials and challenges still to be endured.

Was she ever going to get any rest from it? Would she ever be at peace for the rest of her life?

She found herself envying her mother's timeless, eternally peaceful joy.

Then her mother turned and walked away, disappearing into the infinite tangle of reflections of Riley.

Suddenly there came a terrible crash, and all the mirrors shattered.

Riley was standing in near-total darkness, up to her ankles in broken glass.

She gently pulled her feet out one by one, then tried to make her way through the wreckage.

"Watch your step," said another familiar voice.

Riley turned and saw a rugged old man with a lined, hard, and weathered face.

Riley gasped.

"Daddy!" she said.

Her father smirked at her surprise.

"You hoped I was dead, didn't you?" he said. "Sorry to disappoint you."

Riley opened her mouth to contradict him.

But then she realized he was right. She hadn't grieved when he had died last October.

And she certainly didn't want him back in her life.

After all, he'd scarcely ever said a kind word to her in all his days.

"Where have you been?" Riley asked.

"Where I've been all along," her father said.

The scene began to change from a vast expanse of broken glass to become the outside of her father's cabin in the woods.

He was now standing on the front stoop.

"You might need my help on this case," he said. "It sounds like your killer's a soldier. I know a lot about soldiers. And I know a lot about killing."

It was true. Her father had been a captain in Vietnam. She had no idea how many men he'd killed in the line of duty.

But the last thing she wanted was his help.

"It's time for you to go," Riley said.

Her father's smirk twisted into a sneer.

"Oh, no," he said. "I'm just settling in."

His face and body changed shape. In a matter of moments, he was younger, stronger, dark-skinned, even more menacing than before.

He was now Shane Hatcher.

The transformation struck Riley with terror.

Her father had always been a cruel presence in her life.

But she was coming to dread Hatcher even more.

Much more than her father ever did, Hatcher had some kind of manipulative power over her.

He could make her do things that she'd never imagined she'd do.

"Go away," Riley said.

"Oh, no," Hatcher said. "We've got a deal."

Riley shuddered.

We've got a deal, all right, *she thought.*

Hatcher had helped her find her mother's killer. In return, she allowed him to live in her father's old cabin.

Besides, she knew she owed him. He'd helped her solve cases—but he'd done much more.

He'd even saved her daughter's life along with that of her ex-husband.

Riley opened her mouth to speak, to protest.

But no words came out.

Instead, it was Hatcher who spoke.

"We're joined at the brain, Riley Paige."

Riley was awakened by a sharp jolt.

The plane had landed in the San Diego International Airport.

The morning sun was rising beyond the runway.

The pilot spoke over the intercom, announcing their arrival and apologizing for the bumpy landing.

The other passengers were gathering their belongings and preparing to leave.

As Riley groggily got up and pulled down her bag from the overhead luggage compartment, she remembered her disturbing dream.

Riley was hardly superstitious—but even so she couldn't help but wonder …

Were the dream and the rough landing somehow portents of things to come?

CHAPTER EIGHT

It was a bright, clear morning by the time Riley got into her rental car and drove out of the airport. The weather really was wonderful, with a temperature in the comfortable sixties. She realized that it would make most people think of enjoying the beach or at least lying beside a pool somewhere.

But Riley felt a lurking apprehension.

She wondered wistfully if she could ever come to California just to enjoy the weather—or go to any other place to relax.

It seemed that evil awaited her wherever she went.

The story of my life, she thought.

She knew she owed it to herself and her family to break out of this pattern—to take some time off and take the girls somewhere just for the sheer joy of it.

But when was that ever going to happen?

She let out a sad, tired sigh.

Maybe never, she thought.

She hadn't gotten much sleep on the plane, and she was feeling the jet lag from the three-hour time difference between here and Virginia.

Nevertheless, she was eager to get started on this new case.

As she headed north on the San Diego Freeway, she passed modern buildings punctuated by palm trees and other greenery. Soon she was out of the city, but the traffic on the multi-laned freeway didn't diminish. The fast-moving procession of closely crowded vehicles wound among rough hills where the early sunlight accentuated a steep, brush landscape.

The scenery notwithstanding, Southern California struck her as less easygoing than she had expected. Like her, everyone in the crush of cars seemed to be in a hurry to get somewhere important.

She took an exit marked "Fort Nash Mowat." After a few minutes, she pulled up to the camp gate, showed her badge, and was allowed to enter.

She had messaged ahead to let Bill and Lucy know she was on her way, so they were waiting by a car. Bill introduced the uniformed woman standing with them as Colonel Dana Larson, the commander of the Fort Mowat CID office.

Riley was instantly impressed by Larson. She was a strong, sturdy woman with intense dark eyes. Her handshake immediately conveyed to Riley a feeling of confidence and professionalism.

36

"I'm pleased to meet you, Agent Paige," Col. Larson said in a crisp, vigorous voice. "Your reputation precedes you."

Riley's eyes widened.

"I'm surprised," she said.

Larson chuckled a little.

"Don't be," she said. "I'm in law enforcement too, and I keep up with everything the BAU does. We're honored to have you here at Fort Mowat."

Riley felt herself blush a little as she thanked Col. Larson.

Larson called to a nearby soldier, who stepped briskly toward her and saluted.

She said, "Corporal Salerno, I want you to drive Agent Paige's car back to the rental station at the airport. She won't be needing it here."

"Yes ma'am," the corporal said, "right away." He got into Riley's car and drove out of the base.

Riley, Bill, and Lucy got into the other car.

As Col. Larson drove, Riley asked, "What have I missed so far?"

"Not much," Bill said. "Col. Larson met us here last night and showed us to our quarters."

"We still haven't met the CO of the base," Lucy added.

Col. Larson told them, "We're on our way to meet Col. Dutch Adams right now."

Then with a chuckle, she added, "Don't expect a warm welcome. Agents Paige and Vargas, that means you especially."

Riley wasn't sure what Larson meant. Was Col. Adams going to be unhappy that the BAU was sending two women? Riley couldn't imagine why. Everywhere Riley looked, she saw men and women in uniform mixing freely together. And with Col. Larson on the base, surely Adams was used to dealing with a woman in authority.

Col. Larson parked in front of a clean, modern administrative building and led the agents inside. As they approached, three young men jumped to attention and saluted Col. Larson. Riley saw that their CID jackets were similar to the ones worn by FBI field agents.

Col. Larson introduced the three men as Sergeant Matthews and his team members, Special Agents Goodwin and Shores. Then they all entered a conference room, where they were awaited by Col. Dutch Adams himself.

Matthews and his agents saluted Adams, but Col. Larson did not. Riley realized that it was because she was Adams's equal in rank. She soon found the tension between the two colonels to be palpable, almost painful.

And as predicted, Adams did look distinctly displeased to see Riley and Lucy.

Now Riley was getting the picture.

Col. Dutch Adams was an old-school career officer who wasn't at all used to having men and women serve together. And judging from his age, Riley felt pretty sure that he wasn't ever going to get used to it. He would probably retire with his prejudices intact.

She was sure that Adams must especially resent the presence of Col. Larson on his base—a female officer over whom he had no authority.

As the group sat down, Riley felt an eerie chill of familiarity as she studied Adams's face. It was broad and long, severely sculpted like the faces of many other military officers she'd known during her life—including her father.

In fact, Riley found Col. Adams's resemblance to her father to be downright disturbing.

He spoke to Riley and her colleagues in an excessively official tone.

"Welcome to Fort Nash Mowat. This base has been in operation since 1942. It extends for seventy-five thousand acres, has fifteen hundred buildings, and three hundred fifty miles of roads. You'll find about sixty thousand people here on any given day. I'm proud to call it the finest Army training base in the country."

At that point, Col. Adams seemed to be trying to suppress a sneer. He wasn't quite succeeding.

He added, "And for that reason, I ask that you not make nuisances of yourselves as long as you're here. This place runs like a finely tuned machine. Outsiders have an unfortunate tendency to gum up the works. If you do so, I promise that there will be hell to pay. Do I make myself clear?"

He was making eye contact with Riley, obviously trying to intimidate her.

She heard Bill and Lucy say, "Yes, sir."

But she said nothing.

He's not my *CO,* she thought.

She simply held his gaze and nodded.

He then shifted his eyes to the others in the room. He spoke again with cold anger in his voice.

"Three good men are dead. The situation at Fort Mowat is unacceptable. Fix it. Immediately. Preferably sooner."

He paused for a moment. Then he said, "There will be a funeral for Sergeant Clifford Worthing at eleven hundred hours. I expect all of you to be in attendance."

Without another word, he got up from his chair. The CID agents stood and saluted, and Col. Adams left the room.

Riley was dumbfounded. Hadn't they all come here to discuss the case and what to do next?

Obviously noticing Riley's surprise, Col. Larson grinned at her.

"He's not normally so talkative," she said. "Maybe he likes you."

Everybody laughed at her bit of sarcasm.

Riley knew that a little humor was a good thing right now.

Things were going to get plenty grim soon enough.

CHAPTER NINE

The laughter subsided, and Larson was still looking at Riley, Bill, and Lucy. Her expression was penetrating and powerful, as if she were assessing them somehow. Riley wondered if the CID commander was about to make some dire announcement.

Instead, Larson asked, "Have any of you had breakfast?"

They all said no.

"Well, that situation is unacceptable," Larson said with a chuckle. "Let's fix it before you waste away. Come with me, and I'll show you some Fort Mowat hospitality."

Larson then left her team behind and proceeded to guide the three FBI agents into the officers' club. Riley could see right away that the colonel wasn't kidding about hospitality. The dining facility was like an upscale restaurant, and Larson wouldn't let them pay for their own meals.

Over a delicious breakfast, they discussed the case. Riley realized that she had definitely needed coffee. The meal was welcome too.

Col. Larson gave them her take on the case. "The most salient features of these murders are the method of killing and the ranks of the victims. Rolsky, Fraser, and Worthing were all drill sergeants. They were all shot from a long distance with a high-powered rifle. And the victims were all shot at night."

Bill asked, "What else did they have in common?"

"Not much. Two were white and one was black, so it isn't a racial issue. They were in command of separate units, so they had no recruits in common."

Riley added, "You've probably already pulled the files of soldiers reprimanded for disciplinary or psychological issues. AWOLs? Dishonorable discharges?"

"We have," Larson replied. "It's a very long list and we have been through it. But I'll send it to you and you can see what you think."

"I'd like to talk to the men in each unit."

Larson nodded. "Of course. You can catch some of them after the funeral today, and I'll set up any additional meetings that you want."

Riley noticed that Lucy was taking notes. She nodded to the young agent to ask her own questions.

Lucy asked, "What caliber were the bullets?"

"NATO-caliber," Col. Larson said. "7.62 millimeter."

Lucy looked at Col. Larson with interest. She said, "It sounds like the weapon might be an M110 sniper rifle. Or possibly a Heckler and Koch G28."

Col. Larson smiled a little, obviously impressed by Lucy's knowledge.

"Due to the range, we're guessing the M110," Larson said. "The bullets all seem to have been from the same weapon."

Riley was pleased to see that Lucy was so fully engaged. Riley liked to think of Lucy as her protégé, and she knew that Lucy thought of her as a mentor.

She's learning fast, Riley thought proudly.

Riley glanced at Bill. She could tell by his expression that he was pleased with Lucy as well.

Riley had questions of her own, but she decided not to interrupt.

Lucy said to Larson, "You're guessing someone with military training, I assume. A soldier on the base?"

"Possibly," Larson said. "Or an ex-soldier. Someone with excellent training, at any rate. Not just an average shooter."

Lucy drummed her pencil eraser against the table.

She suggested, "Someone who has it in for authority figures? Drill sergeants especially?"

Larson scratched her chin thoughtfully.

"I've been considering it," she said.

Lucy said, "I'm sure you're also considering Islamic terrorism."

Larson nodded.

"These days, that simply has to be our default theory."

"A lone wolf?" Lucy asked.

"Maybe," Larson said. "But it could be that he's acting on behalf of some group—either a small cell near here, or something international, like ISIS or Al-Qaeda."

Lucy thought for a moment.

"How many Muslim recruits have you currently got at Fort Mowat?" Lucy asked.

"Right now, three hundred forty-three. That's obviously a very small percentage of our recruits. But we've got to be careful about profiling. In general, our Muslim recruits have been exceptionally dedicated. We've never had any problems with extremism—if that's what this is."

Larson looked at Riley and Bill and smiled.

"But you two are being very quiet. How would you like to proceed?"

Riley glanced at Bill. As usual, she could tell that he was thinking the same thing as she was.

"Let's go have a look at the murder scenes," Bill said.

*

A few minutes later, Col. Larson was driving Riley, Bill, and Lucy through Fort Mowat.

"Which of the locations do you want to see first?" Larson asked.

"Let's see them in the order they happened," Riley said.

As Larson drove, Riley noticed soldiers drilling, running obstacle courses, and practicing marksmanship with various weapons. She could see that it was rigorous, demanding work.

Riley asked Larson, "How far along in their training is this round of recruits?"

"The second phase—the White Phase," Larson said. "We've got three phases—red, white, and blue. The first two, red and white, are three weeks each, and these recruits are in their fifth week overall. Their last four weeks will be the Blue Phase. That's about as tough as tough can get. That's when the recruits find out if they've got what it takes to be an Army soldier."

Riley heard a note of pride in Larson's voice—the same pride she'd often heard in her father's voice when he talked about his military service.

She loves what she does, Riley thought.

She also had no doubt that Col. Larson was excellent at what she did.

Larson parked near a footpath that led through the camp. They got out of the car, and Larson led them to a spot on the path. It was in an open area, free of trees that might block a view.

"Sergeant Rolsky was killed right here," Larson said. "Nobody saw or heard it happen. We couldn't tell from the wound or the position of his body where the shot came from—except that it must have been a considerable distance."

Riley looked all around her, studying the scene.

"What time was Rolsky killed?" she asked.

"At about twenty-two hundred hours," Larson said.

Riley mentally converted that to civilian time—10:00 p.m.

She imagined what this place would look like at that time of night. There were a couple of lamps standing within thirty feet of the spot. Even so, the light here would have been pretty dim. The shooter must have used a night scope.

She turned slowly around, trying to guess where the shot came from.

There were buildings to the south and north. It was unlikely a sniper would have the opportunity to fire from within any of those places.

To the west, she could see across camp to the Pacific Ocean, faint in a hazy distance.

There were rough hills to the east.

Riley pointed to the hills and said, "My guess is that the shooter positioned himself somewhere up there."

"That's a good guess," Larson said, pointing to another spot on the ground. "We found the bullet right here, so that indicates the shot must have come from somewhere up in those hills. Judging from the wound, the shot was fired from between two hundred fifty and three hundred feet. We've scoured the area, but he didn't leave any evidence behind."

Riley thought for a moment.

Then she asked Larson, "Is hunting allowed on Fort Mowat grounds?"

"In season, with permits," Larson replied. "Right now it's wild turkey season. Shooting crows by day is also allowed."

Of course, Riley knew that these deaths were anything but hunting accidents. As the daughter of a man who had been both a Marine and a hunter, she knew that no one would use a sniper rifle to kill crows and turkeys and such. A shotgun was the more likely hunting weapon of choice around Fort Mowat at this time of year.

She asked Larson to take them to the next location. The colonel drove them up into some low hills at the edge of a hiking trail. When they all got out of their vehicle again, Larson pointed to the spot on a trail that wound its way uphill.

"Sergeant Fraser was killed right here," she said. "He was taking an after-hours hike. The shot seems to have been about the same distance as before. Again, no one heard or saw it happen. But our best guess is that he was killed at about twenty-three hundred hours."

Eleven o'clock at night, Riley thought.

Pointing to another spot, Larson added, "We found the bullet over here."

Riley then looked in the opposite direction, toward where the shooter must have been. She saw more scrubby hills—and countless places where a shooter might have hidden. She was sure that Larson and her team had combed the area thoroughly.

Finally they drove down to the area where the recruits' living quarters were. Larson took them behind one of the barracks. The first thing Riley saw was an enormous dark splotch on the wall near the back door.

Larson said, "This is where Sergeant Worthing was killed. He seems to have come out here for a cigarette before his platoon's morning formation. The shot was so clean that the cigarette never fell from his lips."

Riley's interest quickened. This scene was different from the others—and much more informative. She examined the blotch and the smear that spread down below it.

She said, "It looks like he was leaning against the wall when the bullet hit him. You must have been able to get a much better idea of the bullet's trajectory than you could for the others."

"Much better," Larson agreed. "But not the precise location."

Larson pointed across the field behind the barracks to where hills began to rise.

"The shooter must have positioned himself somewhere between those two valley oaks," she said. "But he cleaned up very carefully afterward. We couldn't find a trace of him in any likely location."

Riley saw that the distance between the small trees was about twenty feet. Larson and her team had done good work narrowing the area down that much.

"What kind of weather was it?" Riley asked.

"Very clear," Larson said. "There was a three-quarter moon out almost until dawn."

Riley felt a tingle down her back. It was a familiar feeling that she got when she was about to really connect with a crime scene.

"I'd like to go out and have a look for myself," she said.

"Certainly," Larson said. "I'll take you there."

Riley didn't know how to tell her that she wanted to go by herself.

Fortunately, Bill spoke up for her.

"Let's let Agent Paige go alone. It's kind of her thing."

Larson nodded appreciatively

Riley strode out across the field. With every step, that tingling grew stronger.

Finally, she found herself between the two trees. She could see

44

why Larson's team hadn't been able to find the exact spot. The ground was highly irregular with lots of smaller bushes. Just in that area, there were at least a half dozen excellent places to squat or lie and fire a clean shot toward the barracks.

Riley began to walk back and forth between the trees. She knew that she wasn't looking for anything that the shooter might have left behind—not even footprints. Larson and her team wouldn't have missed anything like that.

She took some slow breaths and imagined herself here in the very early hours in the morning. The stars were just starting to disappear, and the moon still cast shadows all around.

The feeling grew stronger by the second—a sense of the killer's presence.

Riley took a few more deep breaths and prepared to enter the killer's mind.

CHAPTER TEN

Riley began to imagine the killer. What had he felt, thought, and observed when he came here looking for the perfect spot to shoot from? She wanted to become the killer, as nearly as she could, in order to track him down. And she could do that. It was her gift.

First, she knew, he had to find that spot.

She searched about, just as he must have searched.

As she moved around, she felt a mysterious, almost magnetic pull.

She was drawn to a red willow bush. To one side of the bush, there was a space between its branches and the ground. There was a slightly hollow place in the ground at that very spot.

Riley stooped down and looked carefully at the ground.

The soil in that hollow place was neat and smooth.

Too neat, Riley thought. *Too smooth.*

The rest of the soil in this area was rougher, more irregular.

Riley smiled.

The killer had gone to such lengths to tidy up after himself that he'd betrayed his exact position.

Imagining the scene by moonlight, Riley gazed down the slope and across the field toward the back of the barracks.

She pictured what the killer saw from this place—the distant figure of Sergeant Worthing stepping out of the back door.

Riley felt a smile form on the killer's face.

She could hear him think …

"Right on schedule!"

And just as the killer had expected, the sergeant lit a cigarette and leaned against the wall.

It was time to act—and it had to be quick.

The sky was starting to brighten where the sun would soon rise.

As the killer must have done, Riley stretched out prone in the hollow place on the ground. Yes, it was the perfect place, the perfect shape for wielding a high-powered weapon.

But how did the weapon feel in the killer's hands?

Riley had never actually handled an M110 sniper rifle. But some years ago she had trained a little with the weapon's predecessor, the M24. Fully loaded and assembled, the M24 had weighed about sixteen pounds, and Riley had read that the M110 was scarcely any lighter.

But the night scope added to that weight, making it a little top heavy.

Riley imagined the view through the night scope. The image of Sergeant Worthing was mottled and grainy.

That wasn't a problem for true marksmanship. For a skilled sniper, the shot would be easy. Even so, Riley sensed that the killer felt vaguely unsatisfied.

What was it that bothered him?

What was he thinking?

Then his thought came to her ...

"I wish I could see the look on his face."

Riley felt a jolt of understanding.

This killing was deeply personal—an act of hatred, or at the very least contempt.

But he wasn't going to put it off on account of his dissatisfaction. He could do this just fine without seeing his prey's expression.

She felt the resistance from the trigger as she pulled it, then the sharp recoil from the rifle as the bullet was fired.

The noise of the shot wasn't very loud. The sound suppressor and the flash hider had muffled the noise and the burst of flame.

Even so, did the killer worry that someone had heard it?

Only for a moment, Riley felt sure. He had shot two other men from much the same distance, and no one seemed to have heard the shots. Or if they had heard them, no one had thought them extraordinary.

But what did the killer do now that he'd fired the shot?

He kept looking through the scope, Riley realized.

He followed the body in its slouch against the wall toward an awkward squat.

And again the killer thought ...

"I wish I could see the look on his face."

As the killer must have done, Riley got to her feet. She imagined the killer taking a wide brush to the soil to smooth it over, then leaving the way he'd come.

Riley breathed a sigh of satisfaction. Her attempt to link with the killer's mind had revealed more than she'd hoped for.

Or at least she had a hunch that it had.

She remembered something that Col. Larson had said earlier about whether the killings were acts of Islamic terrorism ...

"These days, that simply has to be our default theory."

Riley's gut told her that that theory was probably wrong. But she wasn't ready to say so to her colleagues. Under the circumstances, she knew that Larson was right to pursue the possibility of terrorism. It was simply good procedure. Meanwhile, it was best for Riley to keep her hunch to herself—at least until she could back it up with evidence.

Riley looked at her watch. She realized that she and the others were due at a funeral.

CHAPTER ELEVEN

As Riley watched the six uniformed men carry Sergeant Worthing's flag-draped casket to the gravesite, she admired the solemn cadence and precision of their actions.

She was also struck by an eerie contrast between this ceremony and his actual death. The murder of Sergeant Worthing had been abrupt and brutal.

His funeral was elegance itself.

The military cemetery was in a lovely place, high on a hill in a remote part of Fort Nash Mowat. Riley could see the Pacific Ocean in the distance.

Riley, Lucy, and Bill were standing off to one side of the ceremony. She could see Sergeant Worthing's widow and family seated on folding chairs beside the grave. She could watch the fifty uniformed young men and women in Worthing's training platoon standing stiffly at attention.

She also spotted civilians of an unwelcome sort nearby—a small group of reporters and photographers crowded behind a rope barrier.

She stifled a groan of discouragement.

After three murders, there was no longer any way to keep the press away from Fort Mowat. The publicity was certainly going to add to the pressure of solving the case. Riley just hoped that the journalists wouldn't make too much of a nuisance of themselves.

Probably too much to hope for, she thought.

Once the coffin was in place over the grave, the chaplain began to speak.

"We commend to the almighty God our brother, Sergeant Clifford Jay Worthing, and we commit his body to the ground, earth to earth, ashes to ashes, dust to dust ..."

Riley was surprised to feel herself choke up at the chaplain's words.

What was it about this funeral that was getting to her?

Then she realized ...

Daddy.

As a Marine captain, her father had been eligible for a funeral with honors like this one.

Had he gotten this kind of funeral? Riley didn't even know. Not only had she refused to go to his funeral, she'd taken no part in its planning. She'd left all that to her estranged sister, Wendy.

She'd never grieved over her father's death. Nevertheless, she felt sad at the thought that he might not have been buried with full military honors. But who would have gone to the funeral, aside from Wendy? Riley's father had died with no real friends as far as she knew. And Riley and Wendy were all he had left of family.

Riley remembered something that one of her father's former buddies recently told her.

"Riley, your daddy was a good man. But he was a hard man too. He couldn't help it, 'Nam made him that way."

Tears welled up in Riley's eyes.

He'd been a terrible father. But he'd been a good soldier. He'd given everything he had to the Marines—including his humanity, his capacity to love.

As the honor guard lifted the flag and held it taut above the casket, Riley thought …

He deserved this.

Riley thought she should have made sure her father had his full honors funeral, even if no one had been there to witness it except Wendy.

She was jolted out of her sad reverie by the firing of guns. A seven-person squad fired three volleys into the still air. Then the quiet was broken again by the mournful sound of a bugler playing taps.

The honor guard ceremoniously folded the flag, and an officer presented it to Sergeant Worthing's widow. The officer whispered something to her—doubtless some word of support of support or solace.

Then the officer gave the family a slow-motion salute, and the service was over.

*

Before Sergeant Worthing's platoon could leave the cemetery, Col. Dana Larson called them together. She introduced them to Riley, Bill, and Lucy and told them that they were here to investigate the three recent murders.

Riley scanned their faces, looking for some telltale sign of emotion. She detected nothing—certainly not grief.

She guessed that many of the recruits had hated Sergeant Worthing's guts and weren't sorry that he was gone.

Riley stepped forward and spoke to the gathered recruits.

"My colleagues and I are very sorry for your loss. We don't

want to disturb you right now, just after the ceremony. But if any of you has any information that might help us, we hope that you'll talk to us."

Then the platoon was allowed to disperse. Riley, Bill, and Lucy broke up and wandered among them, hoping to draw somebody out. Pretty soon two recruits, a young man and a young woman, approached Riley. They introduced themselves as Privates Elena Ludekens and Maxwell Wilber.

They seemed to be uneasy and reluctant. Riley thought she understood why. Informing on a fellow recruit couldn't be easy.

Riley said, "Look, I get the feeling that Worthing wasn't the most popular drill sergeant at Fort Mowat."

The two recruits nodded and mumbled in agreement.

Riley continued, "But we're looking for someone whose animosity was out of the ordinary. If you know anyone like that, please tell me."

Ludekens and Wilber looked at each other.

The young woman said, "The sarge really rode one of us especially hard."

"His name's Stanley Pope," the young man added.

"Tell me about him," Riley said.

The young man said, "He's got a real mouth and a bad attitude. The sarge busted him for it."

Riley felt a surge of interest.

"Busted him?" she said. "Explain that to me."

The young woman said, "Almost all of us in the platoon are PV1—private E-1. Just 'fuzzies,' they call us, because of this."

She pointed to a blank Velcro patch on her shoulder.

The young man said, "When we get through basic training, we'll get our 'mosquito wings'—chevrons—to show that we've become second-class privates. But Pope had his mosquito wings already when he came to Fort Mowat."

"How?" Riley asked.

The young man shrugged.

"You can come in as a second-class private if you have an associate's degree. Or if you've got a Boy Scout Eagle badge. That's how Pope got his."

"But he talked back to the sarge once too often," the young woman said. "So the sarge busted him, took away his chevron, demoted him to PV1—a fuzzy just like the rest of us. He didn't take it too well."

Riley's curiosity was rising by the second.

"Where can I find him?" she asked.

Private Wilber pointed to the gravesite.

"He's right over there," he said.

A young man was standing alone beside the grave, looking down at the casket with his arms on his hips.

Riley thanked Privates Ludekens and Wilber, who wandered off. Riley saw that Bill and Lucy had each found some recruits to talk to.

Riley walked toward the private who was standing beside the grave. He was a lanky young man with an intense, brooding expression on his face.

What's on his mind? she wondered.

She planned to find out.

CHAPTER TWELVE

As Riley approached Private Pope, she decided not to let on that that she knew anything about him—certainly not that he'd been demoted by Sergeant Worthing. She thought it would be best to see what the young soldier would be willing to reveal.

She stepped right beside him, but he didn't seem to notice her presence. His bitter expression remained unchanged and his eyes stayed fixed on the grave.

Finally, she asked, "Taking the sarge's death kind of hard?"

He turned his head and looked at her and then his expression shifted for a moment. He regarded her with obvious distaste, but he didn't reply to her question. Then he turned and stared down into the grave again, brooding as before.

"Not everyone seemed to like him," Riley said. "Did you?"

Private Pope still said nothing.

Riley said, "It's probably a hard thing to talk about. But I think maybe I understand. I lost my dad recently—and he was a Marine, a captain who served in Vietnam. Folks didn't like him much either."

Then she added with a lie …

"Still, I miss him."

Pope didn't look up from the grave.

"You don't know anything about it," Pope said. "How could you? You're not one of us."

His resentment of Riley was practically radiating off of him.

"I might surprise you," Riley said. "I know a thing or two about comradeship. There's a deep bond among FBI agents. And I've lost colleagues in the line of work. I know it's hard."

He didn't reply at all.

"Come on," Riley said. "Let's take a little walk."

Riley turned and walked away. Pope didn't move at first. Riley wondered if maybe he wasn't going to come with her. But then she heard his footsteps behind her, and then he was walking at her side. He kept looking at the ground as he walked.

"Tell me about the sergeant," she said.

"What's there to tell?" Pope said. "He was a hard-ass."

"Did you ever have any special trouble with him?"

"Everybody had trouble with him. That was his job."

Riley noticed the evasion. Whatever bitterness he may have felt toward Sergeant Worthing, he didn't want to talk to her about it. She'd have to coax it out of him.

She led the way along a paved path at the edge of the cemetery. As she followed the walkway over a rise, Riley found herself looking down on the Pacific Ocean. It wasn't far away. She could actually hear the surf.

Occasional benches indicated that the path had been designed as a restful place to contemplate the view. It didn't feel restful to her right now.

And she sensed that it didn't feel restful to Private Pope either.

At the moment, she figured the trick was simply to get him talking.

Riley asked, "So how far are you along in basic training? You're in the White Phase, right?"

"Yeah," he said.

"How long have you got left? Including the Blue Phase, I mean?"

"Five weeks and three days," Pope said. "Nine more days of white, twenty-eight more of blue."

Riley found his precision to be revealing. She remembered what Private Wilber had said about Pope.

"He's got a real mouth and a bad attitude."

Riley had no doubt that that was true. But she also sensed that serving in the Army was important to him—perhaps the most important thing he could ever hope to do. To get him to open up, Riley needed to dig at his pride.

"I'll bet you're looking forward to getting your mosquito wings," she said. "You won't be a fuzzy anymore. How will it feel, to have those chevrons on your shoulders?"

Pope didn't reply. She glanced at him and saw a sharp grimace cross his lips.

Of course she knew that Pope had had those chevrons until Sergeant Worthing had taken them away. The recruits she'd talked to had told her. But Pope had no way of knowing that, and it gave her an advantage over him.

She said, "It's too bad Sergeant Worthing won't be here to see you get those chevrons. He'd be proud."

Now Riley saw that his fists were clenched at his sides, and his jaw was tight.

She kept walking. The path was taking them to higher ground, but the sound of crashing waves was getting louder. After a few more steps, she could see that on one side of the path a cliff dropped down to the water. A guardrail was placed to keep viewers well back from the edge.

"Have you ever killed anybody?" Pope asked.

Riley was startled.

Why is he asking that?

But she saw no point in lying about it.

"Yes. Have you?"

She knew that she was asking a loaded question. As a recruit in basic training, he shouldn't have killed anybody.

But maybe he has, Riley thought.

Instead of answering her question he asked, "How many people have you killed?"

"I don't talk about it," Riley said.

She felt a creeping uneasiness.

It wasn't something she liked to think about, much less talk about. If she ever stopped to think about it, she could surely remember the exact number of people she'd killed in the line of duty. But she tried to stay away from that dark part of her psyche.

What bothered her at the moment was that she was letting him get to her. She had wanted to open him up, but he was pushing her buttons.

And he was surprisingly good at it.

She needed to turn the tables.

She said, "Tell me more about Sergeant Worthing."

"What do you want to know?" he asked.

"Well, I didn't see any of the other recruits shedding any tears over him."

"What makes you think I felt different?"

"You stayed behind after the ceremony. You stood over his grave."

He let out a grunt of irritation.

Then he said, "I guess a BAU agent like you has seen a lot of danger in your life, right?"

Again, Riley felt a little bit taken aback. She sensed that he was up to something. She didn't reply.

Pope said, "So I'll bet you're pretty fearless, huh?"

Riley felt increasingly uncomfortable, but she still said nothing.

Pope chuckled under his breath.

"Nice view of the ocean from here, isn't it?" he said.

"Very nice," Riley said.

"I know where it's nicer," Pope said. "Want me to show you?"

Riley didn't reply.

"Come on," Pope said. "Let me show you."

He veered around the end of the guardrail, walking between it and the drop to the ocean. He stepped across a weedy patch of ground and then out onto a wide projection that hung over the water.

Riley followed him.

They stood side by side on the edge of a precipice that dropped straight down. She could hear the waves crashing on the rocks below. She looked down queasily. It was at least sixty or seventy feet to the bottom.

"Quite a view, huh?" Pope said.

Riley still said nothing. She realized that she was actually afraid. She wasn't particularly afraid of heights. But in a place like this, she knew it was a perfectly natural reaction.

And yet he was standing closer to the edge of the cliff than she was—and she sensed that he wasn't frightened at all.

That's what he wants, she thought.

He wanted her to be scared of something that didn't scare him.

Riley took a deep breath to calm her nerves. Moving carefully, she stepped back from the edge, back toward the guardrail.

The man moved back beside her.

Then she felt his hand on her shoulder.

CHAPTER THIRTEEN

Riley didn't wait to find out the soldier's intent. She stooped over and hurled herself headfirst into Private Pope's abdomen. He toppled to the ground, and she planted her foot on his chest.

She was about to draw her weapon when he grabbed her leg and threw her to the side. By the time she regained her balance, he was on his feet, and she was in a violent clinch with him.

As they staggered back and forth in the space between the guardrail and the cliff, Riley realized that she didn't know where the edge was. If they stumbled off it together, it would mean both their deaths.

He's strong, she realized.

In fact, he was much stronger than he looked—wiry and muscular. And he was a skilled fighter too. He had lots of potential.

She pushed sharply against his chest, breaking out of his grip. This time, he was the one who was caught off balance.

And now Riley could see that he was right at the edge of the cliff. She reached out and grabbed his hand just in time to stop him from falling. Then she swung him around to safety, slamming him into the rail beside them.

Riley shuddered with relief. The last thing she wanted right now was to get him killed. She just wanted to teach him some manners.

Disoriented, Pope fell to his knees. Before he could get up again, Riley whipped out her cuffs and pulled one of his arms up behind his back. He struggled to get away, but she slapped the cuff on that wrist and rammed her knee into his back, pushing him face down in the dirt. Before he could move again, she had his other arm pulled back and cuffed too.

Pope turned his head.

"Pretty good—for a chick," he sneered.

She snapped, "Don't go overboard thanking me for saving your piece-of-shit excuse for a life."

She grabbed the back of his collar and dragged him along the ground between the cliff and the guardrail.

He scrambled to get his feet under him, but each time he got to his knees she slammed him forward on his face again.

Finally Pope grew quiet and stayed still.

Riley realized that they were both panting for breath. She let go of Pope and looked out across the ocean. It was still a lovely view.

After a few moments, Pope asked weakly, "Are you going to arrest me?"

Riley didn't reply.

"It would destroy my career," he said.

"Do you really care about your army career?" she asked him.

There was a brief silence. Then he said, "More than anything."

"Then trying to kill me was a bad idea."

"I wasn't. Really, I wasn't."

Riley was starting to understand that this was a familiar situation. He was just a macho, misogynist jerk who hated the very idea of a woman with a badge and a gun.

He'd had no intention of really killing her. He'd only wanted to give her a good scare and teach her a lesson.

That hadn't worked out very well for him.

She reached down and released the cuffs. Then she stood back as Pope got shakily to his feet.

"You damn near got us both killed," Riley said. "You're an idiot. You won't live long if you keep pulling this kind of stunt. God help you if you ever see combat."

This time Pope didn't reply. He brushed mechanically at his uniform, trying to clean the dirt off.

Riley said, "Tell me about Sergeant Worthing."

"What do you want to know?" Pope asked.

"How angry were you with him?"

Pope's mouth dropped open with surprise.

"What's this all about?" he said. "Do you think I killed him?"

"Did you?"

Pope looked offended now—and even hurt.

"He was a good man," he said. "I wouldn't have killed him for the world."

Riley was starting to feel confused.

"He busted you down a pay grade," she said. "Took away your mosquito wings."

Pope shrugged and smirked.

"Heard about that, did you?" he said. "I should have figured that was why you got so nosy. Yeah, he busted me. And let me tell you, I sure as hell had it coming. When I came to Fort Mowat, I thought I was some sort of a rebel. Do you know what he told me when he busted me? *'I* was a rebel at your age. You're not even a pimple on a rebel's ass.'"

He laughed. There was a note of admiration in his voice.

"And he was right," he said. "I'm damned glad he straightened me out."

Riley's gut told her that his admiration was perfectly genuine.

Pope hadn't killed Sergeant Worthing. In fact, he might well be the only recruit in Worthing's platoon who truly missed him.

Pope said, "So what are you going to do? Are you going to arrest me?" He was getting a bit of his spirit back. "I didn't attack you. I didn't plan to attack you. In fact, I'm pretty sure you attacked me."

Riley knew that her action was perfectly justified. She also knew that he'd never meant to kill her.

There's no law against being an asshole, she thought.

Besides, arresting him would distract her from the case at hand.

When she made no reply, he asked pleadingly, "Can I please go?"

"You can go," Riley said.

He wheeled and started to walk away. Then he turned toward Riley again.

He said, "I hope you catch the bastard who killed the sarge. And when you do, I hope you'll give me five minutes alone with him. I've got to admit, though—the son of a bitch is one hell of a marksman. I hope I can shoot like that someday."

He held Riley's gaze for a moment. Then he said, "Sergeant Worthing was more than a soldier. A whole lot more. He ran with the pack."

The phrase puzzled Riley.

"What does that mean—ran with the pack?" she asked.

"You wouldn't understand," Pope said. "Never in a thousand years could you understand. You can't even imagine. Not many of us can."

"Try me," she said.

Then he looked her straight in the eye and said, "You're pretty gullible, aren't you? It doesn't mean anything at all."

He turned again and walked away laughing.

Riley stood there thinking, turning what he'd said over and over in her mind.

"He ran with the pack."

It meant something. Pope knew something.

She planned to keep her eye on him.

CHAPTER FOURTEEN

Riley's shock at what had happened on the cliff didn't kick in for a while. A deep shudder finally shook her at the oddest possible moment.

She was staring across the wide beach to the ocean, a scene that was streaked red and gold in the fierce light of the evening sun. It was an incredible view from one of a line of small cottages that the base provided for some of its temporary visitors. She wondered whether Col. Adams had given them this cottage to keep them happy or to keep them distracted.

She heard Bill ask, "Are you OK?"

He'd obviously noticed her spasm of fear.

They were both sitting on the patio drinking margaritas that Lucy had made. The younger agent had taken it upon herself to pick up groceries and stock the kitchen. Right now Lucy was in the kitchen fixing a special dinner.

Riley took another sip of the salt-rimmed, fruity drink. Although she seldom drank tequila, she appreciated the relaxing effect. She had already told her companions about her encounter, but it had felt like describing something that had happened to someone else. The terror hadn't struck until now.

"Yeah, I'm OK," Riley told Bill. "It was a close call, though."

Bill shook his head.

"I don't know, Riley," he said. "I'm not sure you shouldn't report what happened to Col. Larson. Or at least the MPs."

For a moment, Riley wondered about that as well. But again, she felt sure that it was best this way.

"Private Pope isn't our killer, Bill," she said. "And he wasn't actually trying to kill me."

"But you said you think he knows something," Bill said.

"Maybe—just maybe," Riley said. "But I really don't think he actually knows about the murders. I think he might know something that he doesn't realize is connected. He might reveal more if we don't push him."

As she and Bill sat quietly watching the sunset for a few more moments, Riley realized that she'd learned a lesson today. She'd faced dozens of truly dangerous psychopaths, many of them bent on killing her in cruel and sadistic ways. But she'd seldom felt the kind of fear that hit her today.

Why is that? Riley wondered.

Of course, her life had been in danger on that cliff. For that matter, so had Pope's.

If one or both of them had gone over that cliff, it would have been an accident—a stupid and pointless accident.

But Riley would be dead, as surely as if she'd been done in by some murderous monster.

He's just a kid, Riley thought. *A really stupid kid.*

And in a way, that made him more dangerous than a seasoned psychopath who had some idea of what he was doing.

On a training base like this, there were probably hundreds of rash, stupid kids just like him—determined to prove themselves men long before they really were men. They needed army discipline to make that transition.

She and her colleagues needed to be careful here.

Riley was surprised by the sound of a gasp behind her. Both she and Bill turned to look. Lucy was standing there with tears in her eyes.

"Lucy!" Riley said. "What's the matter?"

Lucy hastily wiped her eyes and smiled.

"Nothing," she said. "Come on in. Supper's ready."

Riley and Bill picked up their margaritas and joined Lucy at the table for delicious tacos. The three agents talked idly for a little while about their day. Aside from Riley's misadventure with Private Pope, it had been pretty uneventful. They had individually interviewed a few more recruits and learned almost nothing. They had also scheduled their work for tomorrow, setting up interviews with the soldiers in the other two platoons that had lost their sergeants.

Lucy seemed fine as they ate and talked, but Riley was curious about her tearful reaction to the ocean. She realized there was a great deal that she and Bill didn't know about their younger colleague.

Riley thought the world of her, of course. She knew that Lucy had accomplished a lot even before coming to Quantico. Riley had seen Lucy's amazing high school and college grades, and she knew that Lucy had aced every challenge at the FBI Academy. And Riley had seen Lucy's achievements as a field agent firsthand.

Now she noticed Lucy cast another wistful glance toward the ocean again as she ate.

Riley asked, "Is there something wrong, Lucy?"

Lucy let out a rather nervous laugh.

"Oh, it's nothing," she said. "It's just that I sometimes get a little emotional at the sight of the Pacific. I haven't been out here in a long time."

Lucy went on eating as if there was nothing to say. But Riley kept looking at her expectantly, and she sensed the Bill was doing the same.

Finally, Lucy began to explain.

"My parents were undocumented way back when they came here from Mexico. They traveled up and down California picking crops and doing other farm work. It was awfully hard work, and it got harder when they started having kids. And they lived in constant fear of deportation."

Lucy paused, looking down at the table.

Then she said, "In 1986 President Reagan signed the Immigration Reform and Control Act. It granted amnesty to some three million undocumented Mexicans—including my parents. That gave our family our first real security. We settled in Sacramento, and my parents went to work for a lawn care business. Eventually they were able to buy the business."

Lucy looked out toward the ocean again.

"It was hard work. We never took family vacations. But Mamá and Papá gave up everything so that my brothers and I would have all the opportunities they didn't have. My brother Carlos is going to take over the family business. Victor is on his way toward becoming a lawyer."

Still looking toward the ocean, Lucy heaved a bittersweet sigh.

"There was always so much work to do. Even though we lived in Sacramento, I never got to see the ocean, not during my whole childhood. I knew that it was there, just about a hundred miles away. But I never went there. When I was accepted in college, I knew my life was changing. I finally drove out to see the ocean on my own. It was …"

Lucy's voice trailed off. She wiped away a tear.

"It was just so beautiful. It still is. Whenever I see it, it reminds me of how lucky I am, and how proud I am to live in this country and to do the work that I do. And I think about all the sacrifices my parents made so I could have this life."

Riley felt herself choking up now.

Bill asked Lucy, "Are your parents still alive?"

Lucy nodded.

"They must be very proud of you," Riley said.

Lucy nodded again. She seemed too overcome to speak.

Riley gazed at Lucy in admiring silence.

She remembered how it had felt to be so young and hopeful.

What a great life she's got ahead of her, Riley thought.

She and her companions finished their meal, talking mostly about little things that didn't matter.

*

After dinner, Riley took a walk alone on the beach. Although the sun had set, it wasn't completely dark yet.

Her phone buzzed with a call from April.

"Hey, Mom," April said. "Crack the case yet?"

Riley sighed a little.

"I wish," she said.

"Jilly's going to be disappointed. She was sure you'd have solved it by now."

Riley laughed.

"Tell Jilly to be patient," she said. "What's going on with you?"

"I just got back from a date with Liam," April said.

Uh-oh, Riley thought. *Is this good news or bad news?*

"We went to a foreign languages fair," April said. "All the local high schools were involved, and Liam wanted to go. He and I went from booth to booth, where we got to try saying something in all sorts of languages."

Riley stifled a chuckle. Not long ago, April would have found the idea of a foreign languages fair to be thoroughly uncool.

All it took was a boyfriend to change her mind.

"It sounds like fun," Riley said.

"Yeah, it was. It really was. It's just that …"

April's voice trailed off.

"What?" Riley asked.

"Well, Liam's got this thing about languages. He's already fluent in Spanish, and he knows a little French and German. He's also dabbled a little with Russian. He's just got a knack for it, and sounded like a native speaker no matter what we tried. As for me— well, I'm still struggling with Spanish. I had a hard time keeping up."

Riley smiled.

First chess, now languages!

She was liking Liam more and more all the time. All the same, she was worried that April was feeling a little intimidated. Riley was glad that Liam was challenging her. But she didn't want April to start thinking she was inferior to her boyfriend.

"Is there anything Liam's *not* good at?" Riley asked.

April giggled a little.

"He's pretty clumsy," she said. "He's not nearly as athletic as I am."

Riley said, "Well, why don't you teach him how to play tennis? That might even things out between you."

April giggled some more.

"Hey, that's a great idea! Thanks, Mom. I'll be sure to do that."

Then as her laughter waned, April added, "Oh, I almost forgot. Crystal called to tell me that Blaine says hello. He's wondering when you're going to be back. Crystal and I are sure he wants to get together with you."

Riley smiled. It was encouraging to hear.

"Tell Crystal to let Blaine know that I'll tell him as soon as I find out when we can return," she said.

Riley and April ended the call.

Riley realized that she had walked quite some distance. She was approaching the rocks below the cliff where she'd almost fallen that day.

She shuddered at the memory.

What next? she wondered.

As if in reply, her cell phone rang. Riley saw that her sister, Wendy, was requesting a video chat. Riley was surprised. After almost a lifetime of estrangement, Riley and her sister had only spoken a few times after their father's death and had never met in person. They'd talked about getting together sometime. But since Wendy lived in Des Moines, a visit never materialized.

Riley accepted the call, and Wendy's face appeared on her cell phone. Riley was instantly reminded of her dream about her mother. While Riley herself looked like their father, Wendy looked startlingly like their mother—or at least how their mother would have looked if she lived to be in her early fifties.

"I'm surprised to hear from you," Riley said.

Wendy shrugged and smiled.

"I'm a little surprised myself," Wendy said. "How are you?"

Riley felt uneasy. Something seemed to be wrong. She wished Wendy would just come to the point.

"I'm fine," Riley said. "I'm in California working on a case."

"And your daughters?"

"They're fine too. How are you and your husband?"

"Loren and I are both well, thank you."

Wendy seemed to hesitate a little.

Then she said, "Riley, I need to talk to you about the house."

Riley's heart jumped up in her throat. She'd offered the cabin to Wendy soon after their father died—and before Shane Hatcher had laid claim to it.

Wendy hadn't wanted the property. Had she changed her mind?

Wendy said, "I keep getting calls from your real estate agent, Shirley Redding. She's saying kind of weird things about you."

Riley sighed as she remembered her last phone conversation with Shirley. The Realtor had just gotten a high offer on her father's cabin—an offer that Riley knew that Shane Hatcher himself had made just to test Riley. Riley had told Shirley that she didn't want to sell the cabin after all, and she instructed her to take it off the market.

Of course, Riley hadn't been able to give Shirley a good reason. And Shirley hadn't taken it very well.

"What's Shirley saying?" Riley asked.

"Well, she says she advertised the cabin in good faith and keeps getting great offers, and that you're being completely unreasonable in taking it off the market. She wants me to talk some sense into you. I told her it was none of my business, and that I respect your decision."

Riley stifled a groan.

"I'm sorry about this, Wendy," she said. "Just ignore her."

"I wish I could, but she keeps calling and leaving messages. She says she's thinking about taking potential buyers up there for a look."

Riley felt a jolt of alarm.

"I'll take care of this, Wendy," she said. "Thanks for letting me know."

Riley ended the call. Then she dialed Shirley's number, but got an answering machine.

After the beep, Riley said, "Shirley, this is Riley Paige. I just got a call from Wendy. I want you to stop pestering her. In fact, you're fired."

When Riley ended the call, she realized that she was shaking. And she knew that it was from more than anger at Shirley.

It was the idea of anyone taking potential buyers to the cabin that alarmed her.

If they found Hatcher there, what might happen?

Of course, Hatcher could probably evade surprise visitors if he chose to.

Riley didn't even try to imagine what might happen if Shane Hatcher didn't choose to.

CHAPTER FIFTEEN

Early the next morning, Riley stepped in front of fifty soldiers seated in a meeting room. As she looked out at her audience, she sensed a range of emotions there.

The strongest of all was fear.

These were the recruits in Sergeant Richard Fraser's platoon, and they'd been assembled so Riley could talk with them about his murder. At this moment Bill and Lucy were in a room elsewhere talking with the members of Sergeant Guy Rolsky's platoon.

The atmosphere here was very different from yesterday's funeral. Riley had sensed little emotion among most of Sergeant Worthing's recruits—not even grief.

Now she understood why.

Worthing's recruits hadn't had time to process what had happened.

These men and women had.

They've had time to get scared, Riley thought.

But she also sensed something else that she hadn't sensed yesterday.

It was actual grief. And it was shared by almost everybody here.

Riley cleared her throat and spoke.

"First of all, I understand how hard this is for all of you. Rest assured that my colleagues and the CID agents on this base are doing everything we can to stop this from ever happening again."

A glance over their young faces showed her that they weren't at all reassured.

Riley continued, "I'm asking for your help. Would anybody care to tell me how your platoon as a whole felt about Sergeant Fraser?"

Hands shot up all over the place.

Riley called on an African-American male.

He said, "Sergeant Fraser was a good man. He trusted us. He cared for us. He was tough, but that was his job."

There was a note of pride in the young man's voice. Perhaps he had taken special pleasure in training under an African-American drill sergeant.

Then he added, "I don't think there's anybody here who doesn't feel the same way."

As he sat down, there were nods and murmurs of what seemed

like near-unanimous agreement. Again, the contrast to yesterday was striking.

Another soldier called out, "They don't make many Americans like Fraser anymore."

That approving chorus of murmurs grew louder this time.

"I'm sorry for your loss," Riley said. "I know it's painful and I know you must have already considered this, but I want you to spend some time thinking hard about who might have wanted Sergeant Fraser dead. Not only him, but Sergeants Rolsky and Worthing as well. We need to find out what the link is among their murders. If anything comes to mind, please contact me or any of my colleagues, including Col. Larson and her CID agents."

She looked out over the soldiers again, seeing no change in their faces, sensing no change in their feelings.

Finally she said, "That's all for now."

As the recruits dispersed, their current drill sergeant pushed among them toward Riley. She already knew that his name was Chad Shoemaker.

Shoemaker said, "Agent Paige, I just got a call from the CO. He wants to see you immediately."

Riley stifled a sigh. She, Bill, and Lucy were due for a meeting with Col. Larson. This wasn't a good time to be harassed by Col. Adams.

As she left the meeting room and headed outside, the sergeant kept walking alongside her.

Finally, in a nervous voice, he said, "Agent Paige …"

Riley stopped and looked at him.

The sergeant glanced away and said, "It's nothing. I beg your pardon, ma'am."

But Riley knew it wasn't nothing. He'd just taken over for a slain drill sergeant. He couldn't help but worry that he might be next. He was too proud to say so out loud.

They were standing outdoors, and it was almost impossible not to wonder if someone might be targeting them right now. With the kind of weapon the killer was using, few places on base could be considered safe.

But so far, no one had been shot in a central area of the base. For the time being, drills weren't being conducted on the outskirts of the base and soldiers had been warned away from peripheral areas.

Besides that, so far the shooter had used the cover of darkness for stalking and killing his victims. The daylight was strong right now and might offer some protection.

Even so, Riley couldn't say anything very reassuring. She couldn't guarantee that this killer's MO would stay exactly the same.

She told Shoemaker, "Sergeant, my colleagues and I are doing everything we can to make sure that this never happens again."

Shoemaker nodded, then turned around to rejoin his platoon.

Riley continued on her way to the administration building.

As she neared the building, her heart sank at what she saw.

The reporters who had been held in check yesterday at the funeral were now swarming at the entrance.

Maybe I can just pass for an ordinary civilian, she thought.

But as she approached, the whole mass of reporters moved toward her with cameras, microphones, and notebooks.

"Are you Special Agent Riley Paige?" several of them asked, almost in unison.

Riley groaned aloud. The reporters had been doing their homework, and they knew that the BAU had been brought in. They even knew that Riley was part of the team—and she had a reputation for success.

"Yes," Riley said, pushing through them. "But I have no comment to make at this time."

Bodies pressed hard around her, along with a cacophony of questions. Riley kept shouting "no comment, no comment," as she pushed her way through. Finally, she managed to make it through the door. The media gang knew they wouldn't be allowed to follow her there, and she drew a breath of relief when the door closed behind her.

She showed her credentials to the guard, who let her continue on into the building. He directed her to take the elevator to the top floor.

Riley used the brief solitary trip to collect her thoughts. When she got off and approached Col. Adams's office, she saw that Bill and Lucy were already waiting there.

She said, "I take it the two of you also had to run that gauntlet out there."

Bill said, "I'm afraid it's going to get worse before it gets better."

Lucy said, "We were just waiting for you to get here. What do you think the colonel wants?"

"Anyone want to bet it's not a hug?" Bill replied.

They all laughed quietly.

Riley was anxious to ask them about their own meeting with the other platoon. But there wasn't time for that right now.

The three agents entered an outer office and announced themselves to the secretary. The woman nodded briskly, then stepped into the colonel's office. She soon came out again.

"The colonel will see you now," she said.

Riley hoped they could get this command appearance over quickly so they could keep the meeting they had set up with Col. Larson.

CHAPTER SIXTEEN

The secretary ushered the agents inside and closed the door behind them.

Col. Adams's office was not at all what Riley had expected. She remembered visiting her own father's Marine office once or twice when she'd been a little girl. His workplace had been small and Spartan, with a few pieces of sturdy old furniture and a cluttered desk. Her father had wanted it that way. As far as he'd been concerned, he was a simple soldier.

By comparison, this one was large and opulent. Its location in the upper corner of the building provided a terrific view of the base and the ocean beyond. Tall shelves were filled with leather-bound military histories that looked old and valuable. The big desk was polished wood with very little clutter, just a lamp, a blotter, family photos, and a pen set in an elegant marble base.

The colonel was standing behind the desk. He was in full uniform just as he had been yesterday. His appearance made a marked contrast to the more comfortable camouflage combat dress most of the other people on the base were wearing.

Although he wasn't at attention, the colonel's body looked rigid.

"Be seated," he said, as if commanding a group of soldiers.

Riley and her colleagues sat down in nearby chairs, and Adams took his place in the big swivel chair behind his desk.

Adams glanced disapprovingly at Riley and Lucy, then locked eyes with Bill.

"Agent Jeffreys, give me a full report on your work so far."

Riley hid her amusement that he directed his question to the male among the three agents.

Bill said, "We all talked to the soldiers in Worthing's platoon yesterday. Just now Agent Paige met with Fraser's platoon, and Agent Vargas and I met with Rolsky's recruits."

While Bill continued, Riley let her attention wander around the carpeted office. It told her a lot about Adams's personality—that he was egotistical and self-aggrandizing.

Portraits and certificates hung on the walls in what looked like expensive frames. She also noticed an old print from some battle scene, a mounted army charging with swords held high.

On one table was an image she'd seen in photographs—a metal sculpture of a cowboy on a rearing horse. She wondered whether it was an original Frederic Remington.

Adams apparently noticed her interest. He interrupted Bill and said to her, "It's real. One of the original castings Remington had made. My father bought it for me when I graduated from West Point with honors."

Riley looked at him.

"Was your father an Army man?" she asked.

Adams nodded proudly. "And my grandfather and great-grandfather before him."

Riley felt as though she were starting to understand Adams better.

Even so, she was liking him less and less.

She asked, "What rank did your father achieve?"

Adams's face twitched sharply.

"Captain," he said.

Riley nodded with approval.

"My father was a captain," she said. "In the Marines."

But she could see that the colonel didn't appreciate the comparison. He clearly thought his father should have reached a considerably higher rank.

He was disappointed in his father, she thought. Now he outranked him and was determined to do a lot better. Perhaps Adams could make brigadier general if his record was good enough. And of course, the current situation wasn't doing anything positive for the colonel's record.

Riley was on the verge of asking him how far away he was from retirement. But she realized that that would only be twisting the knife. Adams obviously disliked her enough already, and there was no point in making things worse.

Now that Bill had finished filling him in on their activities, Adams was visibly angry.

"What the hell do you three think you're doing?" he asked. "You're out there badgering perfectly good recruits, and this is an open and shut case of Islamic terrorism. You ought to have cracked it by now."

Riley hid her anger at the colonel telling the agents how to do their job.

She asked, "If it's terrorism, why hasn't anybody taken credit? Usually in cases of Islamic radicals, some group is anxious to take credit—ISIS or Al-Qaeda, say. Nobody has done so at this point."

Adams's eyes snapped from Bill to her. The colonel's lips twisted into a grimace.

He said, "Do you propose that we all sit on our hands until more soldiers get killed, and somebody's proud enough of the casualty rate to take credit?"

Riley bristled a little.

She said, "You've got three hundred forty-three Muslims on this base. Col. Larson and her CID team are doing their best to screen them. Do you want us to personally profile all of them?"

"Why the hell not?" Adams said with a snarl.

Riley's mind boggled at the idea. The logistics would be staggering—to say nothing of the disastrous PR implications. It wouldn't take long for the reporters outside to get wind of what they were doing. Then there would be hell to pay.

Nevertheless, she knew that Adams had a point. Although her gut told her otherwise, Riley knew that Islamic terrorism was the most obvious theory they had to work on at this point.

She could see anger building up in the colonel.

"This whole thing is a PR disaster," he snapped. "I can't control the reporters anymore. The three of you got here just yesterday, and already you've made things even worse."

Riley was dumbfounded by the accusation.

Bill said what she was thinking.

"With due respect, Colonel, what are you talking about? Do you think we're responsible for all those damned reporters? We're just out here doing our job. And as far as I'm concerned, you're wasting our time right now."

Riley added, "And our time is as valuable as yours. In fact, if you expect to end this string of murders, our time is more valuable."

Adams stood up behind his desk, his face red.

"You know nothing about the military. You're accomplishing nothing here."

Riley stood up and faced the colonel across his desk. "We are too well trained to waste our time trying to interview hundreds of suspects without any actual indication that someone among them is to blame."

The colonel was shouting now. "A Muslim fanatic is killing sergeants on my base, and you're too politically correct to track him down and stop him."

Bill was standing now and his voice was angry too. "We follow real leads, not prejudices."

"He's right," Riley added. "You're too isolated up here in your fancy office to know what's happening on your base."

"It *is* my base, and don't you forget it. You don't have the authority here. I should have all of you removed from *my* base right now."

By that time, Lucy was out of her chair as well. The smallest of them all, she stepped forward and spoke up firmly. "Colonel Adams, we understand how much you want this killer caught. We are highly trained to do just that. You won't find better investigative skills anywhere. Please give us the opportunity to get our job done."

A silence fell in the room. For a long moment the colonel stared down at the diminutive Latina FBI agent. Finally he swallowed hard and grumbled, "I will expect you to do that."

Riley nodded and stepped back from the colonel's desk.

He said in softer but still commanding tone, "Now clear out of here. All three of you."

As she and her colleagues headed for the door, Riley turned back and said as politely as she could, "Just one more thing, sir. Does the phrase 'running with the pack' mean anything to you?"

Adams squinted.

"Nothing in particular," he said. "Should it mean something?"

Riley studied his expression. He certainly didn't seem to be lying.

"Just something I heard," Riley said. "It can't mean anything."

She turned and left the office, with the other two agents close behind her.

As they walked down the hall toward the elevator, Riley could feel her temper receding. She focused her thoughts on the phrase that Private Pope had used. Yesterday she had mentioned it to Bill and Lucy.

As they waited for the elevator, she asked her companions, "Did both of you ask the soldiers you talked to about 'running with the pack'?"

"I did," Lucy said. "I got nothing."

"Me too," Bill said to Riley. "Are you sure it means anything at all?"

Riley didn't reply. The truth was, she couldn't be sure. She had no real reason to keep thinking about it.

But something about Private Pope's voice and expression when he'd said it had stuck in her mind.

When they all got into the elevator, Riley's phone buzzed.

She shuddered when she saw that the caller was Shane Hatcher.

CHAPTER SEVENTEEN

Riley fought down her panic. She definitely didn't want to talk to this caller while she was in the elevator with Bill and Lucy. Finally, the sound stopped as her outgoing message kicked in. Riley hoped that Hatcher would either leave a message or give up. But after a brief silence, the annoying signal started up again.

She wondered why Hatcher was so anxious to talk to her.

What would happen if she simply turned her phone off?

She didn't want to find out.

"Don't you want to get that?" Bill asked as the elevator door opened on the ground floor.

"I'd better," Riley said, walking away from Bill and Lucy to talk alone.

When she took the call, Hatcher sounded angrier than she'd ever heard him.

"You broke our deal," he said.

Riley felt her panic rising.

"What do you mean?" she asked.

"Don't pretend you don't know. Your real estate agent was here just now, showing the cabin to a married couple. This is supposed to be my place now. We agreed to that. You promised not to sell it."

Riley was starting to understand. Shirley Redding had disobeyed her once again.

Hatcher continued, "I managed to stay out of sight. I don't think they know anybody's living here. But you'd damn well better make sure nobody else comes around here. I'm not hiding in the woods again. I'm a city person."

"Hatcher, listen to me," Riley said. "I fired her. Yesterday."

"Don't lie to me," Hatcher said.

"I'm not! I swear to you—"

But Hatcher ended the call. The phone was shaking in Riley's hands.

What can that woman be thinking? Riley wondered.

She hastily typed in a text to Shirley.

I fired U yesterday. I meant it.

Riley paused. What else could she say? She couldn't tell Shirley anything resembling the truth.

She typed …

I know U took people to my father's cabin. Don't ask me how I know. Just don't do it again. I repeat. U are fired.

She sent the text, then heard Bill call out to her, "A problem at home?"

She saw that Bill and Lucy both looked a little worried.

"Nothing," she said with a forced smile. "Just some teenage drama."

She immediately hated herself for lying. She'd told too many lies on Hatcher's behalf already. But she doubted that this one would be the last.

Anyway, she told herself sternly, she had to put Hatcher out of her mind for now. She, Bill, and Lucy were already late for a meeting with Col. Larson.

They hurried on to the smaller CID building, ignoring several reporters who still straggled along with them. The guard in the lobby viewed their credentials and let them in, shutting the reporters out. He directed them to Col. Larson's office. Larson's secretary escorted them inside.

Riley was immediately struck by the contrast between this office and Col. Adams's more regal accommodations. Larson's office was comparatively small and businesslike, with no fancy or expensive decor.

It was also at the moment a bit crowded.

Col. Dana Larson was sitting at her desk, flanked by her CID team, Sergeant Matthews and Agents Goodwin and Shores. They were all poring over materials spread out on the desk.

"We're sorry to be late," Riley said as she and her colleagues sat down in waiting chairs facing Larson.

Larson said, "Don't tell me—you were held up by Col. Adams."

"How did you guess?" Riley said, laughing a little.

But Larson didn't look amused. At the moment, she seemed to be all business.

"What have you found out?" she asked Riley and her colleagues.

Riley said, "This morning we met with the recruits in the platoons of Sergeants Rolsky and Fraser."

"Do you think any of them might be viable suspects?" Larson

asked.

Riley said, "It's hard to tell just from one meeting. None of Fraser's recruits stood out as especially hostile. In fact, he was pretty unanimously well liked."

Lucy said, "Agent Jeffreys and I talked to Rolsky's recruits. Our impression was that he wasn't especially popular. One told me that Rolsky was an 'Arab.' I didn't know what that meant. I mean, Rolsky was white and Catholic, wasn't he?"

"ARAB is a military slang acronym," Larson explained. "It means 'Arrogant Regular Army Bastard.'"

Riley was struck by that phrase.

Lucy continued, "Still, Rolsky was nothing if not respected. We didn't sense that any recruits in that platoon actually wanted him dead."

Larson tapped her pencil on her desk impatiently.

"Where does this get us?" she asked.

Sergeant Matthews spoke up.

"I don't think we've seen anything to contradict our original theory—that these were acts of Islamic radicalism. In fact, I think we can be pretty sure of it. We still don't know whether it's a single man or a small cell."

Larson nodded in agreement.

"We've already been investigating on-base Muslims," she said. "We'll put extra surveillance on both Muslim recruits and on-base Muslim civilians."

Agents Goodwin and Shores nodded in agreement.

But a new idea was starting to take shape in Riley's mind

Riley said, "I'm not so sure that's the right approach."

Larson looked surprised.

"Why not?" she asked.

Riley thought for a moment.

Then she said, "Just now, Agent Vargas said that one of Rolsky's soldiers called him 'Regular Army.' A recruit in Fraser's platoon said, 'They don't make many Americans like Fraser anymore.' Fraser's other recruits seemed to agree with him almost unanimously. And yesterday I talked with a recruit that Worthing had busted in rank. The recruit was actually grateful. He admired Worthing all the more for imposing discipline."

Riley paused again, trying to organize her thoughts.

Then she said, "The three dead sergeants were very different men, and they inspired very different feelings among their recruits. But they had one thing in common. They were old-school traditionalists—men who might feel out of place in today's Army."

Larson knitted her brow.

"So what are you saying? That the killer has it in for old-school soldiers?"

Riley gulped. She knew that she was about to say something that might not make sense to Larson.

"No," she said. "If anything, I think it's possible that the killer might have been even more old school than any of his victims."

A murmur of surprise passed among the CID agents.

Agent Matthews spoke again.

"With all due respect, Agent Paige, that doesn't make any sense."

Riley understood why he and his colleagues would feel that way. Her hunches often didn't make sense until they turned out to be true. Right now, she couldn't explain her feelings rationally. But she had to try.

"It's hard to explain," Riley said. "But I got a strong feeling at the spot where Worthing's killer had been when he fired."

Larson's eyebrows rose.

"A feeling?" she asked.

Riley hesitated. Bill and Lucy were used to her unorthodox methods. But it was always difficult to explain what she had felt to people who had never worked with her before.

She was relieved when Bill spoke up.

"Agent Paige has unusually strong intuitions, Colonel. In the BAU, she's known for getting into a killer's mind. When she visits a crime scene, she often gets a sense of the situation, like she did yesterday."

Riley hoped Bill's explanation had helped.

She said, "I got the feeling that the shooter is a soldier's soldier. He might feel more out of place here at Fort Mowat than the sergeants did. He might feel like an outright anachronism."

Agent Matthews looked genuinely puzzled.

He said, "But why would one old-school soldier decide to kill others like himself?"

Riley knew that it was a good question. And at the moment, she had no answer for it.

Larson shook her head warily.

"I don't know what to think of this," she said. "Agent Paige, like I said yesterday, your reputation precedes you. I've admired your achievements. But your methods—well, they're awfully subjective for my taste."

Bill spoke again.

"Colonel, I've been working with Agent Paige for many years, and her hunches are very seldom wrong."

Larson tapped her pencil against her desk again.

"'Seldom' isn't the same as never, Agent Jeffreys. And 'hunches' aren't the same as facts. From what little we know so far, I'm pretty sure that Agent Paige is wrong this time. We're dealing with Islamic extremism. Period."

The words stung Riley. She'd liked Larson when she met her. She'd thought they could work well together. But Larson was clearly offended by Riley's odd skills. It even seemed that the colonel was becoming a new adversary.

I've got enough of those back in Quantico, she thought.

Bill still seemed determined to stand up for Riley.

He said, "Respectfully, Colonel, you brought in BAU agents to work as profilers. That's exactly what Agent Paige is doing. And my guess is that you'll ignore her insights at your peril."

Larson looked angry now.

She said, "This is still my base, Agent Jeffreys. And if 'profiling' is all about acting on half-baked subjective feelings, I'm afraid I don't have much use for it. Now if you don't mind, I'd like the three of you to leave. Let me and my agents get on with our work."

Riley, Lucy, and Bill looked at each other, dumbfounded.

Then they stood up and left Col. Larson's office without a further word.

As they walked away from the building Bill said, "Did I just imagine it, or did we just get fired?"

"You didn't imagine it," Riley said.

"So what do we do now?" Lucy asked. "Go back to Quantico?"

Riley scoffed at the idea.

"Not on your life," she said. "There's too much at stake here and we're just getting started."

CHAPTER EIGHTEEN

Riley and her colleagues went straight from the CID building to the car that the base had assigned them. As they drove back to the beach cottage, Riley sensed that Bill and Lucy were both discouraged.

She didn't feel discouraged.

She felt energized.

She felt more determined than ever to solve this case. In fact, she was beginning to feel downright competitive about it.

Col. Larson had called Riley's skills "half-baked subjective feelings." Of course, Riley had dealt with that kind of criticism before. But she had been a successful agent long enough to know that her profiling talent was real.

When they got to the cottage, they sat around the kitchen table. Riley imagined what they must look like. Here they were, a middle-aged man and woman whose personal lives had been badly battered during their years of FBI service. And a young Latina who had only been out on a few assignments.

But Riley knew that she and Bill were among the most successful of FBI agents. They had proved their profiling and investigative skills again and again. And that young Latina was among the best that Riley had seen come through the academy.

Riley wanted her three-agent team to beat Col. Larson and her brilliant CID agents to the end of this case.

"You're a glum-looking pair," Riley said.

"I don't see what we can do," Lucy said.

"I don't either," Bill said. "We're cut off from the base's CID resources. We've got no access to their data or resources. Or personnel."

Riley smiled.

"Maybe not," she said. "But BAU resources can beat CID resources any day."

Her colleagues' eyes lit up with interest and surprise.

"But we just got fired," Lucy said.

"Yeah," Bill said. "And by the very officer who requested our help."

Riley chuckled mischievously.

"She didn't say that exactly, not in so many words," Riley said. "She asked us to leave the room. I'm not sure we need to interpret that as being 'fired.' In fact, right now I'm inclined to think rather differently. All she wanted was a chance to confer with her CID agents alone. If she reports otherwise to Meredith—well, maybe we misunderstood."

Bill let out a grunt of uneasy laughter.

"You're going to get us all into trouble, aren't you?" he said.

Riley looked each of her colleagues in the eyes.

"Look, I know the two of you aren't used to going rogue. I am."

Bill sighed a little.

"Yeah, and you're used to getting suspended and fired."

Riley said, "If you two feel skittish about this thing, I understand. I'll go it alone."

"Huh-uh," Lucy said, shaking her head. "We're better than that."

"Count us both in," Bill said.

"OK, then," Riley said. "How do we proceed?"

They all thought in silence for a moment.

Finally Bill said, "We've got to play catch-up. They've already had time to pore over complete records of all personnel who come and go at Fort Mowat—military *and* civilian."

Riley had to admit that sounded pretty daunting.

She said, "On a base like this, there have got to be more civilian personnel than military. Larson has got civilians working with the CID. And there are civilian attorneys, contractors, and engineers at any big military base."

Bill shook his head warily.

He said, "And a lot of the base's computer and information tech people are civilians. And some of the medical staff and social workers. It's a long list. They've all got ID passes, and they've been through background checks and various levels of security clearances."

Riley said, "But don't forget—we've got access to BAU sources, including a crack technical department."

"It sounds like we should call Sam Flores," Bill said.

Riley nodded in agreement. This definitely seemed like a job for the head of the Quantico technical analysis team.

Before Riley could speak, Lucy let out a squeal of delight.

"Oooh! Can I call him!"

Riley was surprised by Lucy's sudden girlish attitude.

"I don't see why not," she said.

Lucy flipped open her laptop and got Flores on video. She looked happy to see his nerdish, bespectacled face. Flores had an unusually wide grin.

"Hey, Sammy," Lucy said.

"Hey, Lucita," Flores said.

Nicknames? Riley thought.

"What's going on in California?" Sam asked.

"Well, just the usual. We're trying to catch a serial killer."

"You don't say," Sam said playfully. "It's those three sergeants at Fort Mowat, right?"

"Yeah," Lucy said.

"I'm impressed."

"Aw, shucks, it's just our job," Lucy said in the same playful tone.

Riley had never known either of the two to be silly. She was surprised by this obvious flirtation.

Lucy told Sam, "We need to do a comprehensive search of all the personnel who have come and gone on Fort Mowat lately, both civilian and military."

"What kind of parameters do you want?" Sam asked.

Lucy looked at Riley expectantly.

Riley thought for a few seconds. Then she said, "Let's start by looking for civilians who work on the base and were once in the Army."

"Anything else?"

Riley paused to think again.

She said, "See if you can narrow it down to people who learned sharpshooting skills in the military."

"Right-o," Sam said, starting to type away.

"How long do you think it will take, Sammy?" Lucy asked.

Sam chuckled.

"Just time me, Lucita."

While Flores's fingers clattered away at his computer, Riley led Bill away from the table.

She asked him in a whisper, "Are Lucy and Sam an item?"

Bill chuckled quietly and whispered back, "You didn't know? I thought everybody did. I'm not sure it's serious yet, but it definitely seems to be a thing."

Bill walked back over to the table.

Riley was dumbstruck. How could she have missed something like this when it had been going on right under her nose?

Some detective I am, she thought.

In the moments that Riley waited for Flores's results, a different concern flashed through her mind. She hadn't heard from

82

Hatcher.

He'd said …

"You'd damn well better make sure nobody else comes around here."

She had also sent another text to Shirley but the woman was erratic and unpredictable.

Riley pulled out her cell phone and sent a text message to the number Hatcher had called from.

I swear to U, I fired that woman.

She sighed. What else could she do or say right now?

She heard Flores's voice from the computer.

"I've got the info. How long did it take, Lucita?"

Lucy grinned.

"Thirty-five seconds on the dot, Sammy," she said.

"Liar. I'll bet you weren't even timing me."

Lucy giggled.

"Sorry. I just couldn't take my eyes off your adorable face."

Riley rejoined Bill at the table. They stood looking at the screen over Lucy's shoulders.

"What have you got, Flores?" Riley asked.

Flores's eyes darted over the information he'd found.

He said, "About an eighth of the civilians who now work on the base once served in the Army. Of those, only twelve seem to have achieved exceptional sharpshooting skills."

Riley's nerves quickened. Flores was definitely narrowing things down.

She asked, "Do any of those twelve stand out in any way?"

Flores peered closely at the records.

He said, "You've got to be considering Islamic extremism, right?"

Riley was startled. In spite of the two colonels insisting that's what they were dealing with, her gut had told her otherwise. But of course, she couldn't say they'd ruled it out.

"Yes," she said.

"Well, I've got one hit if I also sort by ethnicity, and he *really* stands out. His name is Omar Shaheed, and his parents emigrated from Yemen. He's been working on a construction team for a couple of on-base building projects."

Riley scratched her chin.

She asked, "What can you tell me about his record?"

Flores said, "He served a three-year term of duty but never saw combat. He had some psych issues during his term. But he was exceptional in most respects, including marksmanship. He got an honorable discharge, and he didn't have any trouble getting civilian clearance."

Riley thought for a few seconds.

"All three murders were at night. Do you know the actual times?" she asked Flores.

"Yes," Flores said.

Riley then said, "Shaheed had to sign in and out on the base whenever he came or went. There must be records of that. See if he was there during those times."

They all waited while Flores's fingers danced on his keyboard again.

"Holy smoke," he said. "He's been working lots of night shifts—including the hours when the three sergeants were killed."

"Have you got an address for him?" Riley asked.

"Yes," Flores said. "He lives in a little town called Cordele. It's near Fort Mowat."

Riley could sense her partners' rising excitement.

"Is he on the base right now?" Bill asked.

Flores typed a bit, then said, "No, this is down time. He's scheduled to be back at work tonight."

"Give us that address," Riley said. "We'll get over there right away."

As Riley and her colleagues got ready to leave, she felt a rush of alarm.

Had Adams and Larson been right that this was a case of Islamic terrorism?

Had Riley's hunch been wrong?

Was she losing her edge?

She felt sure of one thing—that Col. Larson and her team would soon narrow their search to the same man, if they hadn't already.

She was determined to talk to this Omar Shaheed before he got swept up by the CID.

CHAPTER NINETEEN

During the drive to the town where Omar Shaheed lived, Lucy couldn't stop thinking about Sam Flores. She'd always found it fun to talk with Quantico's head techno geek, and took every chance she got to do so.

She told herself sternly to get her head into the game at hand.

We've got a bad guy to catch.

And it seemed likely that they were going to pick him up very soon. They could go back to Quantico and she could turn her attention to Sam. She'd found it obvious for a while now that he was just as interested in her as she was in him.

But they still hadn't gone out on a date yet.

Sam seemed too shy to ask her, so it was going to be up to her to ask him.

When Lucy had first noticed the spark between them, she checked the FBI rules about fraternization. She found no rules at all against FBI personnel dating each other.

She'd been surprised—and relieved.

Lucy studied Agent Paige's face as Agent Jeffreys drove. Lucy couldn't tell what she was thinking. Agent Paige had obviously been surprised back at the cabin at the way she and Sam talked with each other. Apparently, she hadn't already figured out that something might be going on between them. She wondered how she felt about the idea.

Did she disapprove?

Lucy's heart sank at the very thought. Agent Paige was her hero, and the last thing she wanted to do was disappoint her.

But maybe Agent Paige wouldn't judge her too hard. After all, Lucy had noticed a certain sexual tension between Agent Paige and Agent Jeffreys from time to time. She wondered, had they ever acted on it? Did they even consciously know about it?

Well, it was none of Lucy's business, and she sure wasn't going to ask them about it.

She just hoped that Agent Paige wasn't going to see her own possible budding romance as a problem.

Well, I just can't let it be *a problem,* Lucy thought. *Starting right now I'm going to be OK with it.*

She decided to put Sam out of her mind as long as they were working on the case.

When she got back to Quantico, she'd make her move.

Right now, Lucy was a little worried about Agent Paige. She'd seemed taken aback by the news that their suspect was a Muslim. That was hardly surprising, since Agent Paige had been so adamant with Col. Larson about her hunch that the killings had nothing to do with Islamic extremism.

Lucy knew that it was an honest mistake—if it was a mistake. It wasn't like Agent Paige's skills were starting to slip.

Lucy wanted to tell Agent Paige not to take it too hard, but of course, that would probably make her feel worse.

When Agent Jeffreys drove them into Cordele, Lucy saw that it was an ordinary little Southern California town. There was no grass in the yards, but there was a variety of decorative plants around the homes, and palm trees towered here and there.

They drove through a neighborhood of upscale housing and finally arrived on a street of smaller homes set closely together. Agent Jeffreys parked in front of the address that Sam had given them.

It was a little manufactured house with a carport on one side. A pickup truck was parked there, with its hood raised. A man was bent over the engine, working on it.

As Lucy and her partners walked toward him, he looked up from the engine. He was dark-skinned and curly-haired.

"Can I help you?" he asked.

Lucy noticed no accent in his voice.

Lucy and her partners produced their badges and introduced themselves.

"Are you Omar Shaheed?" Agent Jeffreys asked.

"Yeah," the man said. "Is something the matter?"

Lucy thought she heard a note of nervousness in his voice. But that didn't necessarily mean anything. Just about anybody would become nervous when approached by three FBI agents.

"We would like to talk with you for a few minutes," Agent Paige said. "May we come inside?"

Shaheed's dark eyes darted about nervously.

"What's this all about?" he asked.

Agent Jeffreys asked, "Are you aware of the three recent murders at Fort Mowat?"

Shaheed nodded.

"Yeah. Terrible thing."

Agent Paige asked, "Can you account for your whereabouts when Sergeant Clifford Worthing was killed?"

Shaheed was shifting his weight from foot to foot uneasily.

86

Lucy felt her suspicion rising. She was sure that her colleagues felt the same.

"I'm not sure," he said. "When was it exactly?"

Agent Jeffreys told him the time and date of the murder.

The man smiled a little. Lucy didn't know how to read that smile.

"I was on the base," Shaheed said. "I've been working construction on two new building sites there. We've been working crazy round-the-clock hours."

"What's the nature of your work there?" Agent Paige asked.

"I drive a truck," Shaheed said. "I move materials from site to site."

Lucy noticed his eyes shifting toward an open tool cabinet along the wall of the carport.

Agent Paige said, "We'd like to come inside and talk."

In a blindingly fast movement, Shaheed reached into the cabinet. Before any of the agents could draw their weapons, he had a semiautomatic pistol in his hand. Lucy recognized it as a Beretta 92.

Lucy saw that Agent Paige had her gun half drawn, but she slid it back in place.

Shaheed swung his weapon back and forth, pointing at one agent and then another.

"Get your hands in the air," he said. His voice had a tone of desperation.

"You don't want to do this," Agent Paige said.

"I said get your hands in the air."

Lucy knew that neither she nor her colleagues could take out a weapon without one of them getting shot. As they all raised their hands, she saw that Agents Paige and Jeffreys each took a step sideways, moving a bit farther away from each other.

"Now get on the ground, face down," he said.

Agent Paige and Agent Jeffreys just stood there, staring at the man. They obviously had no intention of complying. They weren't going to put themselves at that much of a disadvantage. Facing Shaheed, sooner or later one of them could make a move.

Lucy also stood her ground. She knew it was a risk. Of course Agents Paige and Jeffreys knew that too. She watched them carefully. When one of them moved she would follow their lead.

"Get down, I said," Shaheed barked.

The agents still did nothing. Lucy felt that the air was crackling with tension. She could see hesitation in the man's face now. He had realized that if he shot any one of the agents, he would immediately be killed by one of the others.

Without a word, Shaheed wheeled around and darted out through the open back of the carport. As Lucy and her partners drew their weapons and followed, he disappeared through a gate in a tall fence.

When the three agents dashed through the gate, they found themselves looking up and down an empty alley.

"Which way do you think he went?" Lucy asked.

"We'll have to split up," Agent Paige said.

He can't have gotten very far," Agent Jeffreys said.

Lucy took off in a run down the alley to the left, and Agent Paige went in the other direction. Agent Jeffreys started checking each potential hiding place nearby.

Lucy ran as fast as she could, looking in all directions as she ran. Most of the fences along the alley were tall, but some were short enough to see over. Over one of those, she glimpsed motion between two houses.

It was Shaheed.

He must have cut through a yard, because he was now running along the sidewalk in front of the houses.

Without pausing to think, Lucy leaped over the fence and tore between the two houses. When she reached the sidewalk, Shaheed was just a short distance away. He was still holding the gun in his right hand.

She drew her weapon.

"Freeze!" she shouted.

Shaheed skidded to a stop.

"Put down your weapon!" she yelled.

Shaheed just stood there facing away from her.

"Put down your weapon, I said."

Instead, Shaheed slowly turned toward her, still holding the Beretta at his side.

Lucy gulped hard. She understood the choice she had to make. She had learned from her training that now was the time to use deadly force.

But she couldn't bring herself pull the trigger. She'd never killed anyone. She'd always known that this day would come. But she had no idea that she'd freeze like this.

Time seemed stop, and Lucy felt frozen.

Am I really going to let him kill me? she wondered.

Suddenly she heard a voice shouting.

"Put down the weapon!"

It was Agent Jeffreys' voice. Then he emerged from between two houses, his weapon drawn.

Agent Paige appeared from behind Lucy. She also had her gun in hand.

Lucy realized that they both had heard her shout. They had come to help.

"Put down the weapon!" Agent Paige yelled. "Now."

This time Shaheed stooped down and put his gun on the sidewalk.

Agent Jeffreys yelled, "Hands behind your back! Now!"

Shaheed complied.

Agent Jeffreys handcuffed him and read him his rights.

"Good work," Agent Paige told Lucy. "If you hadn't been alert and made it here so fast, he'd have gotten away."

Lucy's hand shook as she holstered her weapon.

"I should have shot him," she said.

"Yeah, you should have," Agent Paige said, giving her a sharp look. "You should have defended yourself. It would have been correct procedure."

"If you hadn't gotten here—"

"You got lucky. But we're all lucky to take him alive. And you caught him. Agent Jeffreys and I will get him into the car. You go take a look inside the house."

As Agents Paige and Jeffreys hustled Shaheed toward the car, Lucy hurried toward Shaheed's little house. The front door was unlocked, so she walked on inside.

The small living room was neat and simple, with abstract Islamic decor here and there on the walls. She continued on into the house's single small bedroom. It was even plainer than the living room, with no decorations whatsoever—just a single bed, a chest of drawers, and a prayer rug on the floor.

But when Lucy stooped down to look under the bed, she saw that seemingly countless weapons were stuffed in there. They looked like military weapons, including sniper rifles, and boxes of ammunition. She went to the chest and opened one drawer. It, too, was full of weapons. Then she went over to the closet and opened it.

It was packed too, with dynamite and what looked like ingredients needed to make other explosives.

Lucy shuddered as she tried to take it all in.

This looked like preparations for something big. What kind of attack had Shaheed been planning?

And who else was involved?

Because he certainly hadn't put together this arsenal by himself, just for his own use.

Lucy wanted to feel relieved that they'd prevented whatever had been about to happen. But somehow, no relief kicked in.

She had a hunch that their work wasn't anywhere near over.

CHAPTER TWENTY

Riley stood with Bill looking through the two-way mirror into the CID's interrogation room. Inside the small, brightly lit room, Lucy was questioning Omar Shaheed. The prisoner was manacled to a table and Lucy sat facing him from the other side. Riley could see the young agent scanning the prisoner's face, watching for any response to her words.

"She's doing good work in there," Bill said.

"She sure is," Riley said. "She's always been good at this kind of thing."

Riley was glad that she'd arranged for Lucy to take the first crack at interrogating Shaheed. She hadn't drawn any information out of him yet, but she was just getting started.

In fact, Lucy's interrogation techniques were quite exceptional. All alone, she was managing to alternate between "bad cop" and "good cop" modes of questioning—by turns insulting and empathetic.

Riley observed that even Lucy's "bad cop" had a disarming sweetness about it.

Lucy said to Shaheed, "I could have killed you, you know."

Shaheed smirked at her bitterly.

"You should have done it," Shaheed said to Lucy.

Lucy smiled across the table at him.

"That wouldn't have been much of a martyrdom, would it— getting nobody killed but yourself? You want to take out as many infidels as you can. And to be killed by a woman ... well, Allah surely wouldn't be very pleased by that, would he? I'll bet there wouldn't be all those virgins waiting for you in paradise."

The man spit at her and said something ugly in Arabic.

Even so, Lucy kept her cool and her smile and continued asking questions.

Riley was proud of her protégé. She was always good at working with people. But Riley was also a bit worried about Lucy. She'd seen the young agent's shakiness after they captured Shaheed.

Riley said to Bill, "I can tell she's taking what happened back there kind of hard."

Bill said, "You mean not shooting when she should have?"

Riley nodded.

Bill said, "Well, it's probably a good thing if she takes it hard.

It was a mistake, after all. She needs to learn from it."

"You're right," Riley agreed. "Just as long as she's not too rough on herself."

Bill said, "Lots of new agents have the same problem early on."

After a pause, he added, "I froze up my first time too."

Riley looked at him with surprise.

"I didn't know that," she said.

"Well, I'm not exactly proud of it. If my partner hadn't been fast and decisive, I wouldn't be alive today. But I learned my lesson."

Another silence fell.

Then Bill said, "It's not easy to kill someone."

Riley felt a shiver deep inside. It was true of course—most of the time and for most agents.

It was usually true even for Riley.

But sometimes it had been all too easy.

She could remember taking pleasure in one vicious killer's death.

In fact, whenever she remembered it she could feel herself smashing his head with a rock, time and time again. She could feel herself liking what she was doing.

Of course, it had been personal then. The man was a sadistic psychopath who had held both Riley and April prisoner and tormented them.

Riley had to wonder—would Lucy ever be seized by that kind of bloodlust?

For Lucy's sake, Riley hoped not. Something like that changed you. She still didn't know all the ways it had changed her. She wasn't sure she wanted to know.

She remembered what Private Pope had asked her on the top of that cliff yesterday.

"How many people have you killed?"

Riley shuddered.

Don't start counting, she told herself. *Don't even think about it.*

As they watched and listened, Lucy shifted into another line of questioning. Now she was really turning on the empathy.

"Look, I know I'm just an infidel, but I know a little about how you feel."

Shaheed looked somewhat disarmed.

"You couldn't possibly know," he said.

"It's a rotten society, isn't it?" Lucy said. "The West, I mean.

In many ways, anyhow. So materialistic. So unjust. No spiritual center. And so intolerant of others. I'm Mexican-American, you know. I've seen lots of prejudice. My family has been through hard times."

Riley could see Shaheed's face soften.

Lucy's getting to him, she thought.

The young agent asked in a gentle voice, "What was it about those sergeants in particular? Rolsky, Fraser, and Worthing? I'm sure that you're planning something much more magnificent than a few isolated killings. Why did you start with them?"

Shaheed was making direct eye contact with Lucy now.

"I didn't kill them," he said. "I swear to you I didn't."

Riley felt a jolt at his tone of voice.

Lucy asked, "Then who did?"

Shaheed smiled slightly. "I don't know who did. Whoever it was, they aren't connected with me. I don't know anything about it."

It sounded as if he were telling the truth.

Riley could tell by Lucy's expression that she felt that too.

Lucy asked, "But you were planning to kill someone. Are you going to deny that was your mission?"

"No," Shaheed said. "I don't deny my mission. But not them. I didn't even know them. I had nothing against them. Those men would only be killed by me if they were in the wrong place at the wrong time."

Lucy paused for a moment. She seemed to be studying Shaheed's face.

Then she said, "We know you have accomplices. You couldn't have put together that arsenal on your own. You couldn't *use* all that firepower on your own. You're going to have to tell us who they are. The sooner you do, the better."

Riley stepped away from the window and said softly to Bill, "Something's wrong here. This doesn't feel right to me. He doesn't seem like our sniper. Does he to you?"

"No," Bill muttered. "I think he was planning an attack, and we just stumbled across him before he could carry it out. His bad luck."

"And good luck for our side. But we haven't found the man we've been looking for. So what do we do next?" Riley wondered aloud.

They were interrupted by Sergeant Matthews, the head of the CID investigating team. He walked up to Riley and Bill and announced, "Col. Larson wants to see you in her office."

Riley's heart sank.

She had a feeling that she wasn't prepared for this meeting.

CHAPTER TWENTY ONE

When Riley and Bill followed the sergeant into the colonel's office, Larson was sitting behind her desk. She was visibly uncomfortable as she gestured to them to sit down.

Riley and Bill seated themselves and waited for the CID head to tell them what was on her mind. Riley's sense of dread was mounting.

"Congratulations are in order," Larson began. Then she frowned slightly and added, "I can't say I much like your methods, Agent Paige—or the way you went over my head. But you got results. You got our man."

Larson drummed her fingers on her desk for a moment.

"I'm not going to announce that the case is closed," she said. "We're not even letting the press know that we've made an arrest."

"Of course," Riley replied. "You don't want to alert any other cell members or sympathizers. You hope to pick them up before the news gets out."

Larson nodded. "I don't want to say I told you so," she continued. "But you *were* wrong about the killer. This man is definitely an Islamic extremist."

Riley had to bite her tongue. She didn't want to get into an argument—at least not yet. But she was sure that some kind of intense disagreement was in the works.

Larson changed the subject slightly. "How is Agent Vargas doing with her interrogation?"

"Very well," Riley said. "She's developing into one of the very best at that."

"Do you think Shaheed is going to give up his accomplices?"

"I'm all but sure of it," Riley said. "He doesn't strike me as especially strong-willed. Maybe the people he's working with are tougher. But he's a weak link, and he'll definitely crack. You should be able to round up the whole cell before long. Just keep Agent Vargas working on him."

Larson looked at Riley for a moment.

Then she said, "That won't be necessary. Your work here is done, all of you. And I really mean that this time. I expect you to fly back to Quantico at the next opportunity."

Riley felt a flash of alarm.

She said, "With all due respect, Colonel, I don't think that's wise."

"Why not? We do have our own interrogators who can do the job."

Riley hesitated.

"I'm sure you do," she said. "But it would be a mistake for us to leave because Shaheed is not the killer we're looking for."

Larson's eyes widened. Riley could tell from the slight flare of her nostrils that the colonel was struggling to hold her impatience in check.

"That just doesn't make sense, Agent Paige. He'd turned his house into an ammunition dump. He's obviously planning some much larger violent attack."

"That's right," Riley said. "He's *planning* it. And he's surely got accomplices for what he's got in mind. But he didn't kill our three sniper victims. I'm all but sure of it."

Larson just stared at her with disbelief.

Riley continued, "He's a fanatic, and he's full of radical ideas, and he's full of hate and rage. He's a *killer*—or at least he hopes to be. But he's not a stalker. Not in the sense of a hunter stalking specific prey. That's a completely different profile."

Larson shook her head.

"This is just a lot of psychobabble," she said.

Riley felt stymied. She couldn't think of any way to convince Larson.

Then Bill said, "Colonel, I've got a feeling Agent Paige is right. If you'll just give us more time on the base—"

"No," Larson said, interrupting. "The case is closed."

Riley's mind raced, trying to think of what to say.

She asked, "Have you checked out Shaheed's alibi? He claims to have been working on the construction sites at the times of the killings."

"We're looking into it," Larson said. "But his alibi is anything but airtight. His job was to drive a truck back and forth between two building sites delivering materials. I doubt that anyone will be able to account for his precise whereabouts during the times of the shootings."

Riley thought some more.

She said, "What about ballistics? Have you matched the bullets to any of the weapons in his possession?"

"He had three M110 sniper rifles in his stash."

"That doesn't answer my question," Riley said.

"We'll run a check in due time," Larson said.

In due time? Riley thought.

She tried to swallow down her frustration.

Larson's voice was starting to shake from anger.

"Agent Paige, I'm starting to feel like there's something personal about all this. Have you got something against me?"

Riley was shocked.

"Personal? No. I'm just trying to do my job."

Larson rose from her chair.

"Well, you've done your job. And I've commended you for it. And now, if you don't mind, you'd better get ready to leave. You've been a great help, and we appreciate it. But my people and I can take it from here. Tell Agent Vargas that she can leave the rest of the interrogation to us."

Riley looked at Bill. His expression told her that there was nothing more to do or say. She knew he was right.

They left Colonel Larson's office and headed back to the interrogation room to get Lucy.

*

An hour later, Riley and her colleagues were back at their beach cottage packing up to leave. Lucy was ready to go and on the patio taking one last look across the sand to the ocean. Bill was loading his gear in the car.

Just as Riley finished putting her things together and closed her bag, she got a phone call from Brent Meredith.

"Col. Larson says you're finished there," Meredith said. "Congratulations. But I get the feeling she's going to be happy to see you gone. Did you have some kind of problems with her?"

Riley sighed.

"Agent Meredith, I think Col. Larson is making a terrible mistake. My gut tells me that Omar Shaheed isn't our killer. He's an aspiring terrorist, and he surely has accomplices. But he's no sniper."

A silence fell.

Riley continued, "I know Col. Larson is under a lot of pressure. The base is swarming with reporters, and the publicity is getting really ugly. She wants to be able to tell them that the case is closed. But I've got serious doubts."

There was another silence.

Finally Meredith said, "Agent Paige, you know I have a world of respect for your instincts. If it were my call, I might tell you to stay. But it's not my call. Col. Larson asked for BAU help, and you're there at her pleasure. She's got the final word."

Riley stifled a groan.

"I understand, sir," she said.

"I want to see you and your team in my office first thing tomorrow," Meredith said.

"We'll be there, sir," Riley said.

She ended the call and drew a sigh of resignation. She would return to Quantico as ordered. But she still didn't believe that this case was over. She believed that an unknown man was still out there, a skilled marksman who would soon be stalking another soldier.

CHAPTER TWENTY TWO

The next morning, Riley got up early to go to the debriefing at Quantico. It was Saturday, and the girls were still sleeping in, but they had both been cheerful when she arrived at home last night. In fact, home had seemed remarkably peaceful after her arguments with authorities at Fort Mowat.

When she arrived at BAU, the only worry nagging at Riley was the sniper she was afraid would strike again in California. But as she walked toward Meredith's office, she ran into Agent Jennifer Roston in the hall.

The younger agent said, "Agent Paige, could I have a word with you for a moment?"

"I'm due for a meeting with Chief Meredith," Riley said, looking at her watch.

"I understand. This will only take a minute."

"OK," Riley said.

As the two women stood talking together in the hallway, Riley again noticed that, although the new agent wasn't large, her very posture signaled competence. Right now her expression was extremely inquisitive.

Roston said, "You know I'm working full time now on tracking down Shane Hatcher."

Riley nodded uncomfortably. She had a sinking feeling about whatever Roston was going to ask her.

Roston said, "You gave me access to all computer files pertaining to Hatcher, and I really appreciate that."

She paused for a moment, then added, "But one file seems to be missing. It was listed in the summary, but I couldn't find it anywhere. It was titled just 'THOUGHTS.'"

Riley tried to hide her alarm.

I should have expected this, she thought.

A bright young agent like Roston was sure to notice that a file had been deleted. She was bound to be curious about it.

"Oh, that one," Riley said. "It was just rough notes that I jotted down from time to time as I worked."

Roston squinted at Riley with curiosity.

"But why did you delete it?" she asked.

Riley's mind raced as she tried to think of an explanation.

"Because it was all just redundant stuff," she said. "All the information in it was duplicated in the other files that you've got.

And it was so rough, nobody but me could have made any sense of it."

Roston looked almost skeptical now.

"Do you have a backup of it?" Roston asked.

"No," Riley said, clenching up inside at yet another lie. She'd kept a copy of that file on a thumb drive at home.

Riley knew that a technician might still be able to retrieve the deleted file if it hadn't been overwritten. She didn't want to stir up any suspicions that might drive Roston to get someone's help on that.

"OK," Roston said. "I just wish there was more information, especially about Hatcher's financial connections. How he manages to stay at large amazes me. He must have considerable resources and dedicated accomplices. But I'll connect the dots sooner or later."

Riley couldn't help but wince at those words—*"dedicated accomplices."*

Was that what she'd become—Hatcher's dedicated accomplice?

She hoped Roston didn't notice her reaction.

Roston smiled and said, "Anyway, I won't keep you. Great work on that Fort Mowat case, by the way. Congratulations."

"Thanks," Riley said. She didn't feel as though congratulations were in order. But she certainly didn't want to get into her misgivings about the case with Roston right now.

Riley added, "And let me know if I can help you out in any way."

"I'll do that," Roston said.

Roston continued on her way, and Riley headed on toward Meredith's office.

When she got there, she found that Bill and Lucy had already arrived. She sat down with them in front of Meredith's desk. She sensed that Meredith had been waiting for her to arrive to start their discussion. She was relieved to see that they all looked relaxed. There had already been enough tension this morning as far as she was concerned.

Meredith sat silently looking among their faces for a few moments.

Finally he said to Bill and Lucy, "I know that Agent Paige has got misgivings about how you've wrapped up the Fort Mowat case. How do the two of you feel about it?"

Bill and Lucy glanced at each other.

Then Lucy said, "I interrogated Shaheed for a while. He's an aspiring terrorist all right—full of resentment and rage and violent ideology. But …"

Lucy's voice trailed off.

"But what?" Meredith asked.

"But I just don't think he's our sniper."

Meredith cradled his fingers together and thought for a moment.

"What about you, Agent Jeffreys?" he asked.

Bill shook his head.

"I don't think he's our killer either. Shaheed was definitely planning some big attack, and we're sure he had accomplices. Our killer is a loner. He picks off his prey one at a time. And he's got personal reasons for it."

Meredith leaned forward toward them.

He said, "I talked to Col. Larson a little while ago. She said that during the night Shaheed cracked under questioning. He gave away his accomplices. The CID picked them all up last night. It might be a while before Larson and her team can learn exactly what sort of attack they were planning. But whatever it was, it's not going to happen. Thanks to the three of you, many lives have been saved."

Riley spoke up quickly.

"Actually, Agent Vargas deserves a lot of the credit. If it weren't for her speed and skill, Shaheed would have gotten away. We might still be trying to track him down."

Bill added, "And the rest of the cell would surely have slipped away."

Meredith nodded.

"Good work, Vargas," he said.

Agent Vargas let out a rather timid "thank you." Riley was sure that Lucy was still angry with herself about freezing when she'd caught up with Shaheed. It had been an important lesson for Lucy and one that might save her life in another encounter.

Meredith spoke next to Riley.

"I don't suppose I need to tell you that Col. Larson complained to me about your attitude."

Riley gulped a little. But there was nothing unusual about Meredith getting complaints about her.

"I'm not surprised, sir," she said.

"What are your impressions of the colonel?"

Riley thought for a moment.

"Well, our differences aside, I've got nothing but respect for her. She runs an excellent CID office at Fort Mowat. I wish we could have hit it off better."

"I wish so too," Meredith said. "But it's not our job to make everyone happy."

He looked at all three agents and added, "It does worry me that none of you think we've got our sniper. And I hope that Col. Lawson doesn't have to regret not listening to you. But it was her call to take you off the case, and I'm not in a position to contradict her."

Another silence fell.

Then Meredith said, "You've done a good job, all of you. You've got no cases pending at the moment. Take some time to relax. That's an order."

Riley and her colleagues got up and left the office.

Sam Flores was standing just outside Meredith's door, obviously waiting for Lucy.

Flores said, "How about some coffee, Lucita?"

Lucy grinned back at him.

"I'd love that, Sammy."

As Riley watched them walk away together she realized that she was smiling. She glanced at Bill.

"Youth," he said, with a grin. "See you in a few days."

Riley nodded, and they headed off to their separate vehicles.

As she was driving home, Riley reminded herself of what Meredith had said.

"Take some time to relax. That's an order."

She was determined to do that. She would love to spend some time with her girls.

But a troublesome image kept forming in her mind. It was a faceless killer lovingly assembling his M110 rifle.

CHAPTER TWENTY THREE

By the time Riley got home, she had almost pushed her concerns about an agent with questions and a sniper with plans out of her mind. She had convinced herself that April and Jilly would be able to distract her from her worries. But when she got home, Gabriela told her that Jilly was at volleyball practice and April was hanging out with Liam. Then Gabriela went to her own apartment, singing cheerfully all the way down the stairs.

Riley sat down in her living room and looked around. It was a typical Saturday—a nice spring day—and it seemed that everyone in her life had something to do except her.

And now she couldn't help thinking about what she'd said to Agent Roston about the missing file …

"It was all just redundant stuff."

She didn't feel good about lying to Roston like that. But Riley's dealings with Hatcher demanded that she lie again and again—often to people who ought to have every reason to trust her.

And now Riley had to wonder …

Did Roston believe me?

Riley remembered the young woman's intense, steady gaze.

Although Roston was new at the BAU, she already had a reputation for being sharp and determined. Normally, Riley would simply admire those qualities in a promising young agent.

But right now, they were only causes for worry. And for a growing sense of shame.

How had she allowed Hatcher to assume so much power over her?

And what was she going to do about it?

She shuddered as she remembered Hatcher's rage the last time she'd talked to him …

"You'd damn well better make sure nobody else comes around here."

The more Riley thought about it, the more bizarre the whole situation seemed. She had an escaped convict living at the cabin she'd inherited from her father, and he had been threatened by an overly enthusiastic Realtor eager to sell it. Well, she'd finally fired Shirley Redding, and that should be the end of it. But why had the Realtor kept showing the cabin to prospective buyers even after Riley said to take it off the market?

What was the matter with that woman?

She realized that she really didn't know much about Shirley. Riley had hired her to sell her father's cabin mostly out of convenience. Shirley's office wasn't far from the cabin, and she had seemed like a good choice at the time. When they had talked over the phone, Shirley had shown a familiarity with properties in that area. In fact, Shirley had sounded exactly like the kind of real estate agent that Riley needed.

But the truth was that Riley hadn't done any research about Shirley before hiring her. Now her curiosity urged her to check the Realtor out.

She went upstairs to her bedroom office and ran an Internet search on Shirley Redding.

She was alarmed at what she saw.

It was a long list of complaints about Shirley from dismayed buyers and sellers.

Many said that she was much too aggressive and didn't know when to quit.

Others suggested that she was emotionally unstable.

Riley's throat clutched.

I should have checked, she thought. *I shouldn't have hired her.*

Until now, Riley had hoped that her blunt text message telling Shirley that she'd been fired was enough to dissuade her.

But now Riley couldn't be so sure.

Riley dialed the Realtor's office number. Again, she got an answering machine, but this time the message informed her that Shirley Redding was on vacation and would not be available for two weeks.

Riley drew a sigh of relief. At least the Realtor would be out of the picture for a while.

She briefly imagined herself driving up to the cabin right now and telling Hatcher that their deal was off, and that he had to leave the cabin.

Or maybe she'd simply arrest him.

Riley sighed as she considered how unrealistic such thoughts were.

She couldn't shake off Hatcher that easily, much less bring him to justice. Her own fate was much too intertwined with his.

She got up from her desk and paced the room, trying to shake off her worries. But other thoughts quickly crowded in. The Fort Mowat case was still nagging at her. Her gut told her that there was still a sniper loose on the base, and that he'd surely act again.

But even if she was right, what could she do about it?

Absolutely nothing that she could think of.

So why was she still obsessing about it?

This is ridiculous, Riley thought.

She was between cases, and she ought to enjoy herself. It was time to get back to a normal life, whatever that meant.

It was time to get out of the house.

It occurred to her that it was actually about time for lunch and she was getting hungry. So it seemed as good a time as any to drop by Blaine's Grill.

She remembered April telling her on the phone the night before last that Blaine wondered when she'd be coming back from Fort Mowat. Riley had promised to let them all know as soon as she did. But in the turmoil over the case, notifying Blaine that she was coming home had slipped her mind.

She was sure Blaine would be working in his restaurant today. Why not drop in and surprise him? Riley left the house and got in her car and drove straight to Blaine's Grill.

The place was extremely busy when she got there. A line of people waited to be seated. Riley realized that she shouldn't be surprised at such a lunch rush on a Saturday.

Not the best timing, she thought.

She decided she'd have to come back when things were less busy. She had turned to go when a voice called out her name.

It was Wesley, a young man who was working as host.

"It's good to see you, Riley," he said, walking toward her with a smile. "Would you like a table?"

Riley looked around and said, "Well, you seem to be awfully busy."

Wesley winked at her and spoke softly so the other customers couldn't hear.

"Don't worry. We just cleared a table. I can get you in right now."

As Wesley escorted Riley past the waiting line he spoke louder. "I'm so glad you have a reservation."

As he seated her at a nice little table just inside the door, he added, "You do have a permanent reservation here."

"Is Blaine here?" Riley asked as she sat down.

Wesley looked around.

"He's around somewhere. I'll find him and let him know you're here."

Riley began to peruse the lunch menu. When she decided to

order a chef salad, she glanced up, looking for a waiter. She caught sight of Blaine across the room. He was walking in from the patio with an attractive woman who was holding onto his arm.

Riley didn't recognize her, but she felt an instant flash of jealousy.

Blaine and the woman walked to the bar and ordered drinks, looking very cozy together. Wesley walked up to Blaine and spoke to him. Blaine looked around and spotted Riley. For a second he looked like he was about to head toward her. Then the woman tugged at his arm and whispered something in his ear.

As Blaine and the woman talked together for another few moments, Riley wished that she hadn't come. She had thought that arriving unannounced might be fun, but it was just embarrassing now.

Finally Blaine left his companion and came toward Riley's table.

As he approached, Riley's discomfort gave way to anger.

He's just going to be Ryan all over again, she thought.

She got up from her table and hastily left the restaurant, not looking back to see if Blaine was startled or relieved or annoyed.

When she reached her car in the parking lot, he caught up with her.

"Riley, what's the matter?" Blaine asked.

"Nothing," Riley said stiffly. "You just seem rather … busy."

Blaine looked confused for a moment. Then he said, "Wait a minute. Is this because of Laura?"

"Is that her name?" Riley asked. Now that she looked at him, she thought that he seemed embarrassed too.

Blaine laughed awkwardly.

"Come on, Riley. Don't tell me you're jealous. Laura and I have been friends since college. She lives in New Jersey, so we don't get to see each other very often. She's in town just for today."

"Then you'd better go spend some time with her," Riley said.

Blaine's expression of incredulity reminded Riley uncomfortably of Ryan. That was how he always looked when he was making excuses for himself. That surprised and innocent look that said, *"How could you have possibly thought … "*

"I wasn't ignoring you," Blaine said. "I didn't even know you were in town until Wesley told me you were here."

"It sure looked like you had other things on your mind."

"Well, am I ignoring you *now*?"

Riley stood with her hand on the car door handle, not looking at Blaine. She didn't know what to say. Was she overreacting? She was tired, and she'd been worrying a lot. Maybe she just wasn't thinking straight.

Blaine said, "Look, this thing with Laura—it's not a date, it's just two friends getting together."

Then after a pause, he added, "But what if it was a date? Riley, I don't know where things are between us. I mean, you're hardly ever available, and you go away for a couple of days and I don't hear a thing from you …"

Riley snapped back, "You could have called or texted *me,* you know."

She felt her face flush. She wished she hadn't said that.

God, I'm acting like a teenager, she thought.

Blaine drew a deep breath and looked down.

He said, "Besides, don't I have a right to date? We've never even discussed being exclusive."

Riley looked hard at him. Those words really stung.

Ryan had said exactly the same thing in almost exactly the same words before he'd left her last time.

"I didn't know we needed to discuss it," Riley said quietly. "I thought …"

Her voice trailed off. What she wanted to say was that she thought there was something special and unspoken between them. She'd sensed that a strong attraction had drawn them together, that a romance was obviously blossoming between them. Everything that had happened between them seemed significant to her.

But maybe she was wrong. If he didn't feel the same way, she was surely wrong.

Anyway, right now he was sure being casual about it.

She was still holding onto the car door handle.

Blaine said, "Look, maybe it's time we sorted all this out. Come back inside. Let's sit down and talk."

Riley felt herself wavering. But before she could decide, her cell phone buzzed. It was a text from April.

I need your help. Right now. It's about Liam.

Riley's heart jumped up in her throat. She knew that April wouldn't send her a message like that unless she was in real trouble.

She opened the car door and climbed inside.

"I've got to go," she told Blaine.

"Wait a minute. Aren't we going to talk?"

"Not now," she said, shutting the door.

As she started her car, Blaine looked shocked and puzzled. Then he turned and walked away.

But Riley couldn't worry about him right now. She dialed April's number on her cell phone.

CHAPTER TWENTY FOUR

When April answered the phone, Riley could hear panic in her daughter's voice.

"Mom, I'm at Liam's house. You've got to get over here right away."

"What's wrong?" Riley asked.

"Just come right now, please."

Now Riley heard noises in the background, including someone shouting. Whatever was going on, Riley knew she needed to get there fast.

"Should I call the police?" Riley asked.

"No, please don't do that. Just come here."

"What's Liam's address?" April told her, but before Riley could ask any more questions, April abruptly ended the call.

Riley pulled the car out of the parking lot. Fortunately, the address wasn't very far away. While she drove, she felt her worry mounting—and also her anger.

She'd had such hopes for Liam when she'd met him. He'd seemed like a perfectly good kid and a great influence on April. But now it seemed that he was just another one of April's bad choices.

Riley remembered all too well April's last boyfriend, Joel Lambert. When April had gone missing, Riley had tracked her down and found her with Joel in a "shooting gallery"—a condemned house occupied by heroin users. Joel had just shot April up with heroin and was about to sell her for sex when Riley arrived.

Riley shuddered at the memory of seeing April lying helpless on a bare mattress, murmuring "no, no, no" over and over again as Joel tried to pull off her clothes.

Riley also remembered her crazed fury as she'd pulled Joel away and smashed his hand with a baseball bat, then crushed the bones further under her foot, making him beg for mercy …

The memory horrified her. It had taken weeks of rehab to get April over the trauma of that terrible experience.

And now was it happening all over again?

And if it was …

The last time, it had taken all of Riley's self-restraint not to kill Joel Lambert on the spot.

She wasn't sure she could control herself again in that kind of situation.

When she parked in front of Liam's house, she saw that it was a nice but somewhat rundown-looking house in a pleasant middle-class neighborhood. Riley gasped with relief when she saw April standing in the open front door. The girl looked physically safe and sound, but her expression was wide-eyed with alarm.

Riley got out of her car and ran toward her.

April shouted, "Mom! Thank God! You got here just in time!"

Riley pushed past April and went inside.

Right in front of her, she was shocked to see Liam lying on the floor doubled over. There was a bruise on his face.

Standing over him was a tall, muscular man. His fists were clenched at his sides. Riley could see the family resemblance immediately. The man was surely Liam's father. His face was red and knotted with fury, and Riley could smell alcohol on his breath even from where she stood.

Now Riley understood. April wasn't in danger from Liam. Liam was in danger from his father.

The man looked over at Riley.

"Who the hell are you?" he growled.

"I'm April's mother," Riley said.

The man then noticed April, who was standing in the doorway.

"You—still here!" he yelled. "I told you to get out of here, you little bitch! This is none of your business!"

Riley turned toward April.

"Did he touch you?" Riley asked.

Trembling all over, April shook her head no.

"He just tried to throw me out," she said. "But he knocked Liam down twice and kicked him. I told him I'd called for help."

The man was snarling at Riley now.

"Take your little girl and get out of here."

He strode toward Riley, grabbed her by the arm, and tried to push her toward the door. Riley shook off his hand easily. Enraged, Liam's father lifted his open hand to strike Riley across the face. Riley grabbed his wrist, stopping the blow in mid-flight.

The man looked startled by Riley's strength.

Still holding his wrist with her left hand, Riley threw a punch to his jaw that sent him reeling backward. She let go of his wrist and just stood watching as he tumbled onto the floor.

Riley's knuckles were stinging with pain from the blow. The pain made her angry.

She flashed back to how she'd pulverized that psychopath who had held both her and April prisoner. That man had tortured them, and Riley had put an end to him for good.

She could feel again the sensation of smashing his head with a rock. She wished she had a rock right now.

But her fists would do.

Rage took Riley over completely. She leaped onto the man on the floor, crouched on his belly, and slammed her fist into his face.

She heard April yell ...

"Mom! Stop! That's enough!"

At the sound of her daughter's voice, Riley's rage ebbed.

The man was staring up at her with horror. Blood was trickling down his face.

Riley knew that if she hadn't been stopped, she probably would have killed him.

Riley climbed off him, feeling shocked by her own actions. The man rose unsteadily to his feet. Moaning and groaning, he staggered to the front door and left.

Riley went to the doorway and watched him lurching away down the sidewalk.

Then she turned around and saw April helping Liam off the floor and into a chair.

"Didn't you call nine-one-one?" Riley asked April.

"No," April said. "Liam didn't want me to. I called you instead."

"It's OK now," Liam said, rubbing his bruised face.

"It's *not* OK!" Riley said.

Riley was feeling a different sort of anger now—anger at Liam and April for not having called for police help.

"I'm sorry you had to see Dad like that," Liam said, crying now. "He hasn't been drinking like this for a long time. He got bad after my mother left, but then he straightened up and didn't drink for years. Now it's started again. But he'll come out of it. I'm sure."

Riley crouched down in front of Liam.

"Liam, listen to me. You've got to do something. You've got to call Child Protective Services. Your father is dangerous."

Still crying, Liam shook his head.

"No, he's not. He'll come home in a little while and sleep it off. I'll talk to him when he wakes up. He'll listen. I'm sure he won't do it again."

Riley's heart sank. Liam's denial was all too typical of abuse victims. And she knew from experience how hard it would be to persuade him to face facts.

He doesn't deserve this, she thought.

Riley barely knew him, but she already liked him. She used to think she'd like to have a son, a brother for April. Things hadn't worked out that way. But Liam seemed to be exactly the kind of boy she would have liked to raise.

As bad luck would have it, Liam had gotten shortchanged on parents. Riley didn't know why Liam's mother had left his father. She might well have had good reason. But her departure had brought out the worst in his father. And now Liam's situation was truly desperate.

April tugged on Riley's arm. Riley stepped aside to hear what April wanted to tell her.

"Let's take Liam home," April whispered through her tears. "He's not safe here."

For a fleeting instant, Riley felt ready to agree. But she knew that it wasn't a decision to make on an impulse.

She turned back to Liam and said, "I'm going to call Child Protective Services."

"No!" Liam said sharply. "Please, please don't! You have to give my dad and me a chance."

Riley knelt down beside him again.

"Then you've got to, Liam. You've just got to."

Liam shook his head miserably.

"Think about it," Riley said. "Please just think about it."

Liam nodded.

"We'll stay here till your dad gets back," Riley said.

"No," Liam said. "Thank you, but no. I'll—Dad and I will work things out."

Riley felt a crushing sadness settling in. There really was nothing she could do here. She got up and led April out of the house. They got into the car and Riley started to drive home.

"We've got to do something," April said, still in tears.

Riley felt the same way. But what were their options? She thought about it for a moment.

Finally she said, "I'm going to call Child Protective Services myself when we get home."

"Mom, no!" April said.

"Why not?"

"Because Liam told us not to! He'd never forgive me—*us*—if we do that. He'd feel betrayed."

Riley said nothing. She didn't know what to say. She remembered Liam's plea, "You have to give my dad and me a chance."

Then April said, "Let's go back and get Liam. Let's take him home. He can live with us for a while."

Riley was able to think more clearly about that option than she could before. Was it possible? Might it help? She held back a sigh as a world of problems dawned on her.

She was just now getting Jilly settled in and stable with her new life. Did she have the resources—financial or emotional—to take care of another teenager, one whose life was already fraught with trouble?

And how would Liam's father react?

Besides, April was in a relationship with this boy. It just couldn't be a good idea to have them both living in the same house.

"We can't," Riley said.

"Why not?" April asked.

"For more reasons than I can count," Riley said. "And if you just stop and think about it, you'll see I'm right."

A tense silence fell between them.

Then Riley said, "If you really want to help Liam, you've got to talk him into calling CPS."

There was another silence.

Then April spoke in a harsh, angry voice.

"You just don't care," she said.

The words cut through Riley like a knife.

"How can you say that to me?" Riley said.

"You don't."

Riley felt on the verge of tears.

"April, I do the best I can," she said in a choked voice. "I can't fix everything in the world. No one can."

April crossed her arms and didn't reply. She maintained a sullen silence during the rest of the ride. When they got home, April stormed up to her room and slammed the door. Riley looked around and didn't see anyone else. She figured Gabriela was probably downstairs in her apartment, and Jilly must still be at volleyball practice.

Riley sat down in the living room feeling very alone.

Just this morning she'd been looking forward to a few days off, especially some time to spend with the girls.

But it wasn't working out very well so far.

What now? she wondered.

She felt sure that April wouldn't talk to her for the rest of the day. Tomorrow maybe Riley could make peace with her. It would be Sunday, so maybe they could all do something together as a family—April, Jilly, and Gabriela too.

Tomorrow will be better, Riley promised herself.

*

The next morning Riley got up and fixed herself some coffee. The girls were still in bed, and the house was quiet and peaceful. Riley sat sipping her coffee, considering what to do with her family today.

April could phone Liam and find out if everything was all right there. And then she and the girls could go out somewhere.

Of course, she automatically thought of going to Blaine's Grill for lunch.

But then she remembered how tense things had been between her and Blaine just yesterday. It didn't seem like a good idea to just drop in at his restaurant until she and Blaine had worked things out.

If we can *work things out,* Riley thought. She couldn't help feeling pessimistic.

Before she could consider any other options, her phone rang, and she answered it.

"Agent Paige, this is Jennifer Roston."

Riley was surprised and uneasy.

"What can I do for you?" Riley asked.

Roston said, "I really need to talk with you. Right away. Something new has come up regarding Shane Hatcher."

Riley's heart jumped up in her throat.

"What's happened?" she asked.

"We can't talk about it over the phone," Roston said. "I need to see you in person. I could come to your house."

Riley gulped. The last thing she wanted was to talk about Hatcher at home with the girls around. And she could hear them stirring around upstairs, starting to get up.

"No, I'll come to Quantico," Riley said.

"OK," Roston said. "I hate to ask you. I know you're supposed to be taking time off. But this is important. Meet me in the conference room."

"I'll be there in a half hour," Riley said.

They ended the call just as Gabriela came up the stairs to fix breakfast.

Riley said, "Gabriela, I've got to go out for a while. Tell the girls I'll be back soon."

Gabriela nodded, and Riley left the house.

What's this all about? she wondered as she started the car.

Whatever it was, she doubted that it was good.

CHAPTER TWENTY FIVE

When Riley arrived at the BAU building, her uneasiness grew. The whole place felt ominously vacant. The FBI didn't close down on weekends, but there were far fewer people around than usual. Riley was pretty sure that Meredith wasn't here today, and of course Bill wasn't either.

She found Special Agent Jennifer Roston already waiting for her in the conference room. The room felt unusually large and forbidding, with only the two of them sitting at a big table with a dozen empty chairs.

Riley wondered why Roston asked to meet her here. Only the most senior agents had private offices, so Roston would just have a desk in an area with several others. But why couldn't they have met in Riley's office?

Riley wondered—did Roston *want* her to feel uncomfortable?

For a few moments, the young African-American agent sat across the broad table just looking at Riley.

Finally Riley asked, "Why were you so eager to see me?"

Roston didn't answer Riley's question. Instead, she took out a notepad and pencil.

She said, "I need to know everything you know about Shane Hatcher."

Riley tried not to show her rising alarm.

"You have all the files," Riley said. "I don't have anything new."

"I need for you to tell me the whole history of your relationship."

Riley felt puzzled.

"Surely you know all that already," she said. "It's all in the files."

"I need to hear it directly from you."

Riley sat studying Roston's face for a moment. She couldn't read her expression at all. It occurred to her that Roston had the makings of a good interrogator. In fact, this meeting was feeling more and more like an interrogation with every passing moment.

Riley spoke slowly and carefully.

"As I'm sure you know, I first visited Shane Hatcher in Sing Sing in August of last year, when I was working on a case in upstate New York. I met with him at the recommendation of Mike Nevins, a forensic psychologist who works for the Bureau from time to time. Hatcher is a brilliant self-taught criminologist whose articles have been published in professional journals. His insights helped me solve that case. I went back to Sing Sing to consult with him on two more cases."

Roston's notebook lay on the table, but she wasn't taking notes.

She asked, "Why did you always go to Sing Sing to see him?"

"He wouldn't talk to me by phone. I had to meet with him in person."

"Why?"

Riley hesitated. How could she explain a living enigma like Shane Hatcher?

"He's a strange man, and he lives by strange rules," she said. "But like I said, he's brilliant, and his insights were always valuable."

"So he was controlling the situation whenever you met?"

Riley squinted at Roston.

"I'm not sure what you mean by 'controlling,'" Riley said. "He was incarcerated at the time. I found my visits to him to be extremely productive."

Roston began to make seemingly random scribbles on the notepad.

She said, "Then in December he escaped and killed a man in Syracuse, New York. An old acquaintance, I believe."

"An old enemy," Riley said, correcting her. "From many years ago, when Hatcher was still a young gangbanger."

Her words sounded strange to her own ears. She surely didn't mean to justify Hatcher killing anyone. But that was how it must have sounded to Roston. And Roston's face showed it.

Roston asked, "When have you been in touch with him since his escape?"

Riley knew that they were moving into dangerous territory. She had to be careful with all her answers.

"He turned up in Virginia in January," Riley said. "You already know that, because it's in the files. You must also know that he rescued my daughter and ex-husband from a vicious killer."

Riley didn't dare tell the story, but she shivered inside at the memory. Hatcher had not only saved the lives of April and Ryan, he had delivered the killer into Riley's clutches bound and gagged, a test to see if she'd kill him out of sheer vengefulness.

Riley could feel afresh the bitter taste of fury in her mouth, could remember how she'd wanted to cut out the killer's beating heart and show it to him. Even so, she had resisted her own murderous urges.

That was also the first time she had deliberately let Hatcher himself escape arrest.

"A 'vicious killer,'" Roston said, echoing Riley's words. "More vicious than Hatcher himself?"

Riley was momentarily speechless.

What could she possibly say?

She collected her thoughts and said, "I know perfectly well how vicious Hatcher can be. I found the mangled corpse of his old enemy hanging in chains. But he's a complex man—not like the obsessed psychopath who threatened my family. He's always been complex. I talked to the cop who first arrested him many years ago. After his escape, some in the FBI were afraid he'd go after her. She said he wouldn't and she was right. He didn't try to kill her because she had stopped another cop from killing him."

Riley hesitated, then added, "He's got a strict code."

Roston raised her eyebrows.

"A code? Could you explain that to me?"

Riley didn't reply. Where could she even begin to explain?

Then Roston asked, "Do you feel that you owe Hatcher something?"

A chill went down Riley's spine. Her entanglement of obligations to Hatcher baffled even her.

When Riley didn't reply, Roston began to push.

"Are you in debt to Shane Hatcher for saving your family?"

"I—I'm grateful," Riley stammered. "But I'm a sworn law enforcement officer. I wouldn't hesitate to arrest him if I had the opportunity."

Riley's alarm was growing. Could Roston tell that this was an outright lie?

She could have arrested Hatcher several times when she'd confronted him in person.

Or at least she could have tried to.

But she hadn't tried.

Roston said, "I've heard that he's got a nickname—'Shane the Chain.'"

Riley nodded uneasily.

"That's right," she said. "He was called that in his early days as a gangbanger."

Riley didn't go on to say how he'd gotten that nickname—because he had a reputation for pulverizing his victims with heavy chains. Roston surely knew that already.

Now Riley noticed that Roston was looking at the gold chain bracelet on her wrist. Hatcher had given it to her.

I should have taken it off, Riley thought.

A code etched on one of its links was a means of contacting him. He wore one just like it to symbolize their bond. For the first time something occurred to Riley—if Roston ever managed to capture Hatcher, he'd probably be wearing his bracelet.

It seemed odd to Riley that she hadn't thought of that before.

Had she never seriously considered the possibility that Hatcher could be captured?

Nevertheless, Riley resisted the urge to move her arm off the table to hide the bracelet. That would only attract more attention to it.

"So you saw him in Virginia," Roston said. "When did you see him next face to face?"

Riley's alarm was escalating into near panic. Some of her interactions with Hatcher were in the records Roston had read. Others were known only to Riley herself.

How was she going to keep her stories straight?

Riley's mind clicked away frantically.

Then she remembered.

She'd communicated with Hatcher several times by phone and video chat. But she'd only encountered him in person two other times. Once was in Seattle when he'd helped her on a poisoning case. The other was when he'd shown up at her father's cabin. Neither one of those encounters were included in the records. She couldn't admit to them.

"I never saw him in person after that," Riley said.

Riley realized that her alarm was starting to turn into anger. Why was she letting Roston treat her this way?

The young agent had an agenda, and Riley still didn't know what it was.

Riley said, "I don't understand what's going on here, Agent Roston. Perhaps you should get right to the point."

Roston smiled a rather insincere smile.

"Relax, Agent Paige. You're being very helpful, and I appreciate it. It's just a complicated case, and I need to get all the details straight. I've got just a few more questions."

Roston kept making random marks on her notepad.

She said, "I understand that a real estate agent, Shirley Redding, is handling the sale of your property—the cabin you inherited from your father."

Riley felt a new wave of worry.

Where was Roston going with this?

Did she know that Hatcher had been living at the cabin?

Riley said, "I originally asked Shirley to sell it. But I changed my mind."

"Was Shirley Redding ever at the cabin?" Roston asked.

Again Riley knew she had to choose her words carefully.

"Of course she saw the property and estimated its market value. I believe that she also showed it to potential buyers."

"When was that?"

"I'm not sure. I was in California during some of this time."

Roston tapped her pencil against the notepad.

Then she said, "I understand that she reported at least one offer to you. Why did you turn it down?"

"I just told you," Riley said. "I changed my mind. I told her to stop showing it."

Roston flashed that insincere smile again.

"That's odd. I checked on it this morning. It's still an active listing."

Riley managed to keep her jaw from dropping.

"It shouldn't be," she said. "I'll have to talk to her about it."

A short silence fell.

"When did you last see Shirley Redding?" Roston asked.

"I actually haven't met her," Riley said. "We've just communicated by phone and text messages. But why are you asking me about this? What does it have to do with the Hatcher case?"

Roston's smile vanished.

"That's what I'm trying to work out," she said. "Shirley Redding was found dead this morning."

CHAPTER TWENTY SIX

The shock of Agent Roston's words hit Riley hard. She couldn't believe she had heard right.

"What did you just say?" she asked.

Roston sharpened her gaze, staring straight into Riley's eyes.

"I said that Shirley Redding was found dead this morning," Roston said.

Riley was completely dumbfounded for a few moments. The real estate agent? Dead?

Finally Roston asked, "Don't you want to know where it happened?"

Riley tried to steady her breath.

She said, "From your manner, I must assume that it was on my property."

"Yes, it was."

Riley struggled to grasp what had happened. In her gut, she knew that Shirley Redding's death must be the work of Shane Hatcher. The Realtor must have turned up at the cabin again. Perhaps she had caught him by surprise. Or maybe he just refused to hide again, as he had threatened.

But she didn't dare say that.

"Why wasn't I notified as soon as she was found?" Riley asked.

"That's why I called you this morning," Roston said. "That's why you're here."

Riley's anger began to rise again. Roston had been manipulating her during this whole conversation.

Riley sputtered, "Why—why didn't you just tell me that right away?"

"I needed to find out as much as I could," Roston said in a flat voice.

"Why?" Riley asked. "Do you suspect me of murder?"

Roston didn't reply.

No, Riley thought. *It's not me she suspects.*

Riley knew that Jennifer Roston also suspected Shane Hatcher. But she wouldn't want to say that yet. Riley had never told anyone that Hatcher had even been to the cabin. But Roston had taken bits and pieces of information and put them together with her own observations of Riley's subtle evasions. And now Roston was dangerously close to connecting the dots in this awful picture.

"How did it happen?" Riley asked.

Roston leaned across the table toward Riley.

She said, "Shirley Redding was scheduled to meet a prospective buyer at the cabin early this morning. When the buyer got there, he saw her car but couldn't find Redding. He walked around a bit and spotted the body in a rocky gully not far from the house. He called the local sheriff, who called us."

A silence fell between Riley and the younger agent.

Then Roston said, "I've got to consider the possibility of murder. I need to you to tell me whatever you can to help me put all this together."

Riley felt ready to explode from a whole range of emotions—anxiety, fear, and shame.

Right now the strongest emotion she felt was anger.

"I don't have anything to say to you," Riley said through clenched teeth.

"Are you sure?" Roston asked.

Riley rose to her feet.

"Don't play games with me, Agent Roston," she said. "From now on, I expect you to be direct and open with me. No manipulation, no deceptions, no trying to play with my mind. Do you have any questions for me? Any *specific* questions? If so, come out with it."

Roston stared at her for a moment.

Then she said, "Who murdered Shirley Redding?"

Riley fought down a last impulse to tell the truth.

"I don't know," she said. "I don't even know if she *was* murdered. And neither do you. Do you have any other questions?"

Roston just stared at her, saying nothing.

"All right then," Riley said.

Riley turned and left the room. She headed out of the building, struggling to bring her nerves under control. She knew where she needed to go next.

*

It was a three-and-a half-hour drive from Quantico to the cabin that Riley had inherited from her father. The trip up into the Appalachian Mountains gave her some time alone to slow down her racing emotions and think things through.

She kept turning the question over in her mind …

What did Roston actually know?

Did she know that Shane Hatcher had been living in the cabin?

Riley couldn't imagine how.

Nevertheless, it seemed that the young agent's instincts were telling her that Shirley Redding's death probably wasn't an accident. And if it was murder, a killer had to be at the cabin. Roston's suspicions had led her to think that it could be Hatcher.

Pretty good instincts, Riley thought with dismay. *She'll make a first-class BAU agent.*

Riley kept trying to hope that the young agent was wrong—that Shirley's death had been an accident, pure and simple. And as angry as Riley felt about Roston's manipulations, she couldn't really blame her. She was acting exactly like Riley herself might under similar circumstances.

Riley sighed. She wished she could simply admire Roston for her work.

She also wished she hadn't left the meeting room so hastily. Many things now puzzled her, and now she felt that she should have asked questions of her own.

She remembered something Roston had said …

"I've got to consider the possibility of murder."

Riley wondered—was there any real reason for considering that possibility? And was Roston the only one thinking along those lines?

What about the local police? The sheriff had called the FBI to report Shirley Redding's death. Why had he considered it an FBI matter?

Even if the sheriff thought that the death had been murder, wasn't it odd that he had immediately called the FBI?

That was hardly standard procedure.

And if a full-scale investigation was in the works, where would it lead?

Steady, Riley told herself. *Don't let your imagination run away with you.*

Anyway, as of now, Riley felt sure that Roston had no proof about Riley's actual relationship with Hatcher.

And Riley knew that she had to keep it that way.

Riley drove through the little Appalachian town of Milladore, then up into the surrounding mountains. After a few miles, she turned off onto a winding dirt road. At the end of the road was her father's cabin—a small wooden structure that was normally out of sight from the outside world.

But Riley saw right away that the world had encroached here today. Three police vehicles were crammed into the small open area in front of the cabin. Riley knew one thing for certain—the police had not found Shane Hatcher here. He was surely long gone by now, hiding God only knew where.

As Riley parked, a big medical examiner's vehicle pulled out and drove away. Riley guessed that Shirley Redding's body was inside. A local cop greeted Riley as she got out of her car.

She showed her badge and introduced herself.

The cop looked a bit surprised that an FBI agent had shown up.

"Show me where it happened," Riley told him.

The cop led Riley down a path that led away from the house. As they walked, Riley studied the ground carefully. She could see one set of footprints from a woman's shoes in the soft earth. Of course, Riley knew better than to expect to also see Hatcher's footprints. He was far too skillful and cunning to leave any trace of himself.

At the end of the path was a steep gully, where several cops were at work. The cop who had met Riley introduced her to the sheriff, whose name was Ben Garland. He was late middle-aged and considerably overweight, and he was chewing a plug of tobacco.

He shook hands with Riley.

"Glad you could make it," he said. "Sorry about the circumstances, though."

"Why did you contact the FBI?" Riley said.

Sheriff Garland shrugged.

"Well, I knew your dad. At least a little. He used to hang around the VFW down the mountain in Milladore, back before he got banned from the place for making trouble. I'm a Desert Storm vet myself, and we had a few drinks together."

Garland chewed his tobacco a bit, as if ruminating over the memory.

"He wasn't a great talker, your dad," he said. "But he did mention you from time to time, said you'd made a decent career for yourself at the FBI."

Those words caught Riley's attention—*"a decent career."*

Riley's father had never once in her life told her that he was proud of her, much less that he loved her. She could imagine him over drinks at the VFW mumbling about Riley's "decent career." It was probably as close as he'd ever gotten to bragging about her.

"Anyway," Garland continued, "I knew this place belonged to him, and figured you must be the next of kin. I didn't know how to reach you directly, so I put in a call to the FBI."

The situation was becoming clearer to Riley. The sheriff hadn't put in the call because he considered this an FBI case. It had been purely to get in touch with Riley—and Jennifer Roston had intercepted the communication and confronted her with it.

But Riley still didn't know whether Garland believed Shirley Redding to be a murder victim.

"What can you tell me about what happened?" Riley asked.

"Well, what have you been told so far?" Garland asked.

"I understand that Shirley Redding came up here to show the cabin to a prospective buyer. After he arrived, he found her body down in the gully."

Garland nodded. Then he led Riley over to the edge of the gully. It was about a twenty-foot drop to a stream below. A couple of cops were still down there examining the big rocks along the embankment. Riley knew that sometimes more water rushed through here right after snow melted. But right now the stream was peaceful.

Garland led Riley down a precarious path toward the stream.

He said, "The way I figure it, she came this way trying to get down to the water. There's watercress growing down there, so she was probably after that. But she wasn't used to this kind of territory, and she wasn't wearing the right shoes for it, so she tumbled headfirst."

"What was the cause of death?" Riley asked.

"Well, her neck was broken," Garland said. "Some contusions from the fall. That's all we know of at this point. The medical examiner still has to do an autopsy. But my guess is that she died pretty much instantly."

Now Riley understood that the sheriff didn't suspect foul play. But she didn't feel relieved.

Standing at the bottom of the gully, she could clearly imagine Shirley Redding's crumpled body lying here, her dead eyes possibly wide open staring skyward.

Riley felt a spasm of guilt.

Ever since she'd talked to Agent Roston, her mind had been occupied with concerns about herself and whether her connections with Hatcher were about to catch up with her.

Now, for the first time, she was confronted with the reality that someone had died a violent death right here.

Shirley Redding had doubtless been a nuisance—nosy and erratic and unstable.

But she hadn't deserved to die like this.

And Riley herself was at least somewhat responsible.

CHAPTER TWENTY SEVEN

Riley stood staring at the spot where Shirley Redding's body had been found. She managed to suppress a shudder.

Then she told Sheriff Garland, "Thanks for reaching out to me. I really appreciate it. I'd have had to hear the news about a death on my property without knowing anything about it."

"Any time," the sheriff replied with a slight tip of his hat.

Riley then retraced her way back out of the gully and toward her father's cabin. The last time she'd been here, the whole area was covered with a layer of snow. Now the surrounding forest was bursting with spring life. Even so, Riley could see that little had really changed. The same pile of firewood was stacked near a tree stump.

She walked up to the cabin and found that its front door was unlocked. That was hardly a surprise. Riley guessed that Shirley had unlocked it in preparation for showing the cabin to her clients.

When Riley stepped inside, she was overcome with an eerie moment of déjà vu.

Everything looked exactly the same as the last time she'd been here—the same wicker chair, the same medals hanging on the wall, the same wooden stool where her father used to sit skinning squirrels.

Riley could swear that nothing had been moved the slightest bit.

Hatcher had managed to spend his time here without changing anything, without leaving any hint of his presence.

Riley shuddered at her memory of the last time she'd been here, shortly after her father's death.

She'd found Hatcher standing outside the cabin—a most unwelcome guest. He had come inside and sat right there, on that wooden stool.

But now it was as if Hatcher had never been here at all. It was as if none of that had ever happened.

For a few moments she tried to convince herself …

Maybe it didn't happen. Not the worst of it, anyway.

After all, how could even she know for sure that Shirley Redding had been murdered?

Wasn't it possible that Sheriff Garland's scenario was entirely correct—that the woman had stumbled and fallen while climbing down into the gully to get some watercress?

Riley sighed with despair.

Yes, it was possible. But her every instinct told her that Hatcher had murdered Shirley.

And her instincts were very seldom wrong.

Riley went outside and got into her car and began the long drive home.

*

Riley arrived home in time for one of Gabriela's typically delicious dinners. But the mood at the table was uncomfortable. Jilly was perfectly pleasant, and chattered about yesterday's volleyball practice. Gabriela asked Jilly questions about the game and about her homework.

But April was sullen and nearly silent. She barely looked at Riley at all.

April was obviously still angry about yesterday. Although Riley had rescued April's boyfriend, she had refused to let Liam come and stay with them.

Riley sighed. It seemed that she could never do enough, could never get everything right. She approached the topic gingerly.

"Have you talked with Liam?" she asked.

"Yeah," April said, poking at her food with a fork.

"Is he OK?" Riley asked.

"Yeah."

An unpleasant silence followed. Jilly and Gabriela looked on with quiet concern.

Riley asked, "Has Liam contacted anybody, like Child Protective Services?"

"No," April said.

"Why not?"

April groaned with irritation.

"Because he says everything's all right now. His dad says he's sorry. He says he's never going to drink again."

Riley didn't know what to say. Of course she knew that this was an all-too-common pattern in abusive families. Liam's father couldn't be counted on to keep his word. But now was no time for Riley to change her mind. Letting Liam stay here would be complicated and might even involve legal issues.

After another silence, April said, "I don't feel like eating anymore. Could I be excused from the table?"

"OK," Riley said.

April got up and went upstairs to her room.

Riley, Jilly, and Gabriela ate in silence for a few moments.

Finally, Jilly said, "You're right, Mom. April told me what happened yesterday, and you made the right call about Liam. It wouldn't do any good having him stay here. It would only make things worse. He's got to deal with his own problems. April just doesn't get it. But I do."

Riley felt a lump in her throat.

"Thanks for saying that, Jilly," she said.

Jilly shrugged.

"You made the right call," she repeated. "You did the right thing."

Then Gabriela said to Jilly, "Maybe you should talk with April about all this. Maybe you can get her to understand."

Jilly nodded.

"I'll go talk to her after dinner," she said.

The rest of the meal passed in silence, but peacefully. Riley felt grateful for Jilly's understanding and Gabriela's good sense. Even so, she couldn't help feeling miserable. She couldn't shake off her sense of responsibility about Shirley Redding's terrible death. And now she felt useless to her own family.

Jilly and Gabriela handle things better than I do, she thought.

What was the point in her even coming home?

*

Later that evening, when the girls had gone to bed and Gabriela had gone downstairs for the night, Riley opened the kitchen cabinet where she kept a bottle of bourbon. She poured herself a large glass, then carried the glass and the bottle to the living room.

She sat down on the couch and took a long sip of the bourbon. The burning sensation was comforting as she swallowed. Rationally, she knew that drinking probably wasn't a good idea. But she could feel a familiar despair setting in. How else could she numb herself against it?

Her mind was crowded with awful thoughts.

She could see the gully with green watercress in the flowing stream. In her mind, red blood rippled through the green. Then she saw Shirley Redding's body, her dead eyes open and following wherever Riley went.

Riley thought that if only she had gone about things differently. If only she'd done more research about Shirley and found out how erratic she was, she'd never have hired her.

And Shirley would be alive today.

She also kept flashing back to her conversation with Jennifer Roston that morning.

Interrogation was more like it, Riley thought, taking another gulp of whiskey.

Roston had treated her like a common criminal.

And Riley couldn't help wondering if that was all she was—a common criminal.

If so, maybe it was time to admit the truth and face the consequences.

Did she dare come clean about her whole relationship with Hatcher—to Roston, or perhaps to Meredith?

That surely would be the end of her career—at the very least.

And Riley wouldn't be the only person to suffer the consequences. She had two daughters who depended on her. She couldn't let them fall victim to her own terrible judgment.

She finished her glass of bourbon. As she poured herself some more, she noticed the gold chain on her wrist.

Why was she still wearing it?

Why couldn't she bring herself to take it off?

What kind of spell did Hatcher have over her?

Fingering the bracelet, she again noticed the one special link with its tiny inscription ...

"face8ecaf"

She'd long since deciphered the inscription's meaning. It meant "face to face," and it was suggestive of a mirror. For that was what Hatcher considered himself to be—a sort of mirror in which Riley couldn't help but see the darkest parts of her own heart.

But the inscription was also something else. It was the video address she'd sometimes used to get in touch with Hatcher.

Should she call him now? Should she confront him once and for all?

She couldn't imagine what she'd say that could free her from his clutches.

But she felt that she had to try.

She flipped open her laptop computer and opened the video chat program. Then she typed in those characters ...

"face8ecaf"

She let the call ring for a whole minute.

Nobody answered.

Riley didn't know whether she felt crushed or relieved.

The truth was, she wasn't feeling much of anything at all. The bourbon was starting to bring on its welcome numbness. And of course, that was exactly what she wanted.

She poured herself another glass and drank it down quickly.

She was also feeling tired, and the couch felt very comfortable.

She lay down and started to doze. But as consciousness faded, a thought crept upon her …

Something's happening. Right now. Something bad.

She fell into a restless, uneasy sleep.

CHAPTER TWENTY EIGHT

Shortly before dawn, the wolf was carrying his weapon higher up into the hills than usual. When he heard the helicopter circling, he scuttled deep beneath an overhanging ledge. He lay perfectly still beneath it. Despite the impending danger, his breathing scarcely changed. Neither did his pulse.

He was a true wolf, after all, and fully in control of his physical reactions.

The helicopter switched on a searchlight to scour the immediate area.

The light didn't especially worry the wolf. But he knew that the searchers could also be using thermal imaging to locate any warm body, especially any that was moving. The heat-seeking technology was ideal for night, when the terrain was cool enough to pick out the heat of a living form. Maybe they'd picked up his body heat and were now checking to find out what was there.

But as long as he stayed under this ledge, he felt sure that he'd be completely invisible to all their devices. The rock formation above him was easily thick enough to mask his body heat.

He was glad it was a helicopter. He knew that the CID agents had also been using drones, and those would be harder to hear and to avoid. They could hunt lower to the ground and might even be able to pick him out beneath this ledge, since he radiated more heat than the rocks did at this time of day.

But even drones had never spotted him. At night he only went into hills he'd hiked by day. He knew every nook and cranny and potential hiding place by heart. He could dodge to safety at any second.

Now that he thought about it, he realized he hadn't seen any drones out today at all. In fact, the search seemed to be less intense. He'd heard a rumor that someone had been arrested, but he didn't know whether they thought they had the nighttime shooter or not.

Of course, they didn't.

Soon the searchlight clicked off and the helicopter swooped away.

The wolf smiled. It had just been a routine check of the area. If the pilots had even detected a heat signature, they'd have thought it was from a coyote or a rabbit.

Even so, the wolf didn't move from the sheltering stones right away. The helicopter could easily circle back. But instead, the sound gradually faded away.

He slid out from under the rock formation and climbed farther up the hill. The terrain grew more risky the higher he went. The closer he got to the top, the fewer places there were to hide.

Finally he reached the promontory he'd been headed for.

For a moment, he basked in the view. This spot was far away from where he'd killed the others. He'd looked down upon Fort Nash Mowat from this particular spot by day, but the base looked especially striking by night. And he could see all that he needed to see perfectly.

He lay down on the rough ground and snapped the night-vision scope to his sniper rifle. Then he stretched prone and peered through the scope down at the open field, looking for the path where he expected Private Kyle Barton to appear.

He found the path easily.

The path wasn't lighted, and the view through the scope was grainy, but that was just how he wanted it. A few nights ago, the wolf inside him had balked at pulling the trigger when Barton had been in the tennis court. The lights there had been too bright, the shot too easy.

But tonight the challenge would be just right.

Soon he glimpsed Private Barton jogging far away on the trail—too far away just yet to take the shot, but coming closer by the second.

The wolf felt his anger surge at the sight of the young man— the same anger he had felt toward Sergeants Rolsky, Fraser, and Worthing.

The wolf couldn't allow any of them to live.

But the wolf knew that his anger was his adversary. His pulse was quickening just a little, and his breathing was slightly unsteady.

He breathed long and slow, relaxing his entire body, assessing his own readiness.

He'd killed the others with clean shots to the head.

Could he do that again tonight?

The air was still, but it was going to be a longer shot than the others, and he felt a little less steady. He wasn't confident about a shot to the head, and he knew better than to risk it.

Tonight he'd aim at the center of the young man's chest.

He'll be just as dead in any case, the wolf thought with satisfaction as he followed Barton through his night scope.

*

Private Kyle Barton slowed from a vigorous jog to a steady walk. His lungs were burning from the exertion, his heart was pounding, and he felt thoroughly invigorated. The pre-dawn air felt cool on his face as he wiped away the sweat.

He liked jogging around the open field at the foot of the hills while most of the base was still asleep. It woke him up and got him ready for the day better than coffee would. He would be awake and limber and ready for his day.

His jog also gave him some private time to think about his future.

He had finished basic training, and now there weren't many more days left in his Advanced Individual Training. Soon he would graduate from combat training, and he would be a full-fledged infantry rifleman.

But then what? he wondered.

That question was a matter of some friction between him and his wife, Ellen.

Ever since Kyle had begun basic training many months ago, Ellen and their little daughter, Sian, had been living with Ellen's mother in the nearby town of Alton. Living separately had taken a toll on his relationship with Ellen. So had the single-mindedness he had shown toward his new career.

And now, as soon as he finished AIT and graduated once and for all, he would be transferred—but he still had no idea where. That information only came after graduation.

Ellen openly resented having such an unclear future.

And the truth was, Kyle resented Ellen for not understanding him better.

Couldn't she appreciate his deepening commitment to the Army—a commitment that was turning into a passion?

No, of course not, he thought with a sigh.

It was a well-known dilemma among his fellow recruits who had wives and children.

Ellen wanted a house full of kids. She wanted them to grow up in a secure community and to have friends who would always live nearby.

Ellen certainly had no idea what Kyle's life was really like or how he felt. Even he was just beginning to realize what he valued most—and that was his standing among men he respected.

Unfortunately, the fresh air and exercise had brought him no solutions to those problems.

Others in Kyle's platoon had warned him against being out here while it was still dark. After all, there had been three murders. But he was sure he was in no danger. The other killings had taken place much farther away on the base. And whoever had killed those men seemed to have a vendetta against sergeants. The shooter would never target a private like Kyle.

But the deaths had troubled him deeply. He had known them. They had all been good men

Kyle was about to break into a jog again when some mysterious force pushed him sharply backward, almost knocking him down.

Then he felt a terrible burning in the center of his chest.

The world started to lose focus.

I've been shot, he thought.

As his consciousness faded, he couldn't help but admire the marksmanship.

The shot must have come from far away—too far away for him to even hear it.

What kind of man had that kind of skill?

With his last ebb of awareness he caught a glimpse of the answer ...

... but it came too late to save him.

He fell dead to the ground.

CHAPTER TWENTY NINE

Riley found herself in a vast, dimly lit expanse. On all sides, the space faded away into darkness.

Where am I? *she wondered.* What is this place?

She looked down and saw that she was standing on a well-worn floor made of broad oak boards.

She knew this floor from somewhere.

Then she realized—it was the floor of her father's cabin.

But why was the cabin now so huge?

She looked around again and a familiar sight caught her eye. Now a rugged man was sitting on a stool facing away from her, skinning a dead squirrel that he was about to toss onto a pile of naked squirrel carcasses.

She'd seen her father do this many times.

"Daddy?" Riley asked.

The man turned to look at her.

But it wasn't her father.

Instead, she saw the darker visage of Shane Hatcher.

He smiled at her wickedly and said ...

"We're joined at the brain, Riley Paige."

Riley shuddered at the familiar words.

Hatcher had told her that in the past. She hated to hear it.

Now the space around her shifted.

"Look behind you," Hatcher said, skinning yet another squirrel.

Riley turned and gasped at what she saw.

It was a young man hanging from a rope tied to tree branch.

This, too, was a familiar sight.

This young man was a killer. Riley had hunted him down. But when she cornered him at last, she hadn't arrested him. She'd stood by and watched with grim curiosity as he slowly strangled to death.

Just as she was now watching him strangle to death again.

She heard Hatcher ask, "Are you going to help him?"

Riley felt paralyzed.

She had no desire to help the young man.

She was too fascinated by how his body writhed its life away.

The space around her was smaller now, and dark. The walls of the cabin were closing in around her.

She couldn't see Hatcher, but she heard him laugh.

"I didn't think so," he said. "You're becoming."

Riley shuddered again.

She knew exactly what Hatcher meant.

He'd asked her a question in the past ...

"Are you already, or are you becoming?"

And now, once again, he answered that question ...

"You're becoming what you've always been deep down. Call it a monster or whatever you want. And it won't be long before you are that person."

Riley wished with all her heart that it wasn't true.

She wanted to turn away from the monster she was becoming.

But when she forced herself to turn away from the young man's body, she saw the broken body of Shirley Redding lying on the floor.

Then that image was gone and there were just the cabin walls closing in ever more tightly, and the space was becoming claustrophobically small.

There was no place to escape.

Soon she would be squeezed down forever to what she truly was deep inside—and hopelessly bound to Shane Hatcher forever.

As if he could read her thoughts, Hatcher laughed and said again ...

"We're joined at the brain, Riley Paige."

Riley was awakened by the sound of her cell phone ringing.

She drew a breath of gratitude to be out of that vanishing dream, to hear something other than Hatcher's voice.

She reached toward the ringing sound and realized that her hand was fumbling around on the coffee table. She saw an empty glass and a mostly empty bottle of bourbon.

Riley tried to clear her head. She was groggy and achy.

She realized that she had slept on the sofa all night. She didn't like to think about the times she had done that before. Those had always been times of despair.

The phone quit ringing just as Riley's hand touched it.

Then it started ringing again, and Riley took the call.

The caller was Brent Meredith.

"Your vacation's over, Agent Paige," the team chief said with his usual bluntness.

Riley stifled a groan.

"What's the matter?" Riley asked.

"There's been another killing at Fort Mowat."

"Like the others?"

"Yes, a sniper. I'm getting the plane ready for you and your team. Get out here as fast as you can. At least this time you'll get there while the crime scene is still fresh."

Riley struggled to put her thoughts in order.

She said, "Tell Larson and the CID people not to move anything—not even the body. And tell them not to tramp all over the area."

"I'll do that," Meredith said.

They ended the call, and Riley rose unsteadily to her feet.

Her head was splitting, and the images of her dream still haunted her.

But now was no time to let that trouble her. She had a case to solve. And maybe that was exactly what she needed to escape her demons.

*

The trip back to Fort Mowat was mostly a blur to Riley. She, Bill, and Lucy boarded the plane in a mad rush, running across the tarmac with their go-bags. They were all a bit disoriented by the early-morning change in plans.

Larson had sent no information to speak of about the murder, so there was little for them to discuss. The flight seemed interminable, and Riley struggled to keep thoughts about Shirley Redding's death and her grim bond with Shane Hatcher at bay.

She was relieved when a CID vehicle picked them up at the airport and rushed them to Fort Mowat, right to the spot where the soldier had been killed. It was on a large open field facing a high, rocky area.

Col. Dana Larson and her CID team were waiting under a canvas shelter that had been placed over the body. The white cloth fluttered in the breeze and kept the corpse in the shade. The dead young soldier lay on his side on the ground, dressed in a jogging outfit. His eyes stared in what appeared to be an expression of surprise.

Larson nodded to Riley and her colleagues.

"I'm glad you could make it," she said. She hesitated a little, then added, "We need your help."

Riley wasn't surprised that Larson didn't seem at all happy to admit it. After all, they had hardly parted on the best of terms.

She said, "The victim this time is Private Kyle Barton. He was shot while taking a pre-dawn jog. His body wasn't found until after sunrise."

Riley was a bit surprised.

"Not a sergeant this time?" she said.

"No, but not a new recruit either," Larson said. "Private Barton was days away from completing his Advanced Individual Training."

Larson shook her head bitterly.

"He had a lot of potential," she said. "What a goddamn waste."

Lucy said, "At least we can rule out the killer being someone who has a thing about authority figures."

Riley stooped down to look at the body. She saw that the bullet wound was directly in the center of the private's chest.

"The others were shot in the head," Riley said.

"Do you think the difference is significant?" Larson asked.

Riley didn't reply. She wasn't sure. But her gut told her that the shooter was the same person who had killed the others.

Riley looked up at Larson and asked, "Is Omar Shaheed still in custody?"

Larson winced a little at the sound of Shaheed's name.

"Absolutely," she said. "But somebody else in his cell might have done this."

Larson was looking her in the eye now, and Riley braced herself for some friction. It seemed that Larson still wasn't ready to let go of her Islamic extremist theory.

"Do you have any reason to think that's true?" Riley asked, meeting her gaze steadily.

"Not yet," Larson said. "Shaheed has rolled over on several cell members, and we've brought four of them in. But there could be others he hasn't told us about. Or maybe he doesn't even know about. And this might be their revenge for Shaheed's capture."

Riley squinted doubtfully.

"A single shot like this? Does that seem like the kind of revenge a religious fanatic would take?"

"We've got to consider all possibilities," Larson said.

Riley looked at Larson in silence for a moment. She sensed that the colonel didn't entirely believe her own suggestion. But she was apparently reluctant to admit it, perhaps out of resentment toward Riley or perhaps just because she had no other working theory.

I've got to get her over this idea, Riley thought.

Until she did, Larson would be no help with this investigation.

She asked, "Where did the shot come from?"

Larson pointed toward the higher ground.

"Somewhere up in those hills," she said. "We couldn't get a specific trajectory. There was no exit wound, and as you can see, Barton twisted as he fell. We sent some MPs up to search the area, but without a more precise position, they couldn't find anything."

Riley looked up toward the nearby hills.

"What kind of overhead surveillance do you have at night?" she asked.

"Some drones—although it's hard for them to cover the whole base. Fort Mowat is seventy-five thousand acres, and most of it is wilderness. We also send out helicopters with night-vision and heat-seeking equipment."

"Did your searchers pick up any heat signatures last night?" Riley asked.

Larson shook her head.

"None of the shooter," she said. "Just a few animals—coyotes and rabbits, probably."

Riley thought for a moment.

"Do you have any records of those positions?" she asked.

Larson turned toward Sergeant Matthews, the search team chief.

"Is that information available?" she asked him.

"I think so," the sergeant said. "Let me check."

He fingered his computer pad and finally showed a map of the base, with several positions where small, fleeting heat signals had been detected. Riley compared the map with the surrounding terrain. She could see that one of the spots was near where she thought the shot might have come from.

She had a strong hunch that something might be found up there.

It might even be enough to make Larson to give up her Islamic fanatic theory.

"Come on," Riley said. "Let's go have a look."

She hoped that what she was about to do would win Larson's confidence.

CHAPTER THIRTY

Riley's expectations rose as she trudged along after Sergeant Matthews on their way into the hills nearest the field where Private Barton had died. Bill, Lucy, and Col. Larson followed close behind. Matthews was using his GPS to find the exact position of the morning's fleeting heat signal.

The group made their way upward through rough, scrubby terrain. These hills were steeper and higher than the spot from which the killer had shot Sergeant Worthing, and there was no path to mark the way.

As they approached a promontory, Matthews came to a stop. He checked his computer pad and then pointed to the ground.

"The heat signature was exactly here," he said. "The searchers said it was just a blip, obviously an animal that ran off as soon as it was spotted."

Riley looked around the area. It truly was an innocuous spot, with just a few small bushes here and there. It didn't offer clear view of the place where Private Barton was shot.

For a moment Riley wondered if her instincts had misled her this once.

Perhaps the heat signature really had just been some animal.

If so, there were literally countless other places in these hills where the shooter might have positioned himself.

But how had he escaped detection by a passing helicopter's thermal imaging?

Riley realized she was in an awkward situation. She'd brought Col. Larson up here on the hunch that she could change her mind about the killer being a part of Shaheed's cell of Islamic fanatics.

What if Riley came up empty?

It would be an unlucky setback for her—and for the investigation.

She had to get into the killer's mind again. But could she do that with Col. Larson breathing down her neck? And with Matthews watching her expectantly?

She breathed slowly and turned all around.

Then something struck her eye. It was an overhanging rock ledge.

Suddenly, the killer's experience became crystal clear to Riley.

She could feel his thoughts and his movements.

All she needed to do was walk and talk the others through it.

She stepped over to the spot on the ground that Matthews had located.

Then she told the group, "This is how it happens. Our shooter is moving along here, on his way to the top of the hill where he plans to take his shot. Then the helicopter appears, its searchlight glaring. But the shooter is not especially alarmed. He knows this area like the back of his hand."

Riley walked over to the overhanging ledge and put her palm against the rock.

"This rocky shelter, for instance," she said. "He already knows it's here, could find it with his eyes closed if he had to. He's had it in mind all along as a possible hiding place. In fact, these hills are littered with protective spots he's prepared to dodge to at any second—dozens of them, probably. He knows them all by heart."

Retracing the shooter's movements, Riley climbed under the ledge and stretched out prone.

Then something else caught her eye.

The rocky soil was scuffed a little. The mark could have been made by a shoe or a boot. The killer hadn't left anything like a full footprint. He would never be that careless. Nevertheless, he'd left a single mark that didn't look natural in these surroundings, a telltale sign that he'd been here.

"Look here," Riley said to Larson, pointing to the spot.

Larson stooped down to see the mark in the dirt. After a second, she glanced at Riley with a startled expression. Then the CID head listened and watched with rapt attention as Riley continued her account.

Riley was still lying under the ledge, imitating the shooter.

"He stays down here while the chopper circles around. He knows they're looking for him. He figures they must have picked up his heat signal, but it would only have been a fleeting sign. He also knows he's safe here—at least for now. The rock above him is as cold as the rest of the ground, masking his body heat from the thermal imaging."

Riley said nothing for a few moments, imagining how the killer felt as he waited.

Then she crawled out from under the ledge. She saw that both Bill and Lucy were grinning. Both Larson and Matthews were very attentive now.

"At last the chopper goes away. And the shooter heads toward his true destination—the only place nearby where he'll have a good view of Barton's jogging route."

Followed by the others, Riley climbed the short remaining distance to the hilltop. Then she stretched out on the ground as if holding a weapon.

She said, "He sees Barton through his night scope. He's got a clean view, but he's farther away than usual. Even with an M110, it won't be an easy shot. He's not reckless, and he's not a fool. He knows that he'd better change his MO just a little. This time he'll shoot at the chest, not at the head."

Riley pantomimed pulling a trigger.

"And that's exactly what he does."

Riley got to her feet and dusted off her hands. Her account of the killer's movements was over.

Bill and Lucy were barely masking their triumphant expressions.

Bill asked Col. Larson, "Does what Agent Paige has been saying make sense to you?"

Larson nodded, her mouth hanging slightly open.

Then Bill asked, "What kind of profile does this give you of the shooter?"

Larson hesitated for a moment.

Then she said, "He's disciplined. He's extremely well trained, but he's gotten his most important training on his own. His whole life is all about becoming a perfect soldier."

She hesitated again, then grimaced slightly and added, "He's not an ideologue, he's not a religious fanatic. He's not part of Shaheed's cell. His motives are more personal. We really are dealing with a lone wolf."

Riley breathed a sigh of relief that Larson finally saw the light. She knew that the colonel was an excellent investigator, and it would have been a shame if she'd let her resentment of Riley cloud her judgment. Now Riley could put that problem behind her.

But as they headed down the hill the way they'd come, Riley thought about Larson's description of the killer as a "lone wolf."

That reminded Riley of what Private Pope had said to her about Sergeant Worthing during their confrontation on the cliff ...

"He ran with the pack."

She felt an odd chill at the memory.

Her gut again told her that those words were somehow very important.

*

Soon Riley and her companions arrived back where Barton's corpse still lay. The CID agents were still there. So was another man wearing a sergeant's insignias. He was staring down at the body with an expression of horrified disbelief. Col. Larson introduced him to Riley and her colleagues.

"This is Lanford Williams, the drill sergeant for Private Barton's advanced individual training group."

Williams's eyes darted dazedly among the BAU agents, then focused on the body again.

Williams's mouth opened, but he couldn't seem to speak for a moment.

Then he said, "I can't believe this happened. I thought … I was afraid …"

His voice trailed off. But Riley could read a world of meaning into his silence and his expression.

Williams had been afraid because he had thought his own life was in danger.

The other victims had been sergeants, after all—not privates. He'd gone to lengths to keep himself safe, especially by staying inside at nights. The last thing he imagined was that one of his recruits would be killed.

And Riley was sure that he was struggling with a terrible surge of survivor's guilt.

Riley touched him on his shoulder and said gently, "You couldn't have known he'd be a target, Sergeant Williams. Nobody did."

Williams shuddered silently.

Riley asked in a quiet voice, "Do you have any idea who might have done this?"

Williams shook his head.

Bill asked, "Did Private Barton have any enemies?"

"No," Williams said. "He was well liked. He was a good man."

Riley thought for a moment, then asked, "Does the phrase 'run with the pack' mean anything to you?"

Williams' forehead crinkled with thought.

"Mean anything? How?"

"I'm not sure," Riley said. "But if you think of anything please let us know."

Williams shook himself, as if trying to throw off the nightmare he thought he was having. But of course, it wasn't a nightmare. It was real.

He said, "My AIT group is very shaken up. Could someone

talk to them?"

Col. Larson nodded and said, "We're going to do that right now."

Then Larson turned to Riley and asked, "Can the medical examiner come and get the body now?"

Riley thought for a moment. The day was getting warmer, and the heat would take its toll on the corpse despite the shade of the canvas shelter. Now that Riley and her BAU colleagues had seen it, the body was serving no further purpose here.

"Yes, that would be fine," Riley said. "But you should send some good CID people up that hill. They should go over every square inch of ground under that ledge and on that hilltop."

Larson sent Sergeant Matthews and his CID team up the hill. Then Larson, the drill sergeant, and Riley and their companions headed toward the barracks where Private Barton had been in training with his AIT group.

On the way, they passed a fence with crowd of reporters behind it. Riley knew that their movements on the base had been restricted, and they hadn't been allowed near any of the crime scenes. But they were here all the time now, and Riley knew that they wouldn't go away.

As soon as the reporters caught sight of the group, they pushed up against the fence yelling out questions.

Larson said, "Let's just pass on by them."

Riley stifled a sigh. She knew that they needed to control the story as much as they could. Otherwise, crazy rumors would run rampant.

"No, we'd better face them," she said.

CHAPTER THIRTY ONE

Riley dreaded the barrage of questions they were about to face from the reporters. Sergeant Williams looked especially nervous. Since this gaggle was held back by a fence, they wouldn't be physically buffeted by the crowd of reporters as they'd been a couple of days ago.

They were, however, buffeted by questions, which hit them all at once.

"Do you have any leads at all?"

"This is the fourth murder inside a month—or have there been more that we don't know about?"

"Is the killer stationed on the base?"

"Who else would have access?"

"What about a motive?"

Col. Larson shouted the voices down.

"We'll take just three questions—one at a time."

Riley was relieved that Larson seemed ready to answer questions. The colonel certainly had access to better information than FBI agents did.

Larson pointed to one reporter, who asked, "Have you thought about evacuating the base?"

"Of course not," Larson said. "Crimes happen on a military base, the same as in a civilian city. You wouldn't evacuate a city, but you do impose precautions. That's what we're doing."

Larson pointed to another reporter, who asked, "Have you restricted access to the base?"

Larson replied, "We've restricted some civilian access, yes. But a certain amount of traffic is unavoidable. And let's keep in mind that these killings may be intended to distract us, to draw our attention away from some other impending attack. If we change our routine too much, we might be falling into a trap."

Riley was impressed by Larson's answers. The colonel really was good at her job.

"We'll take one more question," Larson said.

Another reporter said, "We've learned that you have a man in custody—an Islamic extremist named Omar Shaheed."

Larson looked somewhat alarmed now.

"Where did you get that information?" she asked.

"Do you deny it?" the reporter said.

Larson hesitated. Riley knew she was trying to decide whether to simply say, "No comment." Riley hoped she wouldn't. Any ambiguity on this issue could release a flood of falsehoods and innuendo.

To Riley's relief, Larson said, "We don't deny it. At this point we are holding several suspects who belong to an Islamic terror cell. The cell appears to have been planning some sort of massive attack. We're still trying to determine the nature of that attack, and where and when it was intended to take place. But we're confident that it has now been thwarted."

The reporter pressed further.

"Is the cell responsible for these four shootings?"

Larson hesitated. Then she looked at Riley, prompting her to speak.

Riley said, "We don't believe that the cell has anything to do with the four shootings. We're pretty sure we're looking for a lone killer. Obviously, an excellent marksman. What his motives are, we don't yet know."

Some of the reporters looked incredulous.

One yelled out, "So a terrorist attack was being planned separately from these shootings, at the same time? Isn't that quite a coincidence?"

Riley nodded.

"That's exactly what it is—a coincidence. When you've been doing our work for as long as we have, you learn that coincidences sometimes happen. In fact, sooner or later they're simply inevitable."

The group erupted into another bombardment of questions. Col. Larson shouted them down again.

"That's all we've got to say for now. We'll keep you informed of any further developments."

The hubbub continued as Riley, Bill, and Lucy followed Larson away from the reporters. The colonel looked somewhat shaken.

"How did they know about Shaheed and his cell?" Larson said. "We were trying to keep that quiet."

Riley realized that Larson had seldom if ever been exposed to this kind of media frenzy.

"You shouldn't be surprised," Riley said. "Leaks are just about impossible to prevent, and reporters are eager to get them. The trick is to cope with what reporters know and don't know, and to answer their questions honestly and yet discreetly."

Larson didn't reply. Riley sensed that she needed a word of

encouragement.

"You handled them fine," Riley said.

"Thanks," Larson said, looking somewhat relieved.

As Sergeant Williams led them on their way among the barracks, Riley could see that the atmosphere of the base had changed since the last time she had been here. Extra guards and MPs were stationed here and there, and the sound of helicopters searching the hills was now constant. Riley also noticed two drones overhead, doubtless with cameras watching all the activity below.

Not surprisingly, the effect on the personnel was palpable. There was a lot of tension in the bodies of soldiers moving around out in the open. They cast suspicious glances all around at each other. No one walked slowly or casually. Everyone kept moving quickly, anxious to get out of sight of the hills as quickly as possible.

As Riley and the others walked by, one enlisted man jostled another. A fight was about to break out when two MPs stepped in to stop it.

Riley said to Larson, "It looks like the killings are taking a toll on base morale."

Larson replied, "Yeah, and the heightened security isn't helping. Also, Colonel Adams has been even more of a hard-ass than usual, cracking down on discipline. Personally, I don't think it's helping. It might be making things worse."

When they neared the barracks they were headed for, Riley wasn't happy to see Col. Adams himself standing just outside the door. Noises were coming from inside the barracks.

Sergeant Williams stopped and saluted. Col. Larson walked straight toward the garrison commander.

"May I ask what's going on in there, Colonel?" she asked.

"Just a routine weapons search," Col. Adams said. "I've got MPs going from barracks to barracks."

Larson looked surprised and dismayed.

"A weapons search seems hardly 'routine,' sir," she said. "And I doubt very much that any recruit is hiding an M110 sniper rifle in his storage locker. Are you sure this search serves any useful purpose?"

Col. Adams sneered a little.

"This is my base, Colonel. I'll be the judge of that. I take it you're here to answer the recruits' questions."

"Yes," Larson said. "I just hope you don't have them too shaken up to be helpful."

146

Col. Adams let out a grim laugh.

"A search like this toughens them up," he said. "We ought to be doing more of this kind of thing routinely."

Larson didn't reply. She appeared to be trying to control her anger.

The MPs who had been searching for weapons emerged from the barracks. Their leader informed Adams that they'd found nothing suspicious. Adams and the MPs then moved on to the next barracks.

"Assemble your recruits," Larson said to Sergeant Williams.

The drill sergeant stepped inside the barracks and called his AIT group together in the formation area. The fifty or so young men and women looked jittery and tense. Williams introduced them to Larson and the BAU Agents, then put the soldiers at ease so the talks could be less formal.

Col. Larson said, "First, I want to share our condolences for the loss of your comrade. This is a hard time for you all. I'm sure you have as many questions as we do. You may ask them now."

One young man held up his hand and asked, "Why did we have a search just now? Are any of us under suspicion?"

Riley could see a flash of irritation in Larson's expression. Riley understood why. Larson was hardly pleased to be left having to explain the garrison commander's arbitrary actions. But Riley also knew that Larson was too professional to undercut Adams with criticisms of her own.

"The search was routine, I assure you," Larson said tersely. "As of now, our search for suspects could lead us anywhere. We need your patience and understanding."

A young woman held up her hand.

She said, "Several of us have been thinking of starting our own search team. Would that be a good idea?"

Larson shook her head.

"I'm afraid not," she said. "It would only add confusion to an already murky situation. Please leave searching to the MPs, CID agents, and these people from the BAU. We know what we're doing."

Then a young man asked, "Wouldn't this be a good time for us all to have personal weapons?"

Larson looked at Riley, referring to the question to her.

Riley was aware that recruits at Fort Mowat normally weren't allowed to carry their own weapons. She could understand why some of these young people might want them now. She also knew that it wasn't a good idea.

Riley said, "You want to be able to defend yourselves. I get that. But personal weapons would only give you a false sense of security. Our shooter is a lone sniper who fires from great distances. Your best precaution right now is to pay attention to your immediate whereabouts. Try not to stand in exposed areas in full view of the hills around this base."

Another recruit asked, "Does that include during the daytime?"

Riley nodded.

"Yes, it does. So far our shooter has only struck at night. But he seems to be adaptable, not unwilling to change his MO. We can't rule out the possibility of a daytime attack. You can't be too careful."

Larson added, "Above all else, we don't want a vigilante atmosphere on this base. We understand that you're scared and mistrustful. Try not to let those feelings morph into paranoia, and don't try to take the law into your own hands. The situation is already dangerous enough, so don't make it worse. Report anything suspicious directly to me."

After a handful more questions from the recruits, Riley said, "We need any information you can give us. Even details that might normally seem insignificant. No details are too small. Come to us right away if you even have the slightest hunch that something is wrong. We especially need to know of any pertinent connections between Private Barton and the other three victims. And if Private Barton had any personal issues or enemies, we need to know that too."

Riley knew better than to hope that hands would shoot up and the recruits would start offering theories. With some luck, maybe some soldiers would approach them privately.

But she needed to ask the same question that she'd asked Sergeant Williams a little while ago.

"Does the phrase 'run with the pack' mean anything to anybody here?"

The recruits looked at each other, some of them shaking their heads. Riley scanned their faces as well as she could. Did she detect any flash of recognition among them? She simply couldn't tell for sure. There was too much tension in the air already.

Riley turned to Col. Larson and said, "I don't have anything else to ask at the moment."

Larson told Sergeant Williams that the meeting was at an end, and he dismissed his group. Some of the recruits went to their barracks while the others milled tensely around the formation area. Riley and her colleagues waited around for a few moments to see if any of the soldiers wanted to speak to them more privately. One did.

He said, "We've got a Muslim in our group. Abdul Sadiq is his name. Don't you think you should bring him in for questioning? I mean, isn't there a chance that this is some kind of Islamic terrorist thing?"

Riley and her colleagues glanced at each other.

We should have seen this coming, Riley thought.

After all, there were 343 Muslim recruits on the base. Suspicions against them were likely to grow.

Riley knew they had to nip these suspicions in the bud.

"There's a lot we don't know yet," she told the recruit. "But we have an extremely high level of confidence that the killer has no links with Islamic extremism. He acts alone, and we don't yet know his motives. Spread that word around."

The soldier went away, and Riley spoke to Larson.

"Could we put out some kind of all-points bulletin, telling personnel not to target Muslims for suspicion? Things could get ugly if we don't watch out."

"I'll get right on it," Larson said.

At that moment, Larson's cell phone rang and she answered it. Meanwhile, another young soldier approached the group.

He said, "This might not mean anything, but Kyle told me he was having some troubles at home. He was kind of tight-lipped about it, so I don't know any details."

Riley doubted that this was significant. For one thing, Kyle Barton's personal problems probably didn't link him to the three slain sergeants. Still, she couldn't discount any feedback.

"Thanks for telling me," Riley told the recruit. "Please alert Col. Larson if you think of anything else. Like I said, no details are too small."

As the soldier went away, Larson ended her call.

She told Riley and the others, "I just got word that Barton's widow and daughter are on the base. We need to go and talk to them."

Riley's heart sank as they walked toward the administration building.

Talking to grieving family members was easily the most painful part of her job. She dreaded it far more, even, than confronting psychopathic killers.

CHAPTER THIRTY TWO

As Riley arrived at the administration building with Bill, Lucy, and Col. Larson, her discomfort mounted. She couldn't imagine what she could say to Private Kyle Barton's widow. What were the right words to say to a young mother whose husband had been killed so abruptly? His death seemed meaningless, and yet it had been no accident. It had been murder.

A female civilian staff member quickly escorted them to a visitors' room where the family was waiting. The staff member introduced them all and quickly left the room.

The widow's name was Ellen, and the daughter's name was Sian.

Riley guessed that little Sian was about fourteen months old. The freckled, golden-haired little girl appeared to have just started to walk and was taking great joy in it. She laughed with delight as she toddled around the room chasing a large sparkly plastic ball with little bells inside.

Riley suppressed a shudder at the sound of the laughter and the bells. Such innocent glee seemed shockingly misplaced at such a horrible moment.

But of course, what did little Sian know about death?

Riley sensed that Sian's mother, Ellen, was also grappling with this emotional dissonance. Ellen shared her daughter's freckles and golden hair, but her eyes were red from crying and her eyes were dazed with shock.

All eyes in the room were on Sian for a few moments. Nobody seemed to have any idea what to say as long as Sian kept bustling noisily around. Then Lucy took the little girl by the hand and said, "Let's go play in another room. Just you and me."

The little girl giggled. Lucy scooped up the ball and led the child out of the room.

Ellen breathed an exhausted sigh when Sian was gone.

Riley was relieved when Col. Larson spoke first.

"We're sorry for your loss, Mrs. Barton."

As always, the words struck Riley as shockingly lame—and as discordant as the toddler's laughter had been.

But what else is there to say? she wondered. Riley would have said those exact words if nobody else had.

Ellen Barton nodded, as if barely aware that anything had been said.

Then Bill got the interview started. "Mrs. Barton, we have to ask you a few questions. We'll try not to take too much of your time."

The woman nodded again. "All right," she whispered. Riley was glad that Bill was taking the lead.

Bill asked, "Did your husband have any enemies that you knew of?"

Riley was shocked anew when what seemed like an involuntary smirk crossed Ellen's face.

"Enemies?" she said. "How would I know? I didn't even know who his friends were."

Riley and Bill glanced at each other.

"Could you please explain what you mean?" Bill asked Ellen.

Ellen breathed another deep, weary sigh.

"Ever since Kyle began basic training, I've felt him slipping away from me. The time we've had to spend apart has been hard. But even the time we've spent together—well, it's been like he wasn't really there. The Army mattered more and more and more to him—mattered more than even …"

Her voice trailed off, but Riley knew where her thought was going.

The Army had come to matter more to Kyle Barton than his wife and daughter.

Riley understood and recognized the situation all too well. After all, this wasn't completely strange territory. Her own father's dedication to his military career had wreaked havoc on his personal relationships—including with Riley.

And of course Riley's own relationships had suffered because of her devotion to the BAU. Ryan had been anything but a perfect husband, but Riley knew that she'd often been absent from the relationship physically or emotionally, sometimes both. And she still worried about how her work was affecting her ability to be a mother. She often had to ask herself whether she was as devoted to Jilly and April as she was to her job.

She hoped she was, but the question kept coming back into her mind.

She knew that Bill's own relationships had suffered in the same way. She remembered something he told her when his own marriage to Maggie was starting to fall apart …

"She thinks I'm having an affair with my job."

Riley felt a pang of sadness.

Infidelity takes many forms, she thought.

And now it seemed almost as though Ellen Barton had lost her husband quite some time before his death.

While Riley was thinking these thoughts, Bill was still asking Ellen more questions. He was being his diplomatic best and Ellen Barton seemed willing to help, but the woman simply didn't know enough to offer any real insights. Finally Bill looked at Riley, silently asking if she wanted to ask anything else.

Riley shook her head and said, "We won't trouble you further, Mrs. Barton. Again, we offer our condolences for your loss."

Col. Larson handed the woman her business card and said, "Please get in touch with us if you remember anything at all—even something that might seem unimportant. Thank you so much for taking some time to talk with us."

Riley, Bill, and Col. Larson left the room. In the hallway, they encountered Lucy and little Sian playing with the ball. Lucy escorted the child back in with her mother, and then the agents all headed for the CID building to regroup.

Instead of considering the rest of the day's activities, Riley found herself still thinking about something that Ellen had said.

"I didn't even know who his friends were."

It was a sad sentiment, but now Riley wondered …

Is it something more than that?

Everybody they had talked to on the base seemed to hold Barton in the highest regard. But had he harbored some mystery that few of them knew about? Had Kyle Barton's secretiveness toward his wife masked some darker riddle—something that had to do with his own murder?

Riley didn't yet know.

But she felt sure that something besides family matters had been amiss in Barton's life—and that whatever it was had everything to do with his death.

CHAPTER THIRTY THREE

As night fell that evening, Riley, Bill, and Lucy sat on the patio of the cottage where they were again staying, looking out over the ocean.

It had been a frustrating day. After meeting with Ellen Barton they had gone on to interview people who had known Private Barton. They had learned nothing.

They had also tracked down and talked to base personnel who had been up and around during the night of Barton's murder. But those people all had alibis that checked out perfectly.

Right now, Riley and her colleagues were enjoying a pizza that they had ordered. Lucy offered Riley a beer, and for a moment Riley hesitated. She wanted a drink badly, but she didn't want a repeat of last night. But after all, the three agents only had a six-pack among them, so she realized that she needn't worry about overdoing it.

As they ate and drank, Lucy asked, "Are we sure the shooter isn't through killing? Serial killers have sometimes been known to just stop."

Neither Riley nor Bill replied for a moment.

Riley found it an oddly unsettling thought. The last thing she and her colleagues wanted was more killings. But if the killer just quit and quietly slipped into the shadows, the case might go cold.

Just last month, Riley had solved a case that had been cold for twenty-five years. And of course a few cases were never solved at all.

She hated the thought of that happening with this one.

At last Bill said, "My gut tells me that he's not finished yet."

"I agree," Riley said. "The question isn't so much whether he's planning to kill again, but when. And we've got to stop him before that happens."

"We might have some time," Bill added. "He's been killing at irregular intervals, and it could be that those intervals will get shorter rather than longer. But I'm not so sure about that. We don't have much to go by."

Riley silently agreed. Security on the base had been heightened, with increased surveillance from drones and helicopters. There also was a new curfew to keep personnel from roaming around at night. But Riley knew that this killer was nothing if not resourceful—a sort of murderous Boy Scout, always prepared for any eventuality. It really bothered Riley that she and her colleagues were making so little progress.

When they finished eating, Lucy got up from the table.

"I think I'll take a walk along the beach," she said.

Riley smiled and said, "You won't be able to see much when it's dark like this."

"It's never completely dark on the water," Lucy said.

The younger agent walked off the patio and onto the beach.

Riley felt moved as she remembered the story Lucy had told about her own life—how she and her family had lived in Sacramento, but had worked so hard that Lucy had no chance to see the ocean until she went to college.

Riley recalled what Lucy had said about the ocean …

"Whenever I see it, it reminds me of how lucky I am, and how proud I am to live in this country and to do the work that I do."

Riley felt her eyes get a little misty.

As if reading her thoughts, Bill said, "That girl's going to do great things with the Bureau. I'm proud to be working with her now, and I know that she's just getting started."

"Me, too," Riley said.

She and Bill fell silent again. Riley realized that she hadn't been in touch with anyone back in Fredericksburg all day. It was too late for phone calls, but not too late for texts. She quickly typed affectionate messages to Blaine, Gabriela, and the girls. She told April and Jilly how much she loved them, and how much she was looking forward to coming home.

Then she sat and stared at the surf and listened to its steady waves.

Anxieties started to crowd into her brain again. The thought of Shirley Redding's pointless death still haunted her. She started looking back over the last few months, thinking about all the decisions she might have made differently.

How did I let all this happen? she kept asking herself.

In the midst of her thoughts, she was startled by the sound of Bill's voice.

"How are you doing?"

Riley looked at him with surprise. It seemed like an odd question for him to ask out of the blue.

"I'm fine," she said.

Bill shook his head.

"You're not fine," he said. "I could tell something was wrong when we met at the plane this morning."

Riley cringed as she remembered how hung over she must have looked.

"I had kind of a rough night, that's all," she said.

Riley knew better than to think that Bill would accept that as an answer. He knew her much too well. But he didn't say anything for a few moments. The only sound was of the surf pounding the beach.

Finally Bill said, "I heard about that woman's death at your dad's place."

Riley shuddered a little. Of course it was hardly any surprise that Bill knew about Shirley Redding's death. Word had surely gotten around the BAU about it by now.

Then Bill asked, "She was your real estate agent, wasn't she?"

"Yeah," Riley said.

"That must have been a tough thing to deal with."

Riley hesitated. What did she dare say about all this to Bill?

Then she said, "I went up there yesterday to see what happened."

She hesitated again.

"The police said it was an accident," she finally said.

As soon as the words were out, Riley somehow knew that Bill wouldn't believe her.

She didn't know why exactly.

Were there rumors that Jennifer Roston was looking into Riley's connections with Shane Hatcher?

Or was it simply that Bill could see right through her?

Again, a few moments passed with no sound but the waves.

At last Bill said, "Riley, you can talk to me about anything. I hope you know that."

Riley turned her head and met Bill's gaze. She could tell by his expression that he had already guessed at least some of what was troubling her.

He probably even knows it has something to do with Hatcher, she thought.

He was her best friend, and he'd seen her through terrible times. He'd also covered for her when she'd done terrible things. He knew perfectly well that she'd deliberately let that young killer hang himself. He'd turned his back when she'd crushed the hand of the young man who had drugged April and tried to sell her body.

He'd remained loyal and silent through all of that.

If there was anybody in the world she could talk to about what was going on with Shane, it was surely him.

But how could she tell him without bringing him into her web of shame and deceit?

Her voice choking a little, she said, "Bill, I can't. I just can't."

Bill nodded and said nothing.

After a few moments, Lucy came back from her walk and went on to bed. Bill also decided it was time to turn in for that night.

Alone on the patio, Riley decided to take a walk of her own.

As she strolled across the wide beach, she saw that Lucy had been right—the water wasn't dark. Moonlight glowed through thin clouds, glistening on the waves. It was all very soothing and peaceful.

As Riley walked along the waterline, she saw another figure further up the beach—a silhouette of a man. Riley wasn't alarmed at first. She saw no reason to be surprised that someone else would want to enjoy a lovely night walk like this.

But when the figure was about a hundred feet away, a voice called out to her.

"Agent Paige?"

Riley felt a rush of adrenaline. She was wearing her sidearm, and her hand hovered near it.

"Who's there?" she called back.

The figure raised his hands.

"Don't shoot. I'm unarmed. I came to help."

Riley recognized the voice now.

It was Stanley Pope, the private who had provoked her on the seaside cliff.

What can he possibly want? Riley wondered.

CHAPTER THIRTY FOUR

Riley turned on her cell phone flashlight to get a better look at the shadowy figure farther down the beach.

It was Private Pope, all right. His hands were still high in the air.

What was he doing here?

What kind of "help" had the soldier who had tried to frighten her come to offer?

Revenge is more likely, Riley thought.

He was surely still stinging from the humiliation he'd suffered at her hands on the cliff a few days ago. She knew that he was arrogant and rebellious and hadn't liked being taken down by a "chick."

Maybe she should have expected him to show up sooner or later for payback.

Riley decided to keep her distance from him this time.

"I'm unarmed," Pope said again.

Riley looked him up and down. It looked like he was telling the truth. But she also knew that he was physically tough and agile.

He began to walk slowly toward her. He moved smoothly, even on the sand.

"Keep your distance," Riley said, her hand still near her weapon.

"I don't want to hurt you," Pope said as he approached, his hands still raised. "Look, you taught me a good lesson the other day. I respect that. I respect you."

Riley wondered whether to believe him.

Then she remembered something he'd said about Worthing, the dead sergeant who had been his drill instructor and had taken away his mosquito wings …

"I'm damned glad he straightened me out."

Now Riley wondered if he felt that way about her too.

It was certainly possible.

"I really want to help," Pope said. "These murders have got to stop."

Pope's voice and expression seemed sincere.

She decided to risk approaching him—but she kept herself alert and ready for anything that might happen.

In a moment, they stood face to face in the beam from Riley's flashlight.

"What do you want to tell me?" Riley asked.

Pope turned his head back and forth, as if to make sure they were really alone.

Riley asked, "Do you know who the sniper is?"

"No," Pope said.

"Then how can you help me?"

Pope locked eyes with Riley.

He said, "I think I know how the four victims were connected."

Riley's attention quickened. So far, any connections among the slain soldiers had eluded both the CID and FBI agents on this case. Perhaps that was about to change.

"What's the connection?" she asked.

Pope seemed to gather his nerve to speak.

"It's hazing," he finally said.

Riley felt alarm bells go off. Hazing was, of course, the first and most obvious theory; and yet it had been ruled out.

"What do you mean?" she asked.

"There have been some serious hazing incidents at Fort Mowat. Some of it has gotten out of hand."

Then Pope fell silent. Whatever he had to say, Riley sensed that he was reluctant to say it.

Maybe even fearful, she thought.

She had to frame her words and questions carefully to draw him out.

"Talk to me about hazing," she said. "Is it unusual?"

"Not really," Pope said. "It happens on all military bases. It's not supposed to happen at Fort Mowat, but it does."

He was looking down at his feet now.

"Look, I think this is a mistake," he said. "I shouldn't be talking to you."

He started to turn away.

"Don't go," Riley said. "Just talk to me."

He turned back toward her and nodded nervously.

"How do you know about hazing?" Riley asked.

"I was hazed. Badly. I can take it. Just like I could take what you dished out after Sergeant Worthing's funeral."

He fell silent again. Riley knew she had to keep him talking.

She asked, "Are there recruits who can't take it?"

"A few. We've had dropouts in my platoon. There was a suicide in another unit."

He shrugged uneasily.

He said, "Like I said, sometimes it can get out of hand.

Physical assault is one thing—beating, getting knocked around. That kind of thing toughens you up, gets you ready for combat. But some of these drill sergeants have been in battle too many times. Some actually suffer PTSD. They get kind of crazy, do crazy things. One recruit's skin was so scarred by bleach that he had to get grafts."

Riley was shocked.

"Nobody mentioned that to me," she said.

"It was a couple of years ago," Pope said. "I heard about it from some guys who were here back then. That drill sergeant was court-martialed. Everybody thought the bad hazing was all over. But it's still going on."

Although Riley was shocked by this news, she sensed that Pope was still being evasive.

"You said you know a connection among the four victims," she said. "What is it?"

Pope looked away again and said nothing.

"Were they hazers?" she asked.

Pope nodded. "They were the toughest of the hazers," he said.

Riley struggled to make sense of what she was hearing.

"I don't understand," she said. "Kyle Barton was a private, not a drill sergeant. Why would he haze anyone? And how?"

Now Pope seemed both scared and defensive.

"Look, he was part of it, that's all I can tell you. And …"

His voice trailed off.

Riley asked, "Is someone taking revenge on hazers?"

"I think maybe so," Pope said. His voice was getting shaky now.

"Why are you so scared?" Riley asked.

Pope seemed to be struggling with himself, trying to decide what to say.

Finally he said, "Look, that's all I can tell you. I've got to get back to the barracks."

He turned and started to walk away.

"Come back and talk to me," Riley said, walking rapidly to keep up with him. "If you're scared, we can protect you."

Pope shook his head and kept walking.

"That's all I've got to say. Please—don't tell anybody I talked to you. Nobody must know. These are people who—"

Without warning, he broke into a run and took off down the beach.

Riley started to run after him, but thought better of it and stopped.

She knew Pope had told her all that he was willing to tell her—probably more than he'd meant to tell her.

Even so, her head was full of questions as she walked back to the cottage.

Why is Stanley Pope so scared? she wondered.

She needed to find out soon—before someone else was killed.

CHAPTER THIRTY FIVE

When Riley woke up Bill and Lucy early the next morning to tell them about her weird and unsettling encounter with Private Pope, her colleagues listened with fascination.

When she finished, Bill said, "We've got to bring this Pope kid in for more questions."

Riley shook her head.

"I don't want to do that," she said. "Not right now."

Bill looked incredulous.

"Why not?" he asked. "Pope is a person of interest, if anybody is. And it sure doesn't sound like he told you everything he knows."

Riley knew that Bill was right. She didn't want to ignore his concerns, but she had worries of her own.

Then she said, "For one thing, I think he's genuinely terrified—and probably with good reason. Bringing him in might make him a target."

"A target for *who*?" Bill asked. "For all we know, he's the one we're looking for."

"I'm sure he's not," Riley said.

Bill sounded incredulous now.

"How do you know? Riley, the guy attacked you."

"He didn't attack me. He just tried to scare me. Apparently he learned his lesson. He was actually trying to find a way to help."

Bill groaned with exasperation.

"I don't know about this, Riley."

The more Riley thought about it, the more sure she was that she was right.

She said, "First I want to talk to Barton's AIT group again. At least for now, we're not telling Larson or anybody else about my meeting with him last night."

She watched Bill's face as he digested her words and somewhat reluctantly accepted her decision. Finally, he nodded his head.

Riley drew a breath of relief. She really didn't want to get into an argument with her partner over this. Once again, she appreciated his willingness to go with her instincts even when she couldn't explain them.

She looked at Lucy, who had been quiet so far.

Lucy said softly, "So what do we do now?"

Riley said, "We go back to Barton's group. We've got to ask more questions," she said.

"Could we ask them at Barton's funeral?" Lucy asked.

Bill said, "No. I've been told that his widow doesn't want a military ceremony, so it's going to be a private funeral for family and a few friends. Few if any of his fellow soldiers will be there. We'd best stay focused on the base."

Riley drummed her fingers for a moment.

She said, "Well, we've got to talk to those trainees right now. Somebody in that group is holding out on us. I feel sure of it."

*

Riley called Col. Larson right away to set up the meeting. About a half an hour later, she, Bill, and Lucy joined Larson and her team head, Sergeant Matthews, at the mess hall. The AIT training group was gathered at a table there. Sergeant Williams explained that Riley and her colleagues had more questions for them.

Riley noticed that their young faces looked markedly more worried than they had yesterday. They also looked more fearful. She wasn't surprised. Now that they'd had a full twenty-four hours to process what had happened to their fellow soldier, the initial shock was giving way to a whole world of dark and troubling feelings—including paranoia, some of it directed at each other.

Riley, Bill, Lucy, and Col. Larson stood in front the group. Sergeant Matthews took his place nearby.

Riley decided to get right to the point.

"I want to ask you about hazing," she said.

A palpable shudder went through the group. Riley sensed surprise, confusion, and alarm.

One young man said, "I don't understand. The victims were shot, they weren't hazed."

"Or *were* they hazed?" a female recruit said.

"Is there something you're not telling us?" another male asked.

A brief hubbub followed until Sergeant Williams sternly quieted the group. The drill sergeant himself seemed shaken by what Riley had just said. That was good as far as Riley was concerned. The last thing she wanted was for the recruits to be comfortable. She was far more likely to get meaningful information now that they were off their guard.

Riley continued, "I know hazing goes on. That's nothing unusual. But I need to hear about your own personal experiences. Has it happened to you?"

Recruits eyed each other anxiously.

Riley knew perfectly well that she'd asked a difficult question.

Sergeant Williams spoke up.

"With due respect, Agent Paige, the Army now has rules against that kind of thing. It says so in the training manual. 'Stress created by physical or verbal abuse is non-productive and prohibited.'"

Riley looked hard at him and said, "Are you telling me that hazing never happens here at Fort Mowat?"

Sergeant Williams didn't answer. His expression grew sullen.

Riley asked, "Do *you* haze your recruits, Sergeant Williams?"

He glared at her, looking insulted now, but still said nothing.

A young man called out, "Sergeant Williams would never do that, ma'am. He sticks to the book. He treats us with respect."

There was a general murmur of agreement. Riley believed them. But she sensed that she was pushing the right buttons.

The young woman who had already spoken said, "Look, sometimes other drill sergeants give us a hard time. My platoon sergeant back in basic combat training used to give us extra workouts. We can deal with it. Anybody who can't deal with it shouldn't be here."

A couple of recruits grumbled in agreement.

Riley pressed on.

"I'm not talking about extra workouts. I'm talking about stuff that pushes the envelope, goes too far. And I need for you to tell me about it right here and right now."

An uncomfortable silence settled over the group.

Then a young man spoke reluctantly, almost in a whisper.

"Something happened in my unit."

Several of his comrades tried to shush him.

Col. Larson said, "Speak up, Private. Agent Paige needs to hear about it. There won't be any repercussions. I guarantee it."

Now there was a barely audibly groan of incredulity from the group. Riley understood why. How could Col. Larson guarantee no repercussions for telling the truth about this kind of thing? The truth was, Riley knew she was asking them to put themselves at risk of retaliation from their peers. Riley didn't like it, but she felt that she had no choice. Lives might well depend on what she learned here today.

She said to the soldier who had spoken, "Go ahead. Tell me."

The young man winced sharply.

"My basic combat drill sergeant assembled our unit and fired a gun in the air. Then he waved the gun at us and said that he was going to take one of us out with the next shot. He pulled the trigger again, but there weren't any more bullets in the cartridge. Scared us half to death."

The soldier sitting next to him looked furious.

"You keep your trap shut, Musser. That's nobody's business."

"But did it really happen?" Riley asked the angry soldier.

"Yeah, it happened," the soldier snapped at Riley. "I was in that unit too. But so what? It gave us a good scare, and we needed it. It was just a taste of what we'd feel in combat. I'm damn glad the sarge did it. He's been in combat, knows what we're in for. We've got to become cold-blooded killers. Coddling us now is a sure way to get us killed later on."

A woman said, "You're full of shit, Parks. It's not like killing's the only thing we're training for. We've got science units, intelligence, engineering, law. I'm going to be a mechanic."

Another soldier barked back at her, "Well, good for you. Some of us are going to be in real combat. We need to be ready. As far as I'm concerned, it's a damn shame hazing's against the rules. You're not really part of a unit until you're broken down mentally and physically."

There was a flurry of voices now, some agreeing, others disagreeing sharply.

She noticed one young man who hadn't said a word so far. From his nametag, Riley saw that his last name was Shealy. He looked especially anxious, sitting rigidly with his hands clenched together. She sensed that it was only a matter of moments before he'd open up with something.

She asked, "What about rumors you may have heard? Kinds of stuff that might even be hard to believe?"

A silence fell. The air felt charged with tension.

Finally, a shy-looking soldier spoke up.

"I've heard stories. About a place called the 'Den.' And things called 'abductions.'"

The tension in the group suddenly felt as though it might explode. Riley started to worry that a fight might break out.

Another private pounded on the mess hall table and pointed at the soldier who just spoke.

"That's just a myth, Daniels," he yelled. "Keep it to yourself."

A few of the others voiced their angry agreement. Others looked like they had never heard of such a thing before. A handful looked truly worried now.

Riley heard a gasp at her side. She turned and saw that Col. Larson's mouth was hanging open from shock.

Riley's nerves tingled. She could tell that Larson had just heard something that meant something to her.

Riley knew that she was about to find out something crucial to solving the case.

She also knew that it wasn't going to be pretty.

CHAPTER THIRTY SIX

Riley kept very still as Col. Dana Larson stepped forward to ask her own questions of the group. She looked truly agitated now and her voice was shaking as she commanded them, "Tell me about these 'abductions.' I don't care if you believe they're real or not. If you know anything talk, damn it. If anybody holds back, I promise there will be consequences."

The private named Daniels shyly spoke again.

"I hear that some privates get snatched up off the base grounds at night. Not by aliens, but strange guys—soldiers, I guess. The privates are put through all kinds of ugly ordeals. When they get broken down enough, they're turned loose. They never understand what happened."

Col. Larson was staring hard at Daniels.

"You said you heard about this," she snapped. "From who?"

Daniels ducked his head, trying not to look at anyone. But Riley could tell whose face he was most anxious to avoid. It was the quiet young man she had noticed just before—Private Shealy.

Riley spoke to him.

"Private, I think you've got something you'd better tell us."

Private Shealy was silent for a moment. Then he mumbled something inaudible.

Riley said, "I couldn't hear you, Private."

Shealy spoke just a little louder.

"I said it happened to me. I was abducted. I told Daniels about it."

Col. Larson folded her arms. Her expression seemed to be growing more troubled by the moment.

"Tell us, Shealy," she said. "Tell us now. Tell us everything."

Private Shealy shuddered.

"It was crazy," he said. "It was awful. It was the worst thing that ever happened to me."

He paused for a moment, as if trying to summon his nerve.

"I was taking a walk one night when a bunch of guys rushed out of the bushes, put a hood over my head, and tied my hands behind my back. I couldn't see anything. They kept turning me around and around as they led me somewhere. I had no idea where we wound up, but ..."

He fell silent. Col. Larson stepped toward him as if she wanted to shake him. Riley motioned her back.

"Take your time, Private," Riley said.

"We wound up inside some building. First they took me to a room, and they bound me to a chair, and they kept my head covered so I still couldn't see anything. The guys around me were pushing and hitting me and yelling insults at me. They made me drink vinegar and eat something hard and tasteless—cardboard, I think. They made me swallow it. I kept throwing up, but they kept making me eat and drink more. And then …"

Beads of sweat broke out on Shealy's forehead.

"They put a different hood on me. This one had eyeholes in it. But it kept flopping around on my head, so it was still hard to see. Then they led me into a big room with a balcony. They told me that this was the 'Den.' There must have been a hundred guys sitting all around, wearing weird masks—clowns, animals, monsters, that kind of thing. A group on the balcony seemed to be overseeing everything, and they wore masks too. And there were five more people like me in an open area. All of us had on those hoods with eyeholes. I didn't know who they were. Our hands were all tied, and they cut us loose, and—"

Private Shealy seemed to choke back a groan of horror.

"They made us fight. They made us beat each other as hard as we could. If we tried not to do it, they beat us up. We had no choice. We pounded on each other like crazy. And the thing was …"

He fell silent again. Riley sensed that he was struggling to find the words to describe what happened next.

Finally he said, "I got into it. The violence made me crazy, and I fought back harder and harder, and didn't want to stop. It looked like we were supposed to keep fighting until there was only one of us standing. And I wanted to be that one guy still left. I wanted to be … part of whatever was going on there."

"Then what happened?" Riley asked.

"I got punched real hard to the side of the head, knocked unconscious. The next thing I knew I was laying in a heap in front of my barracks, and it was long after lights out. I went to my bunk and collapsed. I was—"

Shealy's face twitched with what seemed to be both horror and anger.

"I know this sounds crazy, but I was so disappointed, so ashamed."

Riley was full of questions she wanted to ask. But before she could speak, a young woman spoke sharply. According to her nametag, her name was Nelson.

"You're an asshole, Shealy. You're a piece-of-shit asshole."

Shealy looked at Nelson as if she'd slapped him.

Nelson continued, "It happened to me too. But I refused to let them make me their bitch—not like they did to you, Shealy. I wouldn't let them make me fight the others. I let them pound me down. Finally they gave up on me and hauled me back to my barracks, hooded up so I couldn't see where I'd been."

She was shaking with fury now.

"I've never been so angry about anything," she said. "I'm still angry. If I could find one of the guys who did that to me, I swear to God, I'd kill him. I wouldn't even blink."

Shealy and Nelson stared each other—Shealy with horror, Nelson with rage.

Riley's head reeled with stunned confusion.

She knew she'd just learned something vitally important.

But what did it mean?

Col. Larson asked, "Do either of you have any idea who any of your abductors were—any idea at all, even one of them?"

Nelson shook her head. But Shealy looked at Col. Larson and nodded.

"Some of their voices sounded familiar," he said. "And I'm sure I recognized one of their voices."

"Who was it?" Larson asked.

Shealy gulped and said, "It was Private Barton. He was one of the guys yelling at me in the room, and he was also in the crowd ordering us to fight. I wasn't sure until the next day. Barton and I had been pals before that. But he never treated me the same afterwards. He acted like I was beneath him. He always kept his distance from me—right up until he died."

Riley felt pieces of the puzzle coming together.

There seemed to be a powerful secret society at Fort Mowat. And its members carried on brutal initiations that few young soldiers ever passed—or even voluntarily signed up for. Those who did survive became proud members of that shadowy elite.

Those initiations took place in a place known as the "Den."

That name kept nagging at Riley.

The Den ...

Then she remembered again what Private Pope had said about Private Worthing ...

"He ran with the pack."

Before Riley could think this through, Col. Larson spoke to the group.

"We have no more questions for now."

Riley was startled. Why had Larson decided to end the meeting completely on her own? Riley had more questions she wanted to ask.

Then Larson added, "Privates Shealy and Nelson, I want you to give full reports of what happened to you to Sergeant Matthews here. If any of the rest of you knows anything, do the same. Don't even think about holding back. We're going to get to the bottom of this."

Then turning to her team head, she said, "Take those reports, Matthews. Don't miss a single detail, or there will be hell to pay."

Looking a bit intimidated, Sergeant Matthews said, "Yes, ma'am."

Without another word, Col. Larson strode out of the mess hall.

Riley, Bill, and Lucy hurried after her.

Riley asked, "Colonel, would you mind telling me what this is all about?"

Col. Larson replied in a breathless voice, "I know who the killer is. Come with me."

CHAPTER THIRTY SEVEN

Col. Larson didn't say another word during the walk to the CID building. Riley was wondering what was about to happen, and she saw that Bill and Lucy were exchanging equally puzzled glances.

Only one thing seemed certain to Riley—there was about to be some kind of break in the case.

When they arrived at the colonel's office, Larson didn't speak right away. She sat down at her computer and started to search frantically through records.

As she typed, she finally said, "I've heard about this 'abduction' thing before. I just didn't believe it."

"What do you mean?" Riley asked. "Actual abductions?"

Larson kept typing as she talked.

"A few months ago, we had to discharge a recruit with psych issues. His name was Brandon Graham."

"A dishonorable discharge?" Bill asked.

"No," Larson said. "Someone convicted in that kind of case would likely be imprisoned. What happened with Graham is called a 'separation,' and it's a kind of medical discharge."

Riley's curiosity was mounting.

"What kind of medical problem did he have?" she asked.

"It was called a personality disorder," Larson said. "He was having nightmares, losing weight because he wouldn't eat, couldn't concentrate on anything. Graham's drill sergeant referred him for a medical examination because his behavior interfered with his ability to continue basic training. The psychologist who examined him concluded that he was delusional, possibly schizophrenic."

"Delusional?" Lucy asked. "How?"

"He kept saying he'd been 'abducted,'" Larson said.

Riley felt a tingle of understanding. Everything was starting to come clearer.

Larson turned her computer around so that Riley and her colleagues could see the records she'd brought up.

"You can see the psychologist's report right here, including transcripts of their sessions," she said.

Riley and her colleagues looked at the transcript. An exchange between Graham and the psychologist caught her eye.

Dr. Sears: Who abducted you, Brandon? What did they do to you?

Private Graham: I'm not telling you anything more about it.
Dr. Sears: Why not?
Private Graham: Because it's none of your damn business.
Dr. Sears: If you want to stay in the Army, you'll have to tell me.

Private Graham: Not a chance. Payback is mine. Revenge is mine. I'll take care of this on my own. The Army be damned. Kick me out for all I care. It won't stop me from doing what I have to do.

As she read, Riley remembered what the female private had said during the meeting in the mess hall.

"If I could find one of the guys who did that to me, I swear to God, I'd kill him. I wouldn't even blink."

Now it seemed that Private Graham had been just as angry as that young woman—and a lot less stable.

And he'd been much more likely to actually seek revenge.

Riley also remembered something Private Pope had told her on the beach last night about the four slain soldiers.

"They were the toughest of the hazers."

While Riley was putting all this together in her mind, Col. Larson added, "Of course, the psychologist thought Graham was simply delusional, maybe having hallucinations. It sounded like he was talking about an alien abduction. Everybody thought so, including me. But as soon as those recruits started talking about abductions, the whole thing suddenly made sense. What happened to Graham was real."

Lucy asked, "Does that mean that he didn't have a personality disorder after all?"

"Oh, I'm sure he did," Larson replied. "After all, not everybody who was exposed to hazing responded the same way. In fact, the psychiatrist concluded that the personality disorder had most likely existed before his enlistment. But now I understand why his problems got so much worse."

Bill scratched his chin thoughtfully.

He asked, "Did Graham have any particular military skills while he was in training?"

Larson typed a bit more.

Then she said, "Yeah. He was a promising sharpshooter."

Riley heard herself let out an audible gasp.

Suddenly the whole case seemed to be open and shut.

She said, "We've got to find this man. Where is he now?"

Larson kept on typing.

"He's originally from South Carolina. But he didn't move back there after his separation. It looks like he lives in Limington, a beach town not far from here. I've got an address for him there."

Lucy asked, "Can we find out what he does for a living?"

Larson said, "I've got his Social Security number, so we should be able to find out."

Larson typed some more.

"He's a delivery man for Oriana's Pizza. I know the place. It's not one of the big pizza chains, just a popular place in Limington. Base personnel order pizzas from there all the time. Food delivery guys routinely check in and out of Fort Mowat. So he had access to the base pretty much all the time."

"Let's go get him," Riley said.

*

A few minutes later, Riley, Bill, and Lucy were driving toward Limington. In a car right behind them were three CID agents— Sergeant Matthews and his two-man team, Agents Goodwin and Shores.

Riley wasn't especially happy to have the CID agents in tow. They were in uniform, of course, which was going to attract attention. In Riley's experience, uniforms tended to generate alarm, which usually made arrests more difficult. But Col. Larson had insisted, and Riley felt that she couldn't say no. After all, Larson herself had supplied the insight that probably was going to lead to the arrest.

Limington was a sparkling, gentrified, coastal tourist town. Its main street was lined with palm trees and expensive-looking stores, cafes, and gift shops. It hardly looked like the kind of place that would be harboring a serial killer, but Riley knew that looks could be deceiving.

The two vehicles parked in front of Oriana's Pizza. Riley and her colleagues got out of their car, and Riley walked over to meet the three CID agents.

"I'd like you to stay in your car for now," she told them.

"Why, ma'am?" Sergeant Matthews asked.

Riley bristled a little. She was sure that Matthews wouldn't question an order from Col. Larson. And she didn't feel like explaining the disruption he and his team would cause simply by walking into the restaurant.

"Just do as I say," Riley said.

172

Matthews and his agents got back into the car, and Riley and her BAU colleagues went into the restaurant. The management had tried to make it look like an old-fashioned Italian *trattoria* with heavy ceiling beams, dozens of small bare light bulbs, and tile roofing hanging over the bar. But everything looked too new to be convincingly quaint.

Riley and her companions were greeted by a stout, middle-aged woman who reminded Riley a little of Gabriela.

"May I get you a table?" the woman asked in a distinct Italian accent.

"We need to talk with the manager," Riley said.

The woman smiled broadly.

"That would be me. I'm Oriana Bellone."

Riley wondered whether the accent was authentic or just an old-world affectation. She and her colleagues produced their badges and introduced themselves. Oriana's smile faded into an expression of concern.

Riley said, "We're looking for an employee of yours—Brandon Graham."

"Is Brandon in some kind of trouble?" Oriana asked.

Riley thought she heard the accent falter just a little bit, but she wasn't sure.

"We just need to talk to him," Riley said.

Oriana shook her head.

"Brandon's not here," she said. "He works mostly at night."

"Doing deliveries?" Riley asked.

"That's right. Most drivers don't like night runs, but Brandon does. He's ex-military, so maybe that's why he feels safer than some of the others."

Bill asked, "Does he carry a weapon?"

"I don't know if he has a gun permit or not. They're not easy to come by in California."

Riley knew that California gun laws weren't likely to deter someone determined to get a weapon. Drug runners and gang members had no trouble getting them.

"Does he drive his own car?" Riley asked.

Oriana nodded.

"It's an old used car that he got cheap. A blue Toyota."

"Do you have any idea where he is right now?" Bill asked.

The woman shrugged.

"At home, maybe. I'll get his address for you."

Oriana went to her office and quickly came back with Brandon

Graham's address written on a piece of paper.

She said, "He lives in the Limington Hotel, just a block down the street to the right."

Riley and her colleagues thanked her and left the restaurant. Outside, Riley noticed the CID agents still sitting in their car—undoubtedly feeling none too patient.

"Should we bring them along?" Lucy asked.

Riley thought for a moment. It seemed likely that they were about to apprehend a dangerous suspect. As conspicuous as the uniformed agents might be, they also might be helpful. She asked Sergeant Matthews and his team to come along.

As the group approached the Limington, Riley saw that it stood out from the surrounding shops and eating places—and not in a good way. It was dingy, three-story building that had obviously been there since long before Limington became a thriving tourist town.

In fact, Riley guessed that it was more a flophouse than a hotel these days, and a barely inhabited one at that. She also guessed that it wouldn't be around much longer in such gentrified surroundings. It was probably long overdue for demolition.

The building seemed even seedier once they went inside, with tattered carpeting and grungy wallpaper in the halls. There was no one at the dusty front desk and the place was deathly quiet. Riley found it almost hard to believe than anybody still lived here.

They found Brandon Graham's room on the third floor.

Riley knocked sharply on the door, but nobody answered.

"Maybe he's asleep," Lucy said.

It seemed possible to Riley. Somebody who worked mostly at night probably slept a lot during the day.

She knocked again and called out, "Brandon Graham, we're with the FBI and the CID. We need to talk to you."

Again came no answer.

Riley told Sergeant Matthews to go look for the manager. She waited impatiently until Matthews returned with a decrepit old man who Riley guessed had been running this place since the hotel had seen much better days.

He was carrying a bundle of keys and seemed to have no qualms about opening up Graham's room.

Riley and the others all crowded into the tiny room. It had a single small bathroom, a tiny refrigerator, and a cooking range. The place was dirty, stuffy, and smelled of mildew. Riley looked all around and saw that Graham appeared to have hardly any personal belongings—no TV or stereo, no trinkets or pictures or decorations.

Then Riley heard Lucy say, "Agents Paige and Jeffreys, you'd better have a look at this."

Riley turned and saw that Lucy was holding a piece of paper gingerly by one corner. Careful not to interfere with any possible fingerprints, Lucy laid the paper on the bed.

"This was tucked under the pillow," Lucy said.

Riley and Bill went over to look at it.

Riley shuddered at what she saw.

It was a handwritten list of about twenty names. Four of the people listed were the murder victims—Rolsky, Fraser, Worthing, and Barton.

All four of those names were crossed out.

CHAPTER THIRTY EIGHT

Riley blinked with amazement as she stared at the list. There seemed to be no question about it—Brandon Graham was their killer.

But where was he right now?

Also looking at the names, Lucy commented, "We know the ones whose names are crossed out. What about the rest of them?"

Riley gasped a little as she recognized one other name.

"There's Stanley Pope," she said.

Lucy said, "That's the guy who attacked you on the cliff—and who approached you again on the beach."

"That's right," Riley said. "This must be a list of hazers—soldiers that Brandon Graham had it in for. They would be members of that society the recruits talked about."

"And Pope is one of them?" Lucy asked.

"He didn't tell me about that," Riley said. "But I knew he wasn't telling me everything."

"For all we know," Lucy added, "he might be Graham's next target."

"Not if we can help it," Bill said. "We've got to stop this guy before he takes anybody else."

Sergeant Matthews held out his hand.

"Let me see that list," he said to Lucy.

Lucy handed it to him, and he stood looking it over. Meanwhile, his CID agents were banging around the apartment looking for more evidence. Riley was fairly sure that they weren't going to find anything—not in this tiny place. If Graham had a weapon stash, he was hiding it someplace else.

A voice in the hallway called through the open door.

"What the hell's going on here now?"

The group turned and saw an unshaved man in an undershirt rubbing his eyes. The man fixed his attention on the uniformed CID agents.

"Hey, is Graham in some kind of trouble?" he said.

Lucy stepped forward and showed him her badge. Riley and Bill showed theirs too,

"Do you know Brandon Graham?" Lucy asked.

"Not really, but I live next door. He's a weird guy—noisy as hell for someone who lives alone. Screaming and knocking things around at all hours—he never seems to sleep, day or night. I thought you guys were him, acting up again."

Riley stepped toward the neighbor.

"Do you have any idea where he might be right now?"

The neighbor scratched his head.

"Down at the fishing pier, I guess. He doesn't talk to me much. We just pass each other in the hall. But whenever he does say anything, it's about how he's either been to the pier or is going there. And I've see him out there pretty much whenever I go fishing."

The agents got directions to the pier and all hurried back to their cars. As Riley got behind the wheel and drove, she was excited about their luck. Maybe they could put an end to these murders right now.

But she cautioned herself not to get too confident. First they had to find Brandon Graham and apprehend him.

That might not be so easy, she reminded herself.

The man had eluded capture before.

*

During the short drive to the pier, Bill watched Riley closely. He'd been worried about her ever since they'd talked about the death of the Realtor at her mountain cabin. Actually, they hadn't talked about much at all. She had just clammed up, saying, *"I had kind of a rough night, that's all."*

Bill was sure that she'd been drinking the night before. He knew she did that when she was deeply upset.

Riley had a reputation for going rogue, breaking the rules, and even disobeying orders. He'd accepted all of that long ago.

But during the last few months, they hadn't had much of a break from demanding cases. He thought their recent jobs had been particularly hard on Riley, with her family threatened several times. He had seen how each attack affected her.

He remembered all too well her vengeful brutality toward the boy who had drugged her daughter and tried to sell her body. Bill had also arrived on the scene the moment after she'd let a serial killer strangle himself to death.

Bill hadn't confronted Riley about these episodes, and he certainly hadn't considered reporting her behavior. He'd been Riley's partner and friend for too many years to do anything like that.

But now, he thought that the work was wearing her down.

He was also sure that something was terribly wrong in her personal life right now.

And he had a hunch that it had to do with Shane Hatcher. But she wouldn't talk to him about that either.

Bill desperately wanted to help her somehow. But was she in too deep for him to help her—deep into something dark and evil?

Bill's thoughts were interrupted as the car pulled into a parking lot within sight of the pier. It was a long, old, jutting wooden structure. The tide was low right now, and the pilings lifted the pier some twenty feet into the air.

The CID agents also pulled into the lot. Both cars parked, the agents all got out and surveyed the scene. Bill took a moment to breathe in the salt air. It was a tranquil spring day on the beach—and a crowded one as well. People were roaming all over the pier and on the sand, including many small children.

Bill didn't like having so many people around when they were about to apprehend a dangerous criminal.

He asked his companions, "What the hell are all these people doing here in the middle of the week? Shouldn't these kids be in school?"

"It's California," Lucy said. "The beaches are always full."

Bill could see that Riley was keenly surveying the situation. She said, "Get out your cell phones. I'll send you the Army's file photo of Brandon Graham. We'll spread out and search along the pier. If anybody sees him, message the rest of us."

She told the three uniformed CID agents, and she added, "You guys, try to be as inconspicuous as you possibly can. Stay back here at the base of the pier. Watch your cell phones too—but if you get a message, don't try to join us. Your first duty is to clear all civilians off the pier. And whatever you do, don't cause a panic."

The three FBI agents headed out on the long wooden structure. Aside from numerous roaming tourists, many people were standing at the rail with fishing poles. Despite the number of people, Bill wasn't especially worried that they'd have trouble spotting Brandon Graham. A glance at the picture on his cell phone showed that the young man had a very distinctive face with a jagged nose and a low, sloping forehead. What they'd do when or if they found him was another matter.

Bill moved through the crowd ahead of Riley and Lucy. The pier was about two hundred feet long and they had to get a look at the face of each adult male on it. In a few minutes he had reached the end without spotting anyone who matched the photographs and was about to give up hope of finding Brandon here. Then the he noticed someone sitting on the railing at the very end of the structure, facing out toward the ocean.

As Bill approached, he didn't need to see the young man's whole face to recognize him. Even from slightly to one side, Bill could make out that distinctive sloping forehead. But he looked considerably bigger and stronger than he did in the Army photograph.

He texted to the others …

He's at the end of the pier.

Then Bill just watched the young man for a moment.

He was staring at the rolling waves, but didn't really look relaxed. His hands were twitching, constantly rubbing together. It was also odd that, on a pleasant spring day like this, he was wearing a rather bulky jacket.

He's got a gun, Bill realized.

Bill knew that he and his colleagues needed to handle this man with extreme caution. He glanced back and saw that Riley was hurrying toward him, while Lucy was quietly approaching others on the pier, flashing her badge and directing them to leave.

He silently motioned for Riley to slow down and keep some distance.

Then Bill drew his own weapon and stepped over to the railing beside the young man, who was still staring at the water, oblivious to any activity around him.

Bill asked, "Are you Brandon Graham?"

Still looking downward, Graham nodded.

"You're a cop, aren't you?" Graham asked.

"FBI," Bill said.

Graham let out what sounded like a moan of despair.

"I wondered when you'd catch up with me," he said.

Then Graham reached inside his jacket.

"Don't do it," Bill said, stepping back and raising his Glock.

But in a flash, Graham twisted around, a semiautomatic pistol in his hand. He was still sitting on the railing and his gun was aimed at Bill.

"Why not?" Graham asked in a bland, expressionless voice. "What have I got to lose?"

Bill's eyes were locked with Graham's. Their guns were pointed at each other's face.

CHAPTER THIRTY NINE

Bill kept his own gun steady as he stared over the barrel into Graham's wild-looking eyes. His brain clicked away, calculating what might happen next. Things looked desperate, but he knew better than to panic.

His feet were planted squarely on the wooden pier. Graham was still perched on the railing, his legs still dangling over the water, his body twisted to aim the gun at Bill.

Graham was in a by far more precarious position. His aim was likely to be shaky.

It would be easy to take him out.

Too easy, Bill decided.

Bill could hear the panicked cries and the fleeing footsteps of other people on the pier. Several nearby fishermen simply dropped their poles and hurried away.

In his peripheral vision, Bill could see that Riley and Lucy both had their weapons out and aimed at Graham. He glanced quickly at Riley and gave a slight shake of his head. He didn't want them to fire. He wanted to see if he could bring in Brandon Graham alive.

He knew it might not be easy.

He was sure that Graham was contemplating suicide by cop.

Bill needed to get him to start talking.

"Tell me about everything," Bill said.

"What do you want to know?" Graham asked.

Graham's eyes were glazed now, as if he was having trouble understanding what was going on. Bill remembered what Larson had said about his psychological assessment—that he was delusional, possibly schizophrenic. Bill guessed it wouldn't be hard to keep him distracted.

"I want to know how you got to this point," Bill said. "You were discharged from the Army. What are you still doing in California? Why didn't you move home to South Carolina?"

"I couldn't afford it," Graham said. "They just threw me out, and I had to get a job quick. I spent everything I had getting a used car."

"Tell me about the list," Bill said.

A flicker of surprise crossed Graham's face. His body teetered slightly on the railing. The gun barrel moved a bit off target.

"What list?" he asked.

"You know what list I'm talking about."

Graham smiled ever so slightly. The gun barrel dipped again. Bill could see that the man's arm was getting tired.

"So you searched my apartment, huh? Well, I'm sure you know about the list already. You know who the crossed out names are. The dead bastards."

Bill felt a tingle of shock shoot through his body.

It was practically a confession.

We've got our guy, all right, he thought.

He was glad that Riley and Lucy were within earshot.

"What did they do to you?" Bill asked. "Tell me about the abduction."

Graham's expression darkened. He raised the gun to aim it directly at Bill's face again.

"It was a test of some kind."

He froze in place, and for a moment Bill thought he might fire that gun. But then he lowered it again. The weapon was still pointed in Bill's general direction, but not well aimed now.

Graham continued talking. "They never told me what it was. But once they'd dragged me into it, I was determined to pull through it. I wanted to be part of whatever was going on, one of *them*. I thought I could handle it. First they hit me and cursed at me, and they made me do things, eat cardboard and drink vinegar. I was fine with that. I could tell they were impressed."

Graham's eyes were darting around now as he remembered.

"Then they put me in a room full of guys and they made us fight. And damned if I wasn't the last guy standing. I thought I'd won, I thought I'd got the best of them, and they'd have to accept me, and I'd be one of them. But …"

His voice trailed off. His face looked pained.

"But what?" Bill asked.

"They hauled me away again, took me up into the hills around Fort Mowat. They hung me by my feet over a cliff—Larry's Leap, it's called. And I—"

He choked back a sob. He couldn't continue.

But Bill understood without being told. Hanging from that cliff, Graham had finally cracked from sheer terror. He'd probably cried like a baby. Maybe he'd even soiled himself. His humiliation had been total and horrible.

"Where did you get the list?" Bill asked.

"I got it all on my own," Graham said. He looked like he was thinking back, remembering. "I'm a pianist. I'm a singer. I've got perfect pitch. I've got tape-recorder ears. I remember every single sound I hear. Those guys had masks on their faces, but I could hear their voices. I didn't forget a single voice. During the next few days, I listened everywhere I went—out walking, in the mess hall, the rec area. I could tell who they were, at least some of them. I wrote down their names."

Bill struggled to grasp what he was hearing.

If this guy was truly schizophrenic, how accurate *was* the list?

But some of the names were obviously right. The names of the soldiers who had been killed were on that list. Pope had identified them to Riley as the worst of the hazers.

Bill sensed that Graham's attention was wandering and his determination was wavering. The gun was wobbling up and down, back and forth.

He said, "Put that gun down, Brandon. Come with me. We'll sort all this stuff out."

Graham blinked a few times, looking confused. For a moment, Bill felt sure that he was going to comply.

But suddenly, still holding the gun, Graham pushed himself off the rail and dropped down into the water.

"Son of a bitch!" Bill yelled, kicking off his shoes.

Riley and Lucy were rushing toward him now.

"What do you think you're doing?" Riley asked.

"I'm going in after him," Bill said.

Riley and Lucy both started to kick off their own shoes. Bill didn't want all of them to be thrashing around in the water with the big ex-soldier.

"Don't even think about it," he snapped. "Meet me on the shore and help me pull him in."

Bill threw himself over the railing, leaping feet first toward the water. The fall seemed longer than he'd expected, and the water was surprisingly hard and cold.

He fought his way to the surface, spat out a mouthful of salt water, and caught his breath.

Paddling frantically, struggling against the weight of his own clothes, he looked around for Graham.

A wave rolled by, and then a bit of Graham's jacket bobbed up on the rough surface. Bill felt sure that Graham was trying to pull himself under. Suicide by cop hadn't worked out for him; now it looked like he was going to resort to deliberate drowning.

Bill was getting mad. He wasn't going to let that happen.

He thrashed his way toward Graham, reached down into the water, and pulled at his clothing. Graham thrashed back at him, trying to push him away. Another wave lifted them both in the water. Bill managed to get a grip on the other man's jacket collar and yanked his head above the surface.

Then Bill punched him as hard as he could.

Dazed by the blow, Graham began to sink. Bill grabbed him by the hair, lifted the man, and turned around. He pulled his right arm over the man's shoulder for a cross-chest tow and started swimming with him.

In a struggling sidestroke, Bill dragged the now quiet man along the pier, from one massive piling to the next. Each wave threatened to take them both under.

Finally they reached shallower water and Bill was able to get to his feet, gasping for breath. But waves were breaking around him now and the undertow tugged at his ankles.

Graham was whimpering now.

"Let me go, let me go."

With great relief, Bill saw Lucy and Riley wading through the water toward him.

And Riley had her handcuffs ready.

"We'll take it from here," she told Bill.

Bill handed his burden over to Riley and Lucy.

"Where are the CID guys?" Bill gasped.

Lucy said, "Up on the dock clearing people away."

Bill let out a snort of disapproval.

"Hell, there's no point in that now," he said. "I'll go tell them to stop."

Bill staggered closer to the shore. More exhausted than he had realized, he collapsed to his knees in the shallows, gasping for breath.

With a deep sense of satisfaction, he heard Riley reading Graham his Miranda rights.

CHAPTER FORTY

When the CID team came down off the pier, the BAU agents turned the handcuffed and drenched Brandon Graham straight over to them. Riley watched with satisfaction as Sergeant Matthews and his CID team dragged the captive across the beach and toward their car.

Graham was raving wildly, "Let me go! There are more guys on that list! They're thugs, not soldiers! You won't stop them, so I've got to!"

Riley watched and listened with curiosity. The suspect was implicating himself with every breath.

They'd surely caught the killer.

But she recognized a nagging doubt that she couldn't quite put into words.

We've finished this case, she tried to convince herself. *It just hasn't sunk in yet.*

Then she heard Bill laughing.

"Look at us," her partner said. "Some fine-looking FBI agents."

Riley looked at the other two and broke into a laugh herself.

They were all soaking wet, straggly hair and saggy clothes still dripping salt water onto the beach. They looked more like survivors of a shipwreck than skilled BAU profilers.

"Let's get back and change before we scare somebody," Lucy giggled.

But as Riley and her soaking wet companions staggered across the sand toward their own vehicle, that odd doubt lingered in her mind.

*

While the CID agents drove the captive to the CID building, Riley and her BAU colleagues went to their cottage, showered, and put on dry clothes. When they finally arrived at the CID building, Larson was right there to greet them.

"Congratulations!" she said. "Excellent work!"

"Has Graham made a confession?" Riley asked.

Larson laughed.

"Several times over. We've got him dead to rights. He's still under interrogation. Come on, let's go see how it's going."

Larson led Riley and her colleagues to the interrogation room, where they stood outside looking through the two-way mirror. Sergeant Matthews was conducting the interrogation. Graham was wrapped in a blanket, still wet and shivering.

Riley didn't think Graham sounded any more coherent than he had on the beach.

"You've got to let me out of here," he said wildly. "It's my responsibility. It's my payback. You've got no right to take it away from me."

Riley found it hard to believe that this guy had already given a lucid confession. She also didn't think keeping him wet like this was a very good tactic. The man seemed to have no idea where he actually was.

As Riley stood wondering, Sergeant Matthews was staring coolly at Graham and snapping out questions.

"Tell us where you're hiding the weapon," Matthews said.

Graham's eyes rolled wildly. "Let me go. I'm a good swimmer." He tried to thrash his arms, but his wrists were cuffed to the table. "You've got no right," he wailed. "It's my revenge. Mine, not yours."

Col. Larson didn't seem to share Riley's uneasiness.

She said, "It might take a while, but he'll eventually settle down. He'll tell us where the weapon is. He'll tell us everything— how he came and went on the base, how he stalked his victims, the whole works. It's going to be quite a story."

Col. Larson looked at Riley and her colleagues, smiled, and shook her head with admiration.

"I have to admit, I underestimated you guys. I won't make that mistake again."

Larson turned and headed back to her office.

As Riley stood watching and listening to the interrogation, she began to realize what was nagging at her. At the two shooting sites, she'd gotten a distinct impression of the killer—an impression of a cool, calm, calculating, ruthless mind.

Could this be the same man?

She tried to convince herself that it was possible. She'd known even the seemingly strongest killers to crack up eventually.

Just then, Bill clapped Riley and Lucy on the back.

He said, "What do you say we get out of this place? I for one am ready to call it a day. Let's go to the cottage and pack up and head back to Quantico."

Riley didn't comment. She followed her colleagues as they left the building. When they got to their car, she said, "I'll drive."

On the way back to their beach cottage, Bill got on the phone to the BAU pilot and told him to get the plane ready right away.

But when Riley pulled up to the cottage, she didn't feel like packing. She stayed in the driver's seat with the motor still running, trying to work out something in her mind.

"You two go on inside," she told Bill and Lucy. "I've got one more thing I want to do."

Bill looked puzzled.

"Riley, what the hell's going on?" he asked.

"Nothing, really," Riley said, trying to sound more nonchalant than she felt. "Just one little loose end."

Bill asked, "Do you want me to come with you?"

She shook her head. "It's not really important," she said.

"Well, make it quick," he said. "Our plane leaves in an hour."

Bill and Lucy got out of the car and went into the cottage. Riley turned the car and drove back into the main part of the base, still not sure of what it was she wanted to do or where she wanted to go.

She flashed back to a moment when she was standing near the end of the pier. Bill and Graham were pointing their guns at each other.

Something that Graham had said came back to her ...

"They hung me by my feet over a cliff—Larry's Leap, it's called."

The terror of that ordeal had been too much for Graham.

He'd never been able to pull himself together after that, and he'd had to be "separated," as the Army called it.

Riley pulled her car over to the curb, rolled down her window, and called out to a passing soldier.

"Can you tell me how to get to a place called Larry's Leap?"

The soldier pointed the way.

"Take the next left and follow that road up into the hills. You can't miss it. Believe me."

Riley followed the soldier's directions. Sure enough, a tall cliff quickly came into view. Riley wended her way along the narrow road toward the very top of the cliff.

She parked her car, stepped out, and walked toward the edge.

The place offered a stunning view of the entire camp.

It was also dizzyingly high—about as high as the cliff over the ocean where she'd encountered Private Pope.

Riley swallowed down a sinking feeling of vertigo.

She pictured the place by night, with the camp lit up far below.

Then she tried to imagine how it would have felt to be held by the ankles over this precipice.

She shuddered. It was a terrifying thought. It seemed small wonder that Brandon Graham had cracked under this hazing ordeal.

And yet ...

She thought back to those two locations where she'd gotten such a powerful sense of the shooter—the coolness with which he'd held Sergeant Worthing in the night scope of his M110, the cunning and skill with which he'd dodged the helicopter's heat-seeking technology just before shooting Private Barton.

If he had actually been put through this test of will and courage, would he really have let it faze him?

Riley tried to imagine what it would feel like for the man whose mind she'd probed.

It was night, and he'd been abducted.

He'd already been subjected to beatings, forced to eat cardboard and drink vinegar, and had been the last man standing in a brutal free-for-all of hazing victims.

And now here he was, suspended by his ankles, looking out over Fort Mowat.

But he wasn't terrified. He was annoyed and offended. In fact, he was deeply pissed off.

These guys had a lot of nerve putting him through this kind of test.

Or anybody else, for that matter.

Even so, he called out to his tormentors ...

"Thanks, guys! Great view!"

His voice was full of laughter and mockery.

After all, he knew perfectly well this was the final test.

He was going to be accepted as one of the elite now—ready to "run with the pack."

He would join their pack.

But he would also reinvent it. This behavior, what had been done to him, and to others, was unacceptable. There was a cancer in this fine organization—a culture of vulgar, pointless, undisciplined hazing.

It was up to him to cut out that cancer.

Now, he had a mission all his own. He would get rid of the guys who were the worst hazers.

Honor demanded it.

Duty demanded it.

Only if the worst hazers were gone, could this organization be the elite, honorable organization it was meant to be.

Riley opened her eyes, stunned.

Her whole body shook with the realization.

We had it wrong all the time, she realized. This was not an act of revenge from a man who was hazed.

This was the act of a man of moral superiority. A man who could tolerate no dishonorable actions. A man who lived for the military. Who wanted it to be perfect. Who demanded it be perfect.

And when he witnessed the hazing of others, it was a stain on his own personal honor.

We've got the wrong man, she realized.

Nobody else was going to like that idea, but she knew she was right.

She hurried back to her car and started to drive.

CHAPTER FORTY ONE

As she drove back down the hilly terrain, Riley felt a sense of certainty that had been missing when they arrested Brandon Graham. With that sense came relief at finally knowing what had been bothering her.

She got Col. Larson on the phone. The CID chief's voice sounded pleasant at first.

"Agent Paige, this is a surprise. Where are you? On the plane back to Quantico?"

"Not exactly," Riley said.

"Where are you, then?"

Riley swallowed hard before speaking further.

"Col. Larson, there's no easy way to say this. But Brandon Graham is not our shooter."

A silence fell.

"What are you talking about, Agent Paige?" Larson finally asked.

Riley hesitated.

How on earth was she going to explain her realization to Larson?

"Look, I just know, OK? You're just going to have to trust my gut about this."

Larson sounded angry now.

"Agent Paige, this is ridiculous. Graham confessed. And even if he hadn't, we've still got plenty of circumstantial evidence. He had a list of targets—and he'd crossed out the ones that he'd already killed. What else would he be doing with a list like that?"

It was good question, and Riley knew it. But she didn't have time to sort it out with Larson right now.

"Col. Larson, I'll get my team and we'll come right by the CID building to regroup."

Larson sounded incredulous.

"To *regroup*? Not a chance, Agent Paige. This is over. Go home, get some rest. It sounds like you need it. I won't have this investigation ruined by irrational doubts. You and your agents are to stay out of this from here on in. Is that clear?"

Riley didn't answer for a moment. She remembered what Larson had said just a little while ago …

"I have to admit, I underestimated you guys. I won't make that mistake again."

Riley suppressed a groan of despair.

Larson sure wasn't keeping her promise.

"Col. Larson, I'm serious about this," Riley said.

"So am I. I expect the three of you to get on that plane and head back to Quantico. Are you going to defy me?"

Riley swallowed hard again.

"I'm afraid so, Colonel," she said.

Larson's voice was cold now. "Then you're going to regret it."

The CID colonel ended the phone call without another word.

Just a few minutes later Riley arrived at the cottage, parked, and rushed inside. She found Bill pacing back and forth talking on his cell phone while Lucy looked on with a startled expression.

Bill was saying on the phone, "I don't understand it, sir. Believe me, it's the first I heard of it."

Then Bill looked across the room and saw Riley.

"She just walked in the door, sir. I'll talk to her. We'll straighten this out."

Bill ended the call and stared at Riley.

"Riley, would you mind explaining to me just what the hell's going on?"

"Who was that on the phone?" Riley asked.

Bill's face was red with exasperation.

"That was Special Agent in Charge Carl Walder. Our boss, remember? He just got a call from Col. Larson."

"That was fast," Riley murmured under her breath.

Bill continued, "Col. Larson told him that you said we've got the wrong guy."

"We did get the wrong guy," Riley said.

Both Bill and Lucy stared at Riley in disbelief for a moment.

Riley said, "Look, I just went to Larry's Leap—that place where Brandon Graham said that he'd cracked from the hazing. Believe me, our killer wouldn't have fallen apart like that. It was someone else, not Graham. I just know it my gut. How often have I ever been wrong about something like this?"

Neither Bill nor Lucy spoke for a moment.

Finally Lucy said, "What about Graham's confession?"

Bill added, "And what was he doing with that list?"

Riley had to stop and think. Col. Larson had asked her that same question. But now that she had a chance to run all of the elements through her mind, she could feel them falling into place. Everything was starting to make sense.

"Graham *wanted* to be that killer," she said. "He had his own grudge against those guys. He was ashamed that he couldn't go through with it. And the fact that somebody else had the guts to do it made him feel even worse. He was desperate to claim credit."

Lucy asked, "So are you saying he's *pretending* to be the killer?"

Riley paused and thought for a moment. The man in the interrogation booth had seemed nothing if not sincere.

"No, there's more to it than pretense," Riley said. "Remember, he's probably delusional, even schizophrenic. He's managed to convince even himself. At this point, he might honestly *believe* that he's the killer." She smiled grimly as she pictured the interrogation room in her mind. "This guy is going to keep his interrogators running around in circles for a very long time."

Riley watched as Bill's and Lucy's expressions began to change. She was starting to get through to them.

She said, "Bill, when you met him on that pier, you were sure he was contemplating suicide by cop. But he didn't go through with it. He jumped instead. Do you honestly think he was capable of shooting you in the head so your partners would take him out?"

Bill slowly shook his head. "I didn't think so at the time. If I'd believed he was going to shoot, I would have fired first."

Riley said, "Think about that wretched man, both of you. Do you really and truly think Brandon Graham is capable of stalking his prey without being seen? Of carrying out a cold-blooded murder?"

Bill and Riley looked at each other.

Lucy said, "No. He might kill someone in some kind of frenzy. But he's not a stalker."

Bill just said, "No."

Riley breathed a sigh of relief.

"OK, then," she said. "We've got to get back to work—without the CID's help. We don't know how reliable that list was, but it's likely that more than a few of those other names are actual hazers. Which means they're still targets. We need to put a stop to this before any of them get killed."

"Easier said than done," Bill said. "We don't have that list anymore. We turned it over to the CID agents as soon as we found it in Graham's room."

Lucy cleared her throat.

"Uh, that's not necessarily a problem," she said.

With a shy grin, she held up her cell phone and showed Riley and Bill a photo of the list. All the names were perfectly visible.

"I took this picture the minute I laid eyes on it," Lucy said.

Riley laughed.

"Good, work, Agent Vargas," she said. "Now we've got to find these guys as fast as we can."

"That shouldn't be hard to do," Lucy said.

She opened her laptop and began to type.

"Fort Mowat's records of active recruits are available on its website. I can find the platoons and groups that each of these guys belongs to."

Riley stood watching Lucy deftly searching for information.

She gets better and better at this job every day, Riley thought.

Lucy turned the laptop screen so that Riley and Bill could see it.

She said, "I've got them. The names fall into six units overall."

Riley looked at the breakdown of names closely.

"OK, then," Riley said. "We need to divide up, pay visits to all these units, and talk to all these soldiers. Maybe we can find out something. At least we can warn them. But remember—we are not only warning potential victims. We are also weeding out a potential killer. He may very well be one of the pack. So anybody we talk to just might be the real shooter. And we know how ruthless he can be. So be careful."

Bill shook his head.

"Col. Larson will never allow this," he said.

"I'll take care of that," Riley said.

"How?" Bill asked.

Riley didn't reply. She was about to do something highly improper, and it was best for neither Bill nor Lucy to know exactly what it was.

She took out her cell phone and typed a text message to Col. Larson:

My apologies. Of course you've got the right man. My team and I will fly back to Quantico ASAP. It's been a pleasure working with you.

Riley looked up and saw Bill staring at her. He obviously had a pretty good idea what she'd just done. But he knew better than to ask questions.

Then Bill said, "I'll call the pilot and tell him to cancel that flight."

"Great," Riley said. "But do it while we drive. We've got no time to lose."

They all hurried out of the cottage and into the car.

If they got things right, they could prevent another murder.

CHAPTER FORTY TWO

A few minutes later, Riley parked the car near the barracks, and she, Bill, and Lucy split up to check out individual names from Graham's list.

Riley's anxiety was rising.

We've got to work fast, she thought.

Word could soon get back to Col. Larson that the FBI agents were still on the base asking questions. There would be hell to pay whenever that happened.

Riley was looking for two privates—Damien Temple and Otto Corbin. She went to their barracks and asked their drill sergeant their whereabouts. The sergeant directed Riley to a skeet shooting range a short distance away.

When Riley walked to the range, she found two young men firing shotguns at their flying targets. It was pretty advanced shooting, and they were hitting the targets consistently.

"Are you Privates Temple and Corbin?" she called out as she approached them.

"Yeah, who's asking?" one of them asked.

Riley produced her badge and introduced herself.

Neither of the young men looked especially impressed.

"Mind if I have a try?" she asked them.

The private with the nametag TEMPLE shrugged at the one with the nametag CORBIN. Corbin just nodded.

"Yeah, be our guest," Temple said. With a cocky grin, he handed her his double-barreled shotgun. "She's loaded and ready."

Riley took the weapon, lifted it, and called, "Pull!"

Two clay targets flew from opposite directions toward each other in the air. Riley fired one barrel, picking off one of the targets, then fired again a split second later, hitting the other target effortlessly.

Both men looked impressed as Riley handed the gun back to Temple.

"What can we do for you?" Temple asked.

Riley knew that she was in uncertain territory. She honestly wasn't sure whether Brandon Graham had even known what he was doing when he put these two guys on his list. Graham had psychotic tendencies, after all. He might only have imagined that he'd recognized their voices during the hazing. Were these guys even members of the secret society?

And how was Riley going to get them to tell her anything?

She would have to bluff it out to learn the truth.

She could say some things that were true, but she had to act like she knew more than she did.

"I'm here to talk to you about the pack," she said.

Temple and Corbin looked at each other.

"We don't know what you're talking about," Corbin said.

"Oh, I'm pretty sure you do," Riley said.

And that was a fact. Their expressions instantly betrayed to Riley that they knew all about the pack.

Temple said, "If we did, why would we talk to you about it?"

"Because one or both of you might wind up dead if you don't," Riley said.

The two men gaped at her with surprise.

Riley said, "I'm sure you know about the recent murders on this base."

Corbin shrugged uneasily and said, "Yeah, but wasn't some guy arrested just a little while ago?"

"It's the wrong man," Riley said.

Corbin shuffled his feet and Temple's eyes darted around.

They're getting nervous, Riley thought. *That's good.*

Riley said, "Let's not play games here. You're both part of the pack. And the shooter is targeting pack members. You're on a list of targets."

She saw them exchange skeptical glances, and added, "The lists exists. I saw it. That's the reason I'm here. Sooner or later, the killer is going to get around to you."

Riley knew that she was playing a kind of verbal poker game, and she had to keep bluffing strategically. To get them talking about the pack, she had to act like she was already an expert. That required some speculation and guesswork.

She said, "Look, the pack is no secret. Maybe you don't realize it, but you're kind of famous. The CID has known all about you guys for a long time. So has everybody in the chain of command here at Mowat, all the way up to and including Col. Adams. They don't talk about it out of respect for what you stand for. It's not like your outfit is illegal. Of course, the abductions do push the envelope a little. But you can't make an omelet without breaking some eggs, right?"

The guys were staring at Riley with fascination.

"I'm from a military family myself," Riley said, "and I respect what you guys are doing. The Army's not what it used to be, is it?

Training's not what it used to be. War is more dangerous than ever, but how are you supposed to get prepared for it these days? Everything's all about sensitivity and political correctness and socialization, all that kind of touchy-feely crap."

"You've got that right," Corbin grumbled.

"The Wolf Pack is here to fix that," Temple said.

Riley knew that her tactic was working. She just needed to stay on the same track.

She said, "Of course, not just anybody can be a true wolf."

"No way," Corbin said, shaking his head. "But we look for guys with potential, whether they know they've got it or not."

Temple added, "And once they've survived the hazing—*if* they survive it—they're ready and eager to join the pack, the elite of the elite."

Corbin was starting to look uneasy now.

He said to Temple, "We shouldn't be talking about this. Even if she knows about it already. We swore an oath. You don't talk about the Wolf Pack. Ever."

"I respect that," Riley said hastily. "I'm not asking you to divulge any secrets. I just need you to tell me anything you can to help me find the killer. After all, he's picking off pack members."

Corbin's brow knitted inquisitively.

"But why? Why are we targets?"

"It's got something to do with hazing," she said. "Somebody thinks you go too far."

"Somebody we actually hazed?" Temple said.

"That's right," Riley said. "But not somebody who cracked. He thinks hazing is unworthy of an elite military society. He's taking out the worst hazers because they offend him."

Corbin and Temple looked at each other.

They both shuddered.

These are a couple of the bad ones, Riley thought.

Temple said, "So the killer actually *is* a wolf? A member of the pack?"

"That's my theory," Riley said. "Look, I'm not asking you to give away your entire membership. But can you think of any fellow wolves who have been disgruntled in any way? Who have seemed hostile toward guys like yourselves?"

Riley could tell that Corbin and Temple were seriously thinking it over.

Finally they both shook their heads.

"I can't think of anybody," Corbin said.

"We're a tight bunch," Temple said. "It's hard to believe that we've got a traitor in our midst. I can't imagine who it might be."

Riley sensed that they weren't holding anything back from her.

"He wouldn't consider himself a traitor," Riley corrected. "He would consider *you* all traitors. In fact, he would consider himself to be the best of you."

They stared in silence, shifting, clearly uncomfortable.

She said, "The killer is using an M110 sniper rifle."

The soldiers' eyes widened.

"Wow, that's some kind of firepower," Temple said.

Riley asked, "Do you know any wolves who might have access to something like that?"

The soldiers shook their heads.

Riley said, "Well, one of the wolves *does* have it. And whoever he is, he must be hiding it somewhere. Can you think of where that might be?"

Corbin and Temple thought for a moment.

Then Corbin pointed off into the distance.

"Probably the old assembly building," he said. "There's a lot of room to hide things there."

Riley almost slipped and started asking questions about the building.

Was it the "Den" that hazing victims had talked about?

Then she remembered—she was in the midst of bluffing, acting as though she knew about this kind of thing already.

Don't tip your hand, she reminded herself.

"Thanks, guys," she said. "I'll check that out."

She walked away from the shooting range, looking in the direction where Corbin had pointed. From what the hazing victims had told her, she knew that it had to be a big building, probably an abandoned one.

It shouldn't be hard to find, she thought.

*

Private Stanley Pope's whole body was tingling with shock. Special Agent Riley Paige was headed straight toward him, and he didn't want to be seen. He'd been following Agent Paige ever since she'd gotten out of the car back at the barracks, wondering what she and her fellow BAU agents were up to.

He'd heard that somebody had been arrested for the shootings. So why were the FBI agents still poking around?

Pope was standing inside a little building that offered a few tables and chairs, water, and a bathroom for those taking a break from shooting. He couldn't get any closer to the shooters without being spotted, but he was too far away to hear what any of them had been saying.

What did those dumb bastards tell her? he wondered.

Last night when he'd found her on the beach, he'd been careful about what he'd said.

He'd never forgotten his oath.

He hadn't breathed a word about the Wolf Pack.

But Pope knew from hard experience that Paige was as smart as she was tough.

She might have tricked Corbin and Temple into telling her a lot more than they should have.

That could be bad—really bad.

But now Agent Paige had left the men on the shooting range and was walking fast in his direction. He could see that she was getting out her cell phone.

Pope stepped away from the window of the building, not at all sure what he'd say if she came inside and found him there. But Agent Paige hurried on by as she talked on her phone, not even looking up.

"How are things going on your end, Bill?" she asked.

She stopped in her tracks, listened for a moment, then continued the conversation. Pope was back at the window, listening.

"That's too bad," she said. "But maybe I've had some luck. Could you take a few minutes away from your interviews to check something out with me? I've found out where the Den is. It used to be an assembly building, and now it's abandoned."

After another pause, she said, "Great. It's over in the southwest corner of Fort Mowat, so it's closer to where you are than where I am. I'll meet you there."

The call ended, and Agent Paige hurried on her way.

The hair on Pope's neck rose.

She's found out about the Den! he thought. *And now she even knows where it is!*

What would happen if she and her partner went there? Who might they find there now?

He couldn't imagine, but it wouldn't be good.

Fortunately, he knew a short cut, and he could get there before they did.

Pope stepped out of the building and broke into a run.

CHAPTER FORTY THREE

Lucy Vargas hesitated outside the door of the big abandoned building. This was where she'd been told she would probably find one of the soldiers on her list—Private Titus Mulligan. His drill sergeant had said that Mulligan did voluntary cleanup work over in the old assembly building.

The three-story brick building loomed over the area like a giant ghost. It didn't look like it had been in use for a long time. She wondered why it hadn't been torn down.

Then she remembered something that Private Shealy had said about his brutal hazing ...

"We wound up in some building."

She wondered—was this it?

There was no way to know. Her job was to find Private Mulligan and warn him that he might very well be a target for murder.

Or, as Agent Paige had warned her, he might actually be the killer.

Lucy placed her hand on her weapon. If that turned out to be the case, this time she wouldn't hesitate to shoot.

*

The wolf climbed the stairs to the balcony overlooking the old assembly area. It was dim in the abandoned building, with only a little light entering through the doorway and high windows that had been mostly painted over.

Wolflike, he sniffed the musty air. Even now when no one else was here, he could almost smell the delicious smoky scent of candles from a recent ceremony.

He liked hanging around the Den, and he had taken it upon himself to keep it as well swept, tidy, and clean as a condemned building could possibly be. After all, this secret haven of the Wolf Pack wasn't going to be here forever. Wealthy and influential wolves of years past continued to do everything they could to keep it from being torn down. But sooner or later, this fine and noble old building was doomed to perish.

After all, that was the sad fate of all things fine and noble. Nothing that was good lasted for as long as it ought.

Meanwhile, as long as the building survived, the wolf had

made it his personal task to keep its dignity intact.

But the physical building wasn't the only thing that needed cleaning. The Wolf Pack membership itself needed scrubbing. Some members were not living up to true military standards.

Those goddamn hazings, he thought.

That stupid, boorish behavior had no place here among the elite. The hazings were the sole source of corruption in the otherwise pristine secret society.

He found it hard to believe that the other wolves couldn't see that. Standing on the balcony, he remembered what had pushed him into action—the hazing of Private Brandon Graham. Just below where he was now standing, Graham had been put to an outrageous test.

He remembered his admiration for Graham's fighting spirit as he took on his fellow initiates. His admiration had grown when Graham remained the only man left standing. That should have been the end of it. In fact, a man like Graham should have been admitted to the Wolf Pack with no initiation at all. Anybody could see that Graham belonged among them. His training record alone had been enough to prove it.

Then it had all come to an end with that stupid ritual on Larry's Leap, an absurd ordeal that proved nothing about Graham as a man or a soldier.

When Graham had finally cracked, the wolf realized that the Wolf Pack required purification. It was up to the wolf—and to him alone—to take out the worst of the hazers, to avenge Private Graham for the injustice done to him.

Standing there on the balcony, the wolf again felt rage burning through his system, fury at stupidity and corruption.

His memories were interrupted by the sound of the front door opening.

No one else should be here at this time of day.

A line from his sworn oath ran through his mind…

I will protect the Wolf Pack from outsiders by any means necessary.

When he heard the voice call out, he stepped back from the balcony and went to retrieve his weapon.

*

As Lucy entered the front door, she called out, "I'm Special Agent Lucy Vargas, FBI. I'm looking for Private Titus Mulligan. Are you here?"

Her voice echoed through the dim, drafty building.

No one answered.

She stood in the hallway, wondering if maybe the tip she'd gotten was wrong.

Then she heard the sound of something moving about farther inside.

She walked forward, following the sound, and found herself in a huge, gloomy assembly hall, with a balcony looming above.

"Titus Mulligan?" she called out again.

"Who's asking?" a male voice replied. The voice sounded like it came from somewhere in the balcony.

"Special Agent Lucy Vargas, FBI," she repeated. "If you're Titus Mulligan, you might be in danger. I want to talk to you."

"What kind of danger?"

Now Lucy could see a shadowy figure moving among the chairs on the balcony.

Her hand reflexively hovered near her weapon.

But she quickly let her hand relax. After all, she had no reason to think she was in danger. She was here to warn someone else that *he* was in danger.

She called to him, "I'm sure you know about the series of killings on the base recently."

"Yeah," the man called back.

"We have reason to believe that you might also be a target."

He didn't reply.

Then Lucy cautiously added, "That is, if you *are* Titus Mulligan."

The figure laughed a little. It sounded like a friendly laugh.

Lucy said, "Come on down here so we can talk."

"I don't think so," the figure said.

He stepped to the edge of the balcony, and a beam of light from an unpainted window fell on him.

Lucy fleetingly thought there was something wrong with his face.

Then she realized—it wasn't his face at all.

It was a mask.

A mask of a snarling wolf.

In the sunlight she could also see a glint of metal—the barrel of a rifle pointed straight at her.

Lucy drew her weapon.

Then, all in the same instant, she heard a sound behind her.

She realized that someone else was coming into the room.

And there was a flash from the balcony, a sharp crack, a violent push, and searing pain.

Lucy fell backward and crashed to the floor.

It took a moment for her to realize that a bullet had torn through her body.

*

Bill had just reached the abandoned assembly building when he saw a figure dash in through the door.

Then he heard a shot from inside.

Bill rushed into the building and charged through a short hallway. He came out into a huge room and saw a man moving toward a woman lying prone on the floor.

The woman was Lucy—and she was bleeding from the chest.

Instinctively, Bill raised his weapon and fired at the man, who spun around and hit the floor.

Only then did Bill see that the man's hands were empty.

He wasn't holding a weapon.

But Lucy had raised herself up on one elbow. She lifted her Glock and fired six rounds toward the balcony.

Bill looked up in time to see another man tumble over the balcony rail and crash to the floor nearby.

*

Riley was outside the building when she heard the series of gunshots.

She fought down a wave of panic as she rushed inside.

What the hell's going on?

She found herself in a large, dimly lit room with a balcony.

Lucy was sprawled on the floor, bleeding from the chest. Bill was holding her in his arms.

Bill's expression was glazed, and he was obviously in a state of shock.

A few feet away, a fallen man was moaning in pain. And just beyond all of them lay another man, bleeding from multiple bullet wounds. That one was wearing a wolf mask and an M110 sniper rifle lay near him.

Her mind registered that someone had taken down the killer, and that two people were wounded. Bill was trying to stop Lucy's bleeding. Riley forced her attention to the man who was moaning.

She saw that it was Private Stanley Pope and that he had been shot in the shoulder.

"What happened?" she asked him.

His face twisted with pain, Pope pointed toward Lucy.

"I was trying to help," he gasped. "But then—"

He was in too much pain to finish his thought.

The private was wounded, but he would live.

"You'll be all right," Riley said. "Just hang on."

Riley turned back to Bill and Lucy.

Bill was staring at the young woman in his arms, his expression one of stupefied horror.

"I—I shot the wrong man," he stammered. "And Lucy …"

Riley shook Bill by the shoulder.

"Get hold of yourself. Call for medics. Right now!"

Bill laid Lucy gently on the floor and took out his cell phone.

Riley lifted Lucy's head with one arm. Her heart sank at the amount of blood that was spreading across the floor. She put pressure on the wound, but she knew it was too late.

Lucy opened her eyes. "Agent Paige …"

"I'm right here," Riley said.

Lucy had a faint, agonized smile on her face.

"I did it this time, didn't I? I didn't freeze … like last time. I didn't screw up. I took the bastard out."

Riley knelt down beside her.

"You did good, Lucy," she said. "You're getting better and better every day."

"So are you proud of me?" Lucy asked.

Riley felt a knot of emotion in her throat.

"Oh, so, so proud. You took out the sniper. You've got a great career ahead of you. Now stay with us, Lucy. Stay with us."

But Lucy's eyes closed and she seemed to lose consciousness.

Riley felt tears running down her face. She felt a terrible agony forming inside her. Then she heard sirens approaching. Bill had called them here, but she knew that it was too late for Lucy.

Riley gently lowered the dead agent's head to the floor.

Standing up and looking around the chaotic scene, she understood at least part of what had happened. Bill had seen Lucy down and had fired at what he thought was her assailant. In the chaos, he had shot Pope. But Lucy had taken out the sniper.

Then she heard another sound and looked toward it. The masked sniper wasn't dead yet. Riley wiped away her tears and stepped over to the fallen man.

He was groping across the floor for his rifle. Just when he almost had it in his grasp, Riley kicked him away from it.

She pulled out her own weapon. Wild eyes stared back at her through the eyeholes of the wolf mask.

In a croaking voice, he said, "I will protect the Wolf Pack … from outsiders … by any means necessary."

"Not anymore, you won't," Riley snarled.

She fired point-blank into the man's forehead. Blood oozed out from under the mask.

"That was for Lucy," Riley said to the dead man.

His nametag told her that the killer's name was Mulligan.

Riley lifted the mask and saw his face.

She didn't recognize him.

But his face had been so ordinary, she doubted that she would recognize him even if she'd seen him before.

He had the blond, blue-eyed looks of an all-American Eagle Scout.

CHAPTER FORTY FOUR

Riley struggled to hold back tears as she listened to FBI Director Gavin Milner speak to the gathering of Lucy Vargas's colleagues, friends, and loved ones. She had cried a lot during recent days, and the ache in her chest had barely subsided at all. She hoped that this memorial service would put some of that pain to rest.

As always, the slight, dapper man spoke in that gentle, distinguished purr of a voice.

"What is it that makes the bravery of young agents like Lucy Vargas so remarkable? I think it's that danger is no secret to them. They spend countless hours in an academy learning how hazardous their work is going to be. And then they take the job anyway. They take the oath and they carry out their duties at all possible costs—sometimes at the ultimate cost."

Riley found it impossible to believe that she had listened to this same man speaking in this same Quantico auditorium less than two weeks ago. Back then he had been talking about Riley ...

"We all owe her a debt of gratitude for her service—and for her example."

Riley didn't feel like much of an example right now.

She certainly didn't feel that she could compare with Lucy. In Lucy's short career, she had performed better than many agents did in a lifetime. Just a few days ago, Riley and Bill had attended Lucy's actual funeral in Sacramento. That had been a day of open mourning, of pain experienced and expressed—and at the same time a celebration of a brave, successful life. The size of the funeral had surprised Riley. Much of the conversation had been in Spanish, and Riley had been glad that her own Spanish was good enough to participate at least a little.

This crowd at Quantico was smaller, and the proceedings more formal. But Lucy's parents and brothers were at this ceremony as well. Riley and Bill had insisted to Meredith that the FBI pay their way.

It did Riley's heart good to see the pride in Lucy's brothers' faces. Even Lucy's parents looked proud beneath their pain. She felt that they might eventually find some peace even after their terrible loss.

Riley felt deeply saddened by the shattered expression on Sam Flores's face. It was heartbreaking to think of the romance that had just been budding between Sam and Lucy.

Now it would never be.

Riley was sitting next to Bill. She slipped her arm through his and could feel him trembling. She knew that he was having trouble dealing with all that had happened. He blamed himself for Lucy's death—for getting there just a second after the fatal shot was fired, and for mistakenly shooting a man who was only trying to help her. At least it looked like Stanley Pope was going to recover fully from his injury.

Nobody blamed Bill for his mistake—least of all Riley.

But she knew that it would take a long time for Bill to stop blaming himself. He had seen the future in Lucy.

And now it had been snatched away.

CHAPTER FORTY FIVE

When Riley got home from the service, she was hoping for a quiet afternoon. But to her surprise, Liam was sitting in the family room with April and Jilly. They were all looking glum.

"What's the matter here?" Riley asked.

April said, "Liam's father kicked him out. He's got nowhere else to go."

April and Jilly looked at Riley with expressions of silent appeal.

Riley knew what her daughters were asking with those looks. They wanted to know—could Liam stay here with them, at least for a while?

Riley resisted the impulse to simply say no outright. She sat down with her daughters and the miserable-looking boy.

"Let's talk about this," she said. "It's all very complicated."

"You like Liam, don't you?" Jilly asked her.

Riley simply nodded. She hadn't known Liam very long, but she liked him a lot. He'd had a good influence on April. Her recent grades had been higher than they'd ever been. Liam had even gotten April interested in playing chess and possibly going to a chess camp. He was also good with languages. He was an unusually gifted boy.

But he'd been dealt a bad hand in life, with an abusive father and a mother who had disappeared long ago.

He deserves a break in life, Riley thought.

But was she in any position to give him that kind of break?

She had too much to deal with in life as it was—a professional life that consumed her time and brought danger into her own home, and a family that was growing much faster than she ever imagined.

Riley didn't know what to say. She couldn't imagine what she could do.

Gabriela walked into the family room with a tray of cold drinks and snacks, then sat down with the others. Riley could tell that Gabriela already knew what the conversation was all about.

Jilly was starting to get emotional now.

"Look, whatever you do, don't turn him over to the foster care system. I know what that's like. It's just awful."

Riley felt a knot of emotion in her throat. Jilly had been through her own kind of hell.

Riley could never wish anything like that on another young person.

"I know, Jilly," Riley said. "But …"

"But what?" April asked.

Riley didn't know what she wanted to say.

April said, "Liam doesn't have any friends who can take him in. We're his only chance."

Riley remembered how she'd felt when she'd first encountered Jilly. The girl had been ready to sell her young body just to survive. Riley hadn't been able to turn her back on Jilly. How could she turn her back on another kid who needed help? How could she leave him without choices about his own life and future?

It just wasn't in Riley's nature.

Riley looked at Gabriela and asked, "What do you think?"

Gabriela smiled that warm smile of hers.

"I think you know what I think, Señora Riley."

Riley smiled back. As far as she was concerned, Gabriela's approval pretty much settled the issue.

She said to Gabriela, "This is going to be one more for you to look after when I'm away."

Gabriela laughed.

"I had six younger brothers and sisters. And more cousins than you could count. This is nothing."

Then Gabriela leaned forward and spoke sternly to the teens.

"But there will have to be rules. You girls keep your own rooms. This end of this room will be Liam's living space, with the couch for him to sleep on. It will be enough space. I'll empty some of those cabinet shelves for him. He can use the first-floor bathroom."

Liam's mouth dropped open with amazement.

"Is this really happening?" he asked.

Riley let out a welcoming chuckle.

"It certainly is, Liam," Riley said.

Gabriela wagged her finger at Liam and April.

"Another thing. Here in this house, the two of you are brother and sister. *Hermanos solamente. ¿Comprenden?*"

April and Liam smiled and nodded.

"Sí, comprendemos," April said.

"Perfectamente," Liam added.

As Gabriela continued discussing the rules and arrangements, Riley felt warmth inside that she hadn't felt for a long time.

I think this is going to work out, she thought.

*

Later that evening, Blaine Hildreth came by unannounced with his daughter. Crystal was carrying a bouquet of beautiful flowers.

As they stood in the front doorway, Blaine said, "Crystal told me what you've been through. She heard about it from April. I'm so, so sorry for what happened to your friend."

He nodded to Crystal, who handed the flowers to Riley.

"Thank you," Riley said, genuinely moved. "Won't you come in for a little while?"

Crystal eagerly headed toward the family room to join April, Jilly, and Liam.

"Would you like a drink?" Riley asked Blaine.

"I'd love that, yes," Blaine said.

Riley went to the kitchen and poured them both drinks. They sat down together in the living room.

Blaine said, "Crystal also told me you've got a new member of the household."

Riley smiled and shook her head.

"Yeah, I just can't seem to help myself. I hope we all can handle it."

Blaine briefly patted Riley's hand.

"You can handle it. You're an amazing, generous person."

Riley felt a surge of emotion. But she was determined not to cry. She had cried so much lately, and she welcomed the chance for happier feelings.

"Thank you, Blaine," she said.

They sat together in silence for a few moments.

Then Blaine said, "Look, about the last time we saw each other—I'm sorry about that."

"I'm sorry too," Riley said, truly meaning it.

"There really isn't anything going on between me and Laura. She was just paying me a visit, and we're really just friends. But I know how things looked, and ..."

He shook his head with embarrassment.

"I guess I was just trying to make you jealous," he said.

"It worked," Riley said with a weak laugh.

Blaine shrugged and looked as though he was searching for the right words to say.

"Look, I really don't care about being free to date others. What about you?"

"Actually, I haven't even given any thought to dating anyone else," Riley said.

Blaine took hold of Riley's hand.

"Is it settled, then? Just you and me?"

Riley squeezed his hand back.

"I'd really like that," she said.

They sat together holding hands, looking at each other in comfortable silence.

This is turning out to be a good day after all, Riley thought.

CHAPTER FORTY SIX

Early the next morning, Riley was awakened by a cell phone call from Brent Meredith.

"Agent Paige, what is your location right now?" the team chief asked in his usual gruff manner.

Riley sat up and rubbed her eyes, trying to understand the question.

"I'm in bed," she said. "I just woke up."

"At home?" Meredith asked.

"Yes."

"Whatever you do, stay away from your father's old cabin."

Riley stood up from the bed, suddenly much more awake.

"What's going on?" she asked.

"We've got Shane Hatcher pinned down there."

Riley's heart jumped up into her throat.

"How?" she asked.

"After that woman's death up there, we asked the Milladore sheriff to keep an eye on the place—to keep a lookout for Hatcher especially. Sheriff Garland was prowling around the property on foot a little while ago when he saw the cabin door standing wide open. He saw an African-American man inside."

Riley tried to keep from gasping

"Hatcher?" she asked.

"From Garland's description, there's no question about it."

Riley started pacing about the room.

"Did Hatcher see the sheriff?" she asked.

"He doesn't think so," Meredith said.

Riley wondered whether that could possibly be true. Could anyone get that close to Shane Hatcher without him knowing about it?

Meredith continued, "I've sent a SWAT team up there. Park rangers are on it too. We're just waiting to get a helicopter on the scene to help track him if he runs. We'll have him completely surrounded. There's no way out for him. Not this time. The team will either arrest or kill him. But I've ordered them to be extremely careful. You and I both know how dangerous that man can be."

Riley couldn't speak for a moment.

"Agent Paige? Are you still there?"

Riley said, "Thank you for letting me know, sir. Please let me know what happens."

Riley ended the call and continued to pace.

She pictured the property in her mind. The thirty acres was mostly wooded, and the cabin was the only building on it. The property adjoined the national park, so an experienced woodsman would find plenty of places to hide.

But what about Hatcher?

Riley remembered something he'd said the last time she'd talk to him on the phone …

"I'm not hiding in the woods again. I'm a city person."

Even Shane Hatcher would surely be vulnerable in that wilderness—at least if the team took him by surprise.

But he might stand a chance with a fair warning.

Riley wondered if she owed it to him. After all, she now knew he was about to get killed or captured. Not warning him would amount to her being complicit in it, complicit in killing or capturing the man who had saved her family more than once.

Who had led her to her mother's killer.

She paced the room, torn. She couldn't let it happen. If he went down, so be it. But she couldn't let it be on her hands.

I've got to contact him, she thought.

She had two ways of reaching him—through his video address or by text.

She sat down at her desk, turned on her computer, and opened the video chat program.

Yet she sat there, hands trembling, and did nothing.

For some reason, she couldn't bring herself to type the address.

She found herself thinking about the woman who died at Shane Hatcher's hands.

Shirley Redding had been guilty of absolutely nothing except being erratic and foolish. She hadn't deserved to die.

And how long could she let this go on with Shane? How much deeper could she be complicit in his freedom? As it was, Agent Roston, it seemed, was close to pinning her. It would mean the end of her career, her reputation, and possibly jail time.

When would this spiral with Hatcher end?

Maybe he doesn't deserve my help, Riley thought. *Not anymore.*

She remembered what Hatcher had said to her …

"We're joined at the brain, Riley Paige."

A swell of anger rose in Riley's throat.

It's time for that to end, she thought.

She stared at the blank screen longer than she dared.

Then, finally, she turned off her computer.

Without a moment's thought, she tore the gold chain bracelet off her arm.

She'd been wearing it for months, but she was through with it now. She threw it in the wastebasket.

In a few minutes, they would catch or kill him. He might implicate her. She might go to jail.

But at least her drama with him was over.

Finally, it was over.

Shaking, Riley took her cell phone down to the kitchen. Gabriela wasn't up yet, so she made herself some coffee and breakfast. She sat there, feeling more on edge than she had ever felt, knowing her future hung in the balance.

Soon, she got another call from Brent Meredith.

His voice sounded heavy with discouragement.

"He got away. Gone before we got there. The park rangers found signs of recent motorcycle use on a national park trail. Apparently Hatcher had kept a motorcycle hidden up there where he could get to it. So he's at large, and he's dangerous. You'd better be careful, Agent Paige."

Riley thanked him again and ended the call.

Almost instantly, her cell phone buzzed again.

She looked down, and her heart sank.

It was a text from Hatcher:

You knew. You had a chance to warn me. And yet you said nothing.

Riley shuddered with terror. Should she reply? Before she could decide, he texted again:

It was a test of your loyalty. And you failed. We're through.

Riley sat staring at the message. Then ten chilling words followed.

You will live to regret it. Your family might not.

Riley fumbled with the phone, typing desperately:

213

We've got to talk.

But when she tried to send the text, it was marked "undeliverable."

Hatcher had broken off communications between them once and for all.

Riley was shaking all over, and her breath was coming in short, desperate gasps.

She had a new enemy—an enemy far more dangerous than all the criminals she'd ever faced.

What did that mean for Riley?

What did it mean for her growing family?

She had no idea what to expect next.

But whatever it was, she knew it would not be good.

ONCE LOST
(A Riley Paige Mystery—Book 10)

"A masterpiece of thriller and mystery! The author did a magnificent job developing characters with a psychological side that is so well described th*at we feel inside their minds, follow their fears and cheer for their success. The plot is very intelligent and will keep you entertained throughout the book. Full of twists, this book will keep you awake until the turn of the last page."
--Books and Movie Reviews, Roberto Mattos (re Once Gone)

ONCE LOST is book #10 in the bestselling Riley Paige mystery series, which begins with the #1 bestseller ONCE GONE (Book #1)—a free download with over 900 five star reviews!

Still reeling from her former partner Lucy's death and from her partner Bill's PTSD, FBI Special Agent Riley Paige does her best to try to keep herself stable and to patch together her family life. She has to decide what to about April's boyfriend, recovering from his abusive father, and about Blaine, who is ready for their relationship to move ahead.

But before she can work it out, Riley is summoned for a new case. In an idyllic suburban town in the Midwest, teenage girls are going missing—and a body has already turned up. The police are stumped, and Riley is called in to catch the killer before another girl goes missing.

Making things worse is that Riley is assigned a partner she does not want—her nemesis, Special agent Roston—who had been interrogating her in Shane's case.

Even worse: Shane is on the loose, he wants revenge—and he has Riley's family in his sights.

A dark psychological thriller with heart-pounding suspense, ONCE LOST is book #10 in a riveting new series—with a beloved new character—that will leave you turning pages late into the night.

Book #11 in the Riley Paige series will be available soon.

Blake Pierce

Blake Pierce is author of the bestselling RILEY PAGE mystery series, which includes ten books (and counting). Blake Pierce is also the author of the MACKENZIE WHITE mystery series, comprising six books (and counting); of the AVERY BLACK mystery series, comprising five books; and of the new KERI LOCKE mystery series, comprising four books (and counting).

An avid reader and lifelong fan of the mystery and thriller genres, Blake loves to hear from you, so please feel free to visit www.blakepierceauthor.com to learn more and stay in touch.

BOOKS BY BLAKE PIERCE

RILEY PAIGE MYSTERY SERIES
ONCE GONE (Book #1)
ONCE TAKEN (Book #2)
ONCE CRAVED (Book #3)
ONCE LURED (Book #4)
ONCE HUNTED (Book #5)
ONCE PINED (Book #6)
ONCE FORSAKEN (Book #7)
ONCE COLD (Book #8)
ONCE STALKED (Book #9)
ONCE LOST (Book #10)

MACKENZIE WHITE MYSTERY SERIES
BEFORE HE KILLS (Book #1)
BEFORE HE SEES (Book #2)
BEFORE HE COVETS (Book #3)
BEFORE HE TAKES (Book #4)
BEFORE HE NEEDS (Book #5)
BEFORE HE FEELS (Book #6)

AVERY BLACK MYSTERY SERIES
CAUSE TO KILL (Book #1)
CAUSE TO RUN (Book #2)
CAUSE TO HIDE (Book #3)
CAUSE TO FEAR (Book #4)
CAUSE TO SAVE (Book #5)

KERI LOCKE MYSTERY SERIES
A TRACE OF DEATH (Book #1)
A TRACE OF MUDER (Book #2)
A TRACE OF VICE (Book #3)
A TRACE OF CRIME (Book #4)

CPSIA information can be obtained
at www.ICGtesting.com
Printed in the USA
LVHW081352041019
633101LV00012BA/592/P